UNDER THE INEFFABLE SKY:
Romances from the Future Earth

Under the Ineffable Sky

Romances from the Future Earth

JEREMY BALFOUR

TENTH STREET PRESS

TENTH STREET PRESS

THIS EDITION

Published by Tenth Street Press 2016
Cover design by Axel for Tenth Street Press

ISBN-10: 0-9942955-5-3
ISBN-13: 978-0-9942955-5-2

TENTH STREET PRESS Ltd.
MELBOURNE LONDON
www.tenthstreetpress.com
contact@tenthstreetpress.com

TABLE OF CONTENTS

CHAPTER ONE:
THE NEXT DAY

Gwynhr etched on the log another day. Every third day was trading day, and so he would bring bread and wine into the dusky forest in exchange for honey. It had been his routine for many years, since he was a child, and he always looked forward to meeting the old hermit.

He also looked forward to the cool of the forest. The weather had been drier and drier, until barely any rains came, and the monastery had formed extra small canals from the tiny stream that ran nearby. At least timber to burn was not at a minimum, as the old forest had sat there untouched except by the monastery. Travelers from elsewhere were unheard of in his time, and all the little enclave could do was wonder at the ways of the world outside of a day's walk or two, as no one ventured any further these days. Once it had been worthwhile, to lure a coney or uncover grubs to roast, but supplies of these sorts became rare and then disappeared altogether. The most the monastery could expect was the occasional mouse or rat for a pie. There was not even milk or clotted cream, as the dairy animals had long since succumbed to one ailment or another.

Yet today was a good day. The abbess had kindly gifted Gwynhr with an extra flagon of wine for his journey, and despite the overweening heat the day seemed full of promise. All Gwynhr had to do was sweep the hearth and shift the logs and he could be on his way.

It was a full day's journey, ten miles each way, so Gwynhr got an early start, not only carrying his satchel of bread and wine but also an extra purse for herbs from the forest, which bloomed abundantly with sage and coriander and parsley and rosemary. To supplement the broth, there were always pine nuts and pine needles to roast, and so make a hearty concoction to warm the bones and ease the stomach.

The path Gwynhr took had been had been trod since time immemorial, since before the era of the nuns and monks, an era consigned to fading and crumbling books in the monastery vaults, an age of people, of bustling industry and many comings and goings entirely unfamiliar to their little lives. To imagine such a world was to depart on flights of fancy akin to science-fiction, where machines flew in the air, people came and went in suits and dresses and other strange garb, and where society meshed in a tangled web of industrial fervor. A long time ago at the monastery some had said this world could come again if they just could labor hard enough, but the real truth was there were not the resources or work force to revive civilization, and untreated epidemics had narrowed down the population such that the keep of the monks and nuns had remained nearly isolated for generations.

The path meandered through meadows flowered with dark-red poppies, thriving dandelions, abundant clover, and fragrant rose-petals, all fit for the table of the monastery, and ripe for the beehives of the old hermit, whose prodigious efforts over long years had produced a collection of the cross-pollinators fit to sustain more than just himself, and which likewise sustained the flowers even as the flowers sustained the bees. Over the ten-mile course to the forest there were still small springs to quench ones thirst, and at last the outskirts of the musty old-growth woods, of pine and oak and alder and birch and poplar, gathering dust in the gloom amidst the occasional glimmerings of sunlight. Gwynhr was confronted with pathways only he knew of, and was guided by the trees of his familiarity, towards the lodgings of his old friend, Jack the hermit.

The log cabin sat in a still, quiet dell between oak roots, emitting a wafting warm smoke from baking honey-cakes.

"Coo-ey!" cried Gwynhr. At first there came no response, but then:

"Up here!" came a gravelly voice. "Nature has blessed us again!" An old wooden ladder was perched against a greening elm, and high above was Jack the hermit. "Robin's eggs!" the hermit cried downwards to his friend. This was a rare find indeed, as birds and animals were virtually unknown. "The abbess shall be well-pleased with this offering!"

"There is extra wine in return!" called Gwynhr.

Jack the hermit climbed down nimbly with his treasure-trove of a bird's nest. His agile person betrayed no hint of his long years, except for his snow-white hair and beard which poured out over his shoulders and hung to his waist. He was unusually well-preserved, not only by a lifestyle at one with nature, but by his diet of honeycomb and pollen, an age-old recipe for longevity.

"Come! The honey-cakes are nearly ready!" he hailed.

"The wine has reached its time!" Gwynhr replied jovially.

"Any time is a time for wine!" came the response, and they both knew their tongues would be loosened with gossip, not the unseemly gossip of vicarious speculation and titillating rumor, but with the gossip of the civil-minded, a talk of weather and bees and even mention of the world outside, which drifted on the shores of a distant legacy, allowing for discussion of ponderous weight and contemplation. There, however, always room for discourse upon the nuns of the abbey, and the latest marriage to fatten the flock. Marriages were always times of high speculation, as to the gender of the child especially, and to the lasting portion of the parent's happiness.

"So this Monsignor Dutton you've mentioned

has at last made a name for himself." Jack grinned through crooked teeth in a spasm of mirth. "I would gladly join the pool and bet it will be a girl. I can feel it." Yet Jack had not been to the monastery in fifty years, preferring his lasting, peaceful solitude, apart from his regular visits from Gwynhr. The elderly hermit dove in and broke off a substantial chunk of honey-cake for his friend, as Gwynhr unpacked the flagons of wine.

"We are always looking for the next abbess," Alvin chirped, "for what are boys worth except work? We thresh the grasses and tend the vines and sweep and mop, but our moral guidance is what keeps us from rebelling. Often it has been said we should go our separate ways and discover whether there aren't other monasteries, but always the abbess has kept us close and cloistered as the better part of wisdom. Even the few young rebel boys see the wisdom in combined forces over the life of the itinerant indigent. Who knows what is out there?"

Jack paused in his chewing. "For a long time I've had some idling purpose in finding out, but I have left well enough alone, and so tend to matters close to the hearth." Jack paused again, and the trees outside the cabin began to rustle with a wind from the East. "In any event, I have long suspected we are due for a visitor, a migrant from the Desolations, a possible interloper. We must not be surprised if a foreign event occurs."

"We've spoken of this many times over the years," Gwnyhr noted. "You seem extra keen on it now."

"The longer something does not occur, the more likely it is to occur. We must remember that even in our humble lives we possess something greatly desirable, food, peace, the comfort of the hearth. Why would not a stranger attempt to ingratiate themselves, bringing with them their strange ways?"

Gwynhr looked long and hard at the aged man, who had subsisted in comfort untold years, since long before Gwynhr had been born. "Your concern piques my worry," Gwynhr admitted. "I shall suggest to the abbess that we make exploratory ventures to intercept such interlopers, if such there be. Better to be safe than sorry."

"Any survivors of the Desolations would have to be guileful, indeed, and profoundly cunning," Jack noted. At this, the rest of the honey-cakes and wine was consumed in a respectful silence, until, with much mutual warmth, the friends parted company until three days time.

The Abbess Eliana was wont to listen to any wisdom from the hermit, who had been an acquaintance of hers in olden times. Upon pondering the matter, she chose six monks of relative fitness to search the perimeters for any signs of strangers, from a campfire pit to a bent branch. "To be forewarned is to be forearmed," she recited to Gwynhr. Gwynhr himself had been chosen as one of the fittest, as he was well-used to long walks and the signs of nature, although he was hardly the physical sort. The scouts were supplied in considerable measure, and a day appointed for their departure. There would be some delay in the honeycomb, but this was of little moment compared to any breach of the security of the tiny enclave, and, while on their mission, the six runners could forage for the rarer foodstuffs, an effort that likewise had not been attempted for many years.

Gwynhr chose a particular dune hill as a vantage point, and after scrabbling his way through heather and gorse found the pinnacle. There, he decided, he would make camp for several days and watch over a significant territory for any newcomers. The hermits words were not lost on Gwynhr: any survivor of the Desolations would have to be cunning, indeed. Gwynhr surmised that this potential individual would be expert at self-concealment, and therefore only light fires at night. So Gwynhr maintained wakefulness and inspected the horizons after sundown for any glimmer of a fire.

Jack the hermit had not been wrong: his long self-imposed isolation had bred in him a special sensitivity, so that the slightest change of air would be a portent. Gwynhr discovered the glimmerings of fire one night, barely discernible on a rocky bluff some few miles away from his own encampment. Gwynhr had directives to risk investigation, and so packed the last of his dwindling supplies with all due haste, and made his way that night in the direction of the fire.

He discovered a few flaming brands initially, but no other evidence that the area had been attended. Gwynhr became acutely aware of the precariousness of his position, a foreign sense of insecurity, and concealed himself in a nearby hedge, after dusting away any evidence of his shoe prints. He waited there in the dark.

What finally appeared was what Gwynhr at first took to be a hideous monster, until he recognized it as a bear, or, rather, a person concealed within a bear skin, complete with head and fangs concealing this persons own visage. Gwynhr had never seen a bear or a foreigner before, and his first instinct was to yield and vanish in the darkness to warn the abbey. Yet some lure of fascination made him pause, the lure of, as it were, looking at a man from civilizations ancient past.

Yet it was not a man. This frightful personage squatted before the fire and unpacked a satchel of grubs, and continued, one by one, to skewer the grubs to a stem of thorns, and carefully roast them, turning the stem with the absorption of one immersed in the most particular task. Upon pulling back the mask of bears-head, it was revealed that this foreigner was a woman, with flaming red hair and a stern visage all her own, on the one hand hard-bitten and wild, and on the other hand of a self-prepossessed sternness. Gwynhr immediately thought the unarmed abbey to be most vulnerable and susceptible, and fearfully contemplated his options, unadvised and ill-equipped as he was. His options were few: he could take flight as best he may, or approach this alien figure as best as able on friendly terms, or take the ultimately most prudent measure and try to kill her. Yet, Gwynhr thought, in failing this last option he might bring a dread retribution upon the abbey. With only his own wisdom to rely upon, Gwynhr chose to compromise. He would reveal himself, yet take no offensive measures. Although he was acutely aware that he himself might be considered a valuable foodstuff, Gwynhr chose to invite this survivor, with a gesture of ultimate friendship, to partake in a feast of honeycomb and wine, and lead her away from the abbey into the woods to the hermit's log cabin. Gwynhr was fraught with the uncertainties and risks, but upon consideration decided this gesture of friendship, as well as protection of the abbey, to be the best weighed option, although he feared for his friend Jack's life, and his own, and indeed still the abbeys existence. The Desolations were well-rumored to breed the savage and unpredictable.

His contemplation was disturbed by a harsh order. "Come out, you!" the bear-woman ordered, in tones of modulation combined with fierce authority. Gwynhr realized she must have detected his presence by a keen sense of smell.

"I have brought you bread and wine and pine nuts," Gwynhr tried timidly as he revealed himself.

"You must sit," came the responding command. Gwynhr had committed himself this far, and had no other option but to obey. His only weapon was a wooden pencil knife which he used for marking the days back at the abbey.

Gwynhr sat in his patched brown robe next to the burning embers, and handed the stranger all his bread and wine. He attempted to remember a prayer or two, but religion, except for obeisance towards the abbess, had fallen out of practice generations ago.

The bear-woman set to consuming with immediate haste. Gwynhr realized that the revelation of his presence, complete with the foodstuffs, was evidence sure of a nearby civilization, which could be taken either way: either the bear-woman was contemplating pillage or fearing for her own life.

"There is honeycomb not far," Gwynhr tried. Yet he realized this might seem a ruse to trick an opponent.

The woman's red hair shone and danced in the firelight. Gwynhr perceived eyes of deep hazel, full yet resolute lips, and the thin yet wiry body of a long struggle for survival, of many years battling the uncertainties of daily living, and he could also feel the intelligence born of the instincts of a true survivalist; an unerring constitution for self-preservation and prudence which had conquered many doubtful circumstance, battled hardships and fought with demons. Yet she had made no move to take his life, but squatted there and continued to eat ravenously. Gwynhr realized their position was mutual: any imposition upon the other might be cause for retaliation from hidden cohorts. Even in their predicament, violence was too uncertain a course of action.

"A mere twenty miles, and much honeycomb," Gwynhr tried again against the silence. The bread was gone, and the bear-woman swiftly quaffed the remaining wine. Gwynhr realized that the wine certainly revealed an entire civilization, and hoped desperately that this woman was alone, and not also a scout like himself.

"We have no more time," the woman stated, pulling down her bears mask over her face. "We will go to the honeycomb."

"I will take you there," Gwynhr promised, although it sounded false and hollow. He prayed on every star he knew that he was not jeopardizing Jack the hermit or the abbey, but again realized the danger of taking a life under such circumstance. He was almost overcome with doubt and insecurity, yet the woman had made no direct aggression.

Clearly, she must be most hungry above all else and perhaps this was some protection from any bestial instincts she might hold.

Once they reached the forest, the way to Gwynhr from this direction was unclear, so he judged by the direction of the newly forming sunlight their path to the hermit. At last, in the distance, was the faint trail of smoke.

Jack seemed to be expecting them. "Come right in," he said in a positively jovial manner, evidently ignoring the bear mask with its fangs. Upon his wooden table sat a lavish spread of all he could supply, bread, wine, honeycomb, and herbal teas in abundance. The woman pulled back her mask to again set to.

"You're not from around here," Jack began. The red-haired woman seemed to almost betray a smirk and a faint smile, but was evidently more in consideration of the feast. Yet Gwynhr and Jack knew she must feel more than fortunate. "Let's see," Jack continued without hesitation, "that's one, two, three, four hundred miles? Two thousand, mayhaps?"

"More," the woman slurped with her mouth full of honeycomb.

"Let's see," Jack continued, "that makes ten thousand, two hundred, and ninety-five grubs, by my estimation."

"You live well here," came the reply.

"Oh," Jack said with his beard wagging, "just tending bees, the usual."

"Take me to your leader," was the woman's only response to this.

"That is a good one," replied Jack, "but we have no leader. However, we are seeking a good seamstress, or perhaps a nanny."

This invoked a chortle from the woman, and an evident sense of relief, finally. "There are none behind me," she assured. "Only by the meat of this bear did I make it so far. None survive the Wilderland, except by rare chance."

"This we believe," Gwynhr interjected. "We haven't seen a stranger in generations."

The woman paused with her mouth full. "I slaughtered only a few."

"Perfectly understandable," said Jack. "Survival of the fittest, after all."

"Fortune was with me. It could have been different. It was in self defense," she explained.

Jack's look could not have been more sympathetic. "The Great Spirit forgives you. Here, have some tea and your stomach will feel better, and have some more wine if you like. The day is getting on: there is a comfortable bed of moss and lichen in the corner for a wee bit of a nap. When you awake, all will seem different."

"Do you have books?" came the woman's unexpected reply.

"Why, yes," Jack responded. "Not in great volume," he jested, "but a few notables. May I ask you a question?"

"That is a question already," said the woman.

"Quite. What is your name?"

"It was Justine. Now I have no name."

"I understand. When you awake things will seem different."

The woman seemed to drop all pretense, and rapidly finished the wine.

"Goodness," Jack noted, "you are most susceptible to drink."

"Twenty years," said Justine. "I must stay."

"Why, this is entirely good news," offered Jack. "We shall be best of friends. All I ask is that you don't frighten the bees with your hide."

Justine was clearly amused. "It held some use for a while. Now the Great Spirit has at last smiled upon me, or am I dreaming?"

"You must be tired," said Gwynhr. "My name is Gwynhr, and this is Jack. We ask nothing of you. Except the bees."

Justine finished her bread with honeycomb. "I thought I was a wild thing."

"Well," said Jack, "misapprehensions happen under the best of circumstance."

Justine stripped off her bear-clothes down to torn and ragged linens, and stumbled to the moss and lichen mattress, and collapsed. Jack looked at Gwynhr, and Gwynhr looked at Jack, and in silence they began clearing the table out to the foyer. The dusky light of a setting sun began to show through the trees and fronds. Gwynhr and Jack spoke together deep into the night.

"For a Survivor," Jack indicated, "she does not have too wild a soul. Some things we can only imagine. It is not for us to judge. By all my imaginings, I see only the victim of circumstance."

"Perhaps," Gwynhr put forward, "she is waiting for opportunity."

"Nay," Jack gainsayed, "she is not cruel. What is cruel is the world she has lived in. Let us not be quick to judge."

"What of the abbey?" Gwynhr queried.

Jack laughed. "Judging by her beauty, the monastic life will be virtually abandoned. Yet seriously, surely this can only be a good thing: here is one adept at foraging, and not too un-tame as to conform, from the looks of things. If she has ulterior motives, then she is still smart enough to know that there is strength in numbers, and that her very own diet partially depends on letting us live. Right now she is just waking up from a very bad dream. I deem, of all survivalists, here is one who has not lost her soul."

"What do I tell the abbess?" Gwynhr queried desperately.

"This much is clear: we, likewise, must conform to new presentiments. The introduction of a new species must be met with flexibility and generosity, as we would hope for if we were in her place. I venture that you take her to the abbess immediately, so that we do not disguise ourselves out of our own distrust. She seems to like books: take her to the library, and feed her well, and she will return to her senses eventually."

"If such be your wisdom," Gwynhr relented.

"Give things time," Jack indicated, "and healing may ensue."

Indeed this seemed to be the case. However, that morning, when Gwynhr arrived at the abbey with Justine, who had stumbled behind him in a stupor, there had been a general uproar at seeing an outsider for the first time. In fact, none there had seen red hair before.

Gwynhr brought Justine before the Abbess Eliana, who smiled broadly and hugged the young stranger. The abbess indicated to one of her retainers that a new robe be brought, and a pail of fresh water. She had Justine sit for a little while in the meantime, and asked her a few polite questions about the outside world, attempting, under the circumstances, to be as tactful as possible, yet Justine was no longer accustomed to socialization, and clearly needed rest, so she was left to her bath, and then provided a stuffed mattress and pillow, and a little more wine.

Over time, and gradually, Justine became more sociable, and was able to teach the cloister useful things regarding cultivating and harvesting certain plants, and proved an invaluable asset. Over time, due to her exotic appearance and eccentric character, her hand was sought by many of the young men, yet she preferred Gwynhr's quiet company. She showed Gwynhr how to make chamomile poultices for aches and pains, and Gwynhr showed her when a grape was just ready for harvest.

Together, they would often go to the woods and visit Jack, who was always delighted for their company. They regularly stuffed themselves on honeycomb.

"It is an odd thing," Justine said one day, "that when hope dwindles there is still new life around the corner."

CHAPTER TWO:
THE ALMOND TREE

The almond tree blossomed early that year in the monastery courtyard. It was a single surviving remnant of an old grove which now was out of living memory and barely discussed. The grapevines were thriving, and more canals were constructed to expand operations. Last year's supply of wine was rapidly dwindling away.

Justine was haunted by her usual nightmares. She would be roasting grubs at night, and hear the echo of strange calls, and the old contradictory impulses would arise automatically: eat for more energy, or flee to, hopefully, find safer ground. Sometimes in the distance she would hear motor sounds, and then she would flee, further and further into the wastelands, across the Desolations of deserts.

In her restless days she would accompany Gwynhr to trade for honey with Jack the hermit. One day they arrived to find him deep in a comb.

"Can't get enough," he explained. "Tastes like it's from clover." He gestured to his back porch where his stockpile of bee hives resided. "They're as busy as bees back there. Now, Gwynhr, do break out the bread and wine, and we'll sop up the one with the other."

"Jolly good idea, as always," Gwynhr replied.

He gave the greater share to Justine, who was still rather slim. This all occasioned a period of silence as the three set to.

"What lies within, Jack?" Justine asked that day.

"The forest, you mean? Nobody really knows. I've been that way on many occasions, and marked out some trails, but it must go on a goodly way, and one doesn't wish to get oneself lost. If you go far enough there are blackberries in summer, and evidence of a ruined, deserted well. Beyond that, I don't really know. The abbey considered forming an expedition, but had doubts about snakes and such things, so abandoned the idea."

Justine was silent. Her restless nature formed a compulsion about the idea, but at the same time she wished to play it safe, and not arouse the wrath of the unknown.

She had trouble making friends of the other young women at the abbey. They seemed to Justine confined and restricted to the average thoughts of everyday, but Monsignor Dutton's wife Honica took a liking to her, and they would sow and harvest grasses, and stomp on grapes together. It was certainly a fair trade for wandering the Desolations, to be sure, yet her restless nature always seemed to reimpose itself. Finally, she went before the Abbess Eliana.

"I wish to enter the cloistered life," Justine told the abbess.

"Well, dear, we don't really have anything like that here. You are of course welcome to the privacy of your room, but our bell only signals meal times, now. Perhaps you might find more time in the library useful..."

"Yes, the books are good, they feed the soul, but I require a special purpose, a mission. May I have your permission to seek out the heart of the forest?"

"We do not go there," the abbess abjured. "Why, what if there was a starving wolf, a snake, or a scorpion?"

"Then they could become food," Justine could not help but say.

"It's the other way around, dear."

"I slaughtered a bear once with only pointed sticks. What if there are wild boar to roast, or pheasant or grouse?"

"Yes, I do see what you mean," the abbess replied hungrily. "Yet you cannot go alone, that would be much too dangerous."

"I can take Gwynhr."

"Hmm. Well, yes. There is rather a dearth of brave warriors here. It is allowed," the abbess decided, "but only for four or five days, two days in and three to make your way back. We have a bucket of whitewash somewhere here to mark your way with."

Gwynhr was against the idea, but Justine was

adamant, and because Gwynhr was overprotective of his beautiful red-haired discovery, he relented. They gathered the few necessities, of blankets and bread and wine and honey, and first made their way to Jack's house.

It was a relief to escape the intense heat of the arroyo for the forest. They found Jack deep in a tankard of wine.

"I thought as much. Young people are too restless. Abide by the strictest rules of caution, especially in regards the Wild People."

"The Wild People?" asked Gwynhr. "You've never mentioned them before."

"Nor have I seen one," replied Jack. "Yet when I was very small and my parents raising me in this very hut, they mentioned it. Perhaps there are no such things..."

"I have sharpened sticks, and a slingshot," Justine declared.

"You can't help but look like food," answered Jack. "Here, have some wine before you depart, and more honeycomb."

Gwynhr and Justine wandered tipsily into the musty old woods of fallen trees and tangled vines. One of the first things they did was make a sled to carry plants in, and very soon they had vine for rope, juniper berries for the wine, and aloe as a salve. As they progressed, many of the plants looked unfamiliar, and soon even the trees began to seem unusual, weeping willows and redwoods and Asian pines planted long ago by forest gardeners long since passed.

At the end of their first day the forest turned damp, and there were trickling springs feeding marshy pools. Justine knew exactly what to do and baited lines with grubs and waited for fish. Gwynhr had never seen this before, nor a fish, but he got the idea and waited patiently. After a few minnows and polliwogs, a sizable trout was had. They cooked them thoroughly for Jack and the abbey to taste, and by then it was nightfall, and, despite the heat, they wrapped themselves in blankets against the night. No sounds of birds or savage animals could be heard.

The second day out, some forty miles into the wild undergrowth, proved to be more eventful. The rambling trail they had chosen lead them to a pool with an old carven stairwell climbing from it towards the mild height of a single hillock. Upon making their way to the top, they discovered a building outside their experience, a dome made of cut stone such as nothing the monastery could produce.

An oaken door stood on rusty hinges, which they creaked back in utmost curiosity. Within the dome was such as they had never imagined, a finely wrought telescope aimed at a gap in the roof. Old, crumbling manuscripts lay about, including a few handwritten journals that the pair discovered.

Gwynhr and Justine began to take to the idea. Here was a lost example of a scientific person whose object was charting the night sky. With the ending of the day the pair set to clearing away brambles and lichen from the roof of the domed structure, and cleaning dust from the telescope lens. Their excitement grew as dusk came, and they had an opportunity to perceive into the night sky in all its brilliance. Venus shone as hadn't been seen in centuries, and the Milky Way was spread out like a glowing heavenly cloud of dust. Gwynhr looked then with his own chocolate-brown eyes into Justine's piercing hazel and they grasped each other's hands firmly in mutual discovery. Civilization had not ended without the race still peering above for inspiration. The stars over Utah twinkled and flashed with the promise of the future, of new discoveries lying latent, of a creeping ascent into the vast unknown, and the slow unfoldment so long lost to the race.

With their renewed wonder, neither could sleep that night. Justine crumbled dry leaves to dust, and Gwynhr assembled dried lichen, and with some effort a roaring fire shone out from the porch of this ancient observatory. The discovery warmed them even as the fire, and each were possessed alike of the excitation of the past pursuits of scientific man, so pertinently begun and so unceremoniously ended. The final journal recorded the last flying of drones that had swept across the Desolations. Now their past had been revealed, and the long centuries of struggle unfolded in their imaginations.

In the early breaking dawn a new warning met them with all the terror of the unknown. A snarling growl met their ears, and they leapt to their feet, not anticipating in any form the plight of this ambush. A savage, snarling, starving cougar faced their encampment. Alvin thought too little too late of any preparations, yet Justine seized the initiative and sought a torch from their dying fire. Alvin had never seen a cougar, but Justine had some familiarity, and jousted with prods of the glowing embers.

Another, different cry rang out, the call of a man, and soon from the underbrush was revealed a savage, a tall, lean man with knotted hair, dressed in rough hides and painted with elderberry juice and mud. He held a long spear at the ready, and did not hesitate to confront the trembling Gwynhr and Justine with feints of his javelin, accompanied by bestial snarls of no language whatsoever, except that of an untamed mercenary long adrift in a world of limited supplies and mental chaos.

With a command from its master the cougar lunged forward, but received an ember in its eye for its efforts that immediately quelled its hostilities. The savage then leapt across the dying fire with his javelin bared, yet Justine had two sharpened sticks at the ready. They collided in the fire, and Justine felt the spear cut at her shoulder, while her own sticks were of little avail. Yet Gwynhr had possessed himself of an unused well of motivation against his terror and confusion, bred of his protective instincts towards Justine, and brought a large stone down upon the back of the savages head.

"Let us flee this place!" Gwynhr urged the injured Justine, and as quickly as they could they gathered their supplies and rushed in the direction of the nearest whitewashed mark they had left to indicate their trail. Justine was bleeding rather much, but her strength did not yield.

They arrived at Jack's hermitage the evening of the next day. "Our past is lost," Justine related, "guarded by untamed demons of the night. Yet we have seen what our forebears witnessed, the night sky as it should be seen, as the Great Spirit sees it, close and glowing and true, and, at least, we have collected many plants."

"Yet we have left a trail," Gwynhr interrupted, "leading from there to this very place. It is not safe here."

Jack heard the story of the encounter with the savage, and merely leaned back and sipped some honey-wine spiced with sage. "The answer is simple, really. I must take up residence at the monastery, and its walls be fortified. Boiling water should be enough to discourage any interlopers, and we shall set snares along our ways to trap any wild things," he said in his optimism.

This encouraged Gwynhr and Justine only somewhat, although it was certainly true that it was the best of options. Gwynhr hugged Justine and Jack and gave them both pats on the back. "To be forewarned is to be forearmed," Jack assured them. "You have done nothing wrong."

Within the year, Jack had instituted himself as the monasteries official librarian, and the monks and nuns were all eager for new cross-referencing and direction. Also that year Justine came to a breakthrough decision: instead of the cloistered life, she would marry Gwynhr, who had so boldly shown dedication in the face of the savage unknown.

The celebrants partook of the usual victuals beneath the almond tree, which was blossoming fully even in the height of the summer's heat. The Abbess Eliana consecrated the place and the day holy, and so a new holiday was born.

Justine would select books for Gwynhr, and together they unfolded the secrets of the lost astronomers, whose eyes had peered up from Earth to the stars in the lost age of peace and security. Again an age of innocence had been lost, but the age of the ancients was slowly being rediscovered.

Jack passed away one Saint Crispin's Day and a special place for his internment was chosen on the arroyo, and sprinkled with wine for good measure.

"What we take with us," the abbess dedicated, "is a store of love and knowledge that can never

34

fail."

Yet Justine brought Gwynhr along to a conference with the abbess and Monsignor Dutton. They described again in detail the fury of the warrior they had met with, and that he possessed a tamed cougar. The abbess and monsignor knew to be fearful, although they had never seen violence before nor a cougar. Jack's advice was discussed in some detail, and fortifications proceeded against the unknown. The walls of the crumbling mission were bulwarked somewhat with bricks of mud and straw, and slowly wooden fences grew up about the vine-lands, although they could not protect all their grasslands.

An enclave was held of all 192 residents of the mission, and the discussion focused on the hunter and his vocation. Many argued it must have been a solitary creature, but Justine indicated that possession of a tamed cougar revealed the idea of a distant tribe of warriors, and that the savage they had met must have been a remote scout staking out new territory.

Gwynhr continued to notch the days upon a log, and greatly missed his friend Jack, but Justine had turned out to be the gentlest of creatures, especially as her traumas subsided, and she became accustomed to the genteel life. Yet it was only at her prodding that the monastery was kept at alert for wild things. She knew the monastery floated like a mirage of peace, an island in the midst of storm, a meagre dedication to a lost past of civility.

Justine slept lightly, and was awakened one night by a distant call. She awoke, and rushed to ring the bell. The monks and nuns were disturbed in their rest without fully comprehending their predicament, but Justine had them fill all the cauldrons to boil water, and haul these to the heights of the bulwarks. The abbess and Monsignor Dutton began organizing the parishioners into some semblance of preparedness, including a supply of heavy stones to drop upon any comers.

Soon, beneath a moonless night sky, low growls and snarls could be heard plainly, and monk and nun alike began quivering with insecurity and fear of these foreign phenomenon, entirely unexposed as they were to wild animals, except for pictures and stories which had almost been consigned to the world of fable, and never included in the daily world they had known.

Justine had donned her old bear skin, and wrapped herself in all her blankets. She grabbed at Gwynhr's trembling hand. "Gwynhr," she whispered with insistence, "there is no more here. The world you know is ceasing to be. They seek for food, and we are virtually defenseless. Come away, we must come away!"

"We cannot desert our friends," Gwynhr persisted with equal insistence.

"There is nothing here, Gwynhr, we must come away! Quickly, gather what you can carry before we are surrounded!"

"What of the abbess, what of the monsignor?" Gwynhr protested.

"They would not understand, they cannot make their way. I shall show you how to climb, how to forage. Quickly, now, or we shall be surrounded!"

Gwynhr was just able to grasp this idea. He fumbled with his bag and his provisions, his food, his wooden knife for cutting plants and digging, and his own blankets. Justine led him by the hand to the rear of the vineyards and stacked loose stones that they might climb over the fence. Gwynhr looked back into the night and said goodbye to what he had known. The couple continued to scramble across the arroyo towards the distant mountains, with cries of despair and futility reaching their ears as though from some nightmare of chaos and violence. They hurried with all their speed, until the cries had faded into the moonless night. Gwynhr did his best to keep pace, and at last the light dawned on rocky shale that rose towards the dry and broken mountains.

It was not many days before their bread and wine and honey were dwindling. Still, the mountains approached, and Justine, in her cunning, turned over rocks for salamanders to roast. After several weeks they came to a remote mountain lake, and fishing was to be had.

Gwynhr was sorely fatigued and worn. Apart from physical exertion, he could not grasp this new life and its hardships of foraging and flight. Yet Justine was like a rock of endurance and dedication and steadfastness.

They paused at the lake for a few days. There were no birds in the sky, no wandering deer, no foxes or stoats or beavers. "What shall find us out?" Justine asked Gwynhr pertinently as she sharpened sticks in a fire.

"Bear," Gwynhr guessed correctly.

"Show no fear, they can sense it," Justine warned.

"Justine," said Alvin, "you must tell me of your past, wife."

"I cannot escape my past. I will tell you of my childhood."

CHAPTER THREE:
DREAD AT THE COMING OF BABYLON

"Please don't send me to the mutants, Papa," Justine pleaded and whined. She could not and would not stay mute.

Barnaby sat staring up from his tin of Spam. "Damn you for your thieving ways, child. There is no more store here." His furrowed brow and long eyebrows bristled in consternation, dour yet resolute.

"Then kill me now and have done," his daughter demanded as a final hope.

"You must go and find your way. There is no two ways. Keep your enemies close, then run and hide. Do not bide your time, but seize the day. All is not lost." Barnaby tossed Justine a suit to protect her sleight pale self from the radioactivity which swirled and swam and dawned outside. "We cannot hold out here. This bunker shall be a slaughterhouse of charnel. Nothing survives the coming of Babylon." Barnaby pressed the air-hatch button. "Go forth and never return, for your footsteps shall be followed. Bring no more misfortune upon the last of the house. I have done well by you, and now you must go."

"How can you consign me to the hinterlands of waste?! Dear Papa, please, please let me stay. They shall enslave, they shall indulge in rapine and carnage. Save me, Papa!"

"It would only delay the inevitable," Barnaby rejected flatly, unscrewing a jar of peanut butter. He handed one spoonful to his bitter, unconsolable daughter. "This is your last. The flowers bloom gigantic, and there are also leaves and pine nuts to eat. Keep your enemies close and feed them, lest they feed upon you, and do not waste salty tears, young child of mine. If you should see me in a years' time, our situation might be reversed."

"Yes, Papa. Thank you, Papa. I take my leave." The inner hatch slid to and all was silent in the bunker for a time. Then Barnaby slowly, ponderously, and with all due reserve lit his long-stem carved deer antler pipe, and not for the last time, for of tobacco he had made good store. This at least he would maintain for some while. His daughter was another matter. No other body must compete indefinitely, until both sat on a waste heap of sardine tins. There was no two ways.

Barnaby broke the seal on a canister of amyl nitrite, and prepared. It had been his trick. Only he knew that he must now follow his daughter outside. He had kept it a secret from her that they were both running out of food. Barnaby would follow Justine into the horrors of radioactive gigantism, disease, and abject poverty at a distance, protecting and hunting for his daughter.

"I shall live on the Other Side," Barnaby grumbled, suiting up while he smoked. "Let all that is food fear my harpoon." He groused about for a few last cigarette stubs then pressed the door. With a few deep breaths he passed into a marshy deep, which slowly emitted thick vapors of poison. Barnaby knew he was now under the rule of the mutants. His automatic harpoon he kept thereafter at constant vigilance, even during sleep.

Justine tried to light a roaring fire in the moist jungle. The chirps of toads and the ribbit of frogs were a steady backbeat and suggestion, and the tweets and caws of birds her companion. Her tinder set, the fire came to under the breathing of her headgear filters. She thought, "The more fire the better." For weeks she had caught rumor of hungry, nay, voracious tourists, the slimy swamp-bear and cats, and she had even discovered scat of the giant human. Her terror was consummate.

The wind brought her a whistle and the familiar call of "Justine!"

"My gemstone, where are you?" Barnaby had successfully traced her down across several weeks time. "Daughter, can you hear me?"

"Father! I thought you were the sound of a ghost! You have changed your mind!"

"Dear Justine, we must hunt beast-flesh before we can go home again. Your time has been difficult, yet it was only necessary, for now you are prepared for the hunt. This is the law."

"Papa, you were right to keep it a secret. Now, I

shall hunt the wild things with you, your trident and my fire shall be one in battle, but yet shall we fear the coming of Babylon."

CHAPTER FOUR:
THE INEFFABLE SKY

Justine and Gwynhr stayed by the lake many days to fish. They enjoyed their minimal comforts, primarily talking to each other. Gwynhr noted with deep regrets the many fine years of the monastery, the flow of good cheer and good wine, and his long conversations with Jack the hermit over honeycomb. Their own supply of bread and honey and wine were now gone, and they sat by the reflection of mountains as though next to the ineffable sky, their acquaintance the looming uncertainty of a vast world of few resources, their companion the possibly rueful choices of direction and limited resources and ultimate fates. The supply of fish was now clearly running low, as well. They could not stay, but where would they go? The debate contained no strong contender, but at minimum they could not return the way they had come.

The land had been dry for a great many years, but their seventh day at the lake brought a radical event: winds began to blow, and very soon a tremendous series of stratospheric cumulus clouds appeared, swiftly approaching on the gale. The couple broke camp and climbed towards a ridge of the encircling mountains, and they managed to locate an overhanging boulder that would provide shelter. Undisturbed for generations were a few stones of a makeshift fire pit, used long ago by some other lonely drifter seeking the meagre subsistence of a land bereft of resources, empty of the usual foodstuffs to be relied upon, which long ago had suffered an inevitable extinction, except for the few fish, some insect species, the rare mouse, and the solitary bear.

Justine and Gwynhr crumbled their last supply of dry leaves towards producing a fire, even as the winds began to whistle between boulders and howl between the surrounding mountain peaks. Yet Justine listened again, and gestured with finger to lips for Gwynhr's silence.

"The Wild People are coming. Now that they have found the monastery, they have the means to continue sending scouts for more food." Justine's face turned to a pall Gwynhr had not seen since they first had met. Justine wrapped her bearskin about her petite frame, which already had lost weight again since their flight from the monastery.

"What does it foretell, wife?" Gynhr asked desperately.

Justine spoke low. "I can hear their own whistles and howls amidst the storm. There are many. If they catch us they will feed upon us." This was still an unfathomable idea to Gwynhr, who had lived so long in the contentment of an isolated and simple life, almost wholly unaccustomed to imagining other cultures or the world outside. "Wrap your blankets about you. We must flee as quick as our feet will carry us, towards that ridge between the two summits. The lowlands behind us are theirs, now. Our only hope is to outpace their searchings. Pray that we find food." Both knew they could not long survive on the supplies they had, a few toasted frogs and toads and a few dried grasses. Both knew the mountains they were fading into were a land of arid outcroppings and few springs, without even a patch of snow to briefly gain sustenance from, for time out of mind the weather had been dry.

Not that night. Even as Justine and Gwynhr fled, the cumulus broke overhead with a great release of thunder and lightning. Gwynhr was terrified by an encroaching sense of apprehension and chaos, but looking upon Justine's own grim visage he knew he must have strength, and cast aside the wilderness of their situation and the great fears of the unknown, and persevere for her sake. From this he did draw some strength, otherwise he would not have wits to survive alone.

Sheets of rain pounded down upon the stony outcroppings, and no trail revealed itself, except to scramble forward, only to have ones way thwarted, and have to turn and go around certain impassable areas. Justine urged Gwynhr forward, insisting that the greedy marauders could not be far behind, that their encampment by the lake was too obvious to be overlooked.

The wind and rain battered and buffeted them

as they climbed forward, and their old shoes of ancient wool became soaked through and their feet sore. Gwynhr thought with some encouragement that at least Justine would remain somewhat dry in her bearskin.

At last, near the ridge-top, they met with a path of sorts. Stacked stones showed the way of some passed denizen of the mountains from the lost years, and the path lead eventually to a long-abandoned mine shaft leading back into one of the outcroppings. Next to the cave was a flat carven stone which read: "This is the final testament of myself, Homer Stack. The world has ended and I am old. May you find this home suitable, and be blessed against the wrath of God."

"We cannot stay here," Justine urged in the thunder and lightning and downpour.

"Do you suppose we shall find people?" Gwynhr asked desperately.

"These mountains hardly provide a subsistence, and those following us are hell-bent on carnage and pillaging. At least they cannot track our foot-traces and scent so easily in this rain, but they have trained the cougar for the outlying searches, and the cougars know how to follow us. All we have is pointed sticks and my slingshot to stave off their viciousness. We must turn here on the bluff and establish higher ground. Daylight shall not be merciful." They consumed the last of their roasted frogs and toads, and, as best they could, followed the ridge upwards. Justine continued to urge Gwynhr onwards, but his strength was not so great as her wiry determination, bred of many desperate circumstance.

In the crackling lightning they could just discern the outlying area from the ridge. The desert mountains of Utah stretched into the distance like a giant graveyard, without mercy or clemency or hope. When strength was nearly failing them both, at some hour nearing daylight, they discovered another cave.

"Bear," Justine whispered. "I can feel it. This is either our final undoing, or our hope. Take these pointed sticks and some stones, such as you can manage. I shall arm myself with my slingshot. It must not be hibernating, but voraciously hungry. It can surely smell us even now. Be at the ready!"

The unlikely couple, the one of bred determination and the other of meekest demeanor, hid themselves behind boulders not far from the cave. Sure enough, a thin, starving brown bear emerged with fangs dripping. Justine let loose a swift volley of stones in the near-dark from her slingshot, some finding the mark of the beasts head, but not its eyes. Their direction was revealed, and without hesitation the beast charged forwards. It leapt over the boulders of their concealment, and, without lightning, the confrontation ensued in near total darkness.

Justine, in her own bearskin, became the bear's

first target. The animal was not so starving that it wasn't swift, and all Justine could do was briefly feint and jab with two fire-sharpened sticks before she was overwhelmed by the grip of the bears claws and fangs upon her covering. She was borne back without defense, and Gwynhr, shivering wet in the pitch darkness, could hardly descry the scene.

There was one saving grace: Gwynhr's love for Justine, which like a lever turning goaded his resolve into heroism, and he sprang forward of a quickened sudden, the urge of an acute primordial instinct, to protect and preserve all that life has.

The bear was slashing and biting upon Justine's covering of hide, as she vainly and uselessly attempted to counterattack with her sticks under the savage momentum of the starving bear. Yet this gave Gwynhr his one opportunity, and he fell upon the beasts back and, before he could be shaken off, with all his swiftness, reached around the bears angry jaws and jabbed at its eyes with his sticks with all his fortitude. The bear was thus disabled, and snarled a last misery before relenting and attempting to clamber back to its cave.

Justine perceived the situation through her own running blood, which poured from a gash left by the fangs on her scalp, which ran into her eyes. "Kill it before it runs off!" she gasped. "It is our only food!"

Gwynhr paused momentarily between this

command and the desire to bring aid to his wife, but he realized the evident truth of what she said, and, as best he could, picked up some of the heavier nearby stones that he could lift. He then pursued the bear into its very lair, and there, without pause, began hurling rocks forward. There came a great snarling and gnashing of frustration and anger from the blinded bear, but it was in too much pain and too sorely disoriented to produce another onslaught. Gwynhr continued his own, not ceasing to grab and throw stones into the depths of the mountain cave. Some he could hear clack against other stones, but some he heard thump as they met their target. Gwynhr's urgency drove him on, and at last no sound came from the interior of the cave. Gwynhr continued his collection and throwing of stones for some while, to be absolutely certain.

Light dawned at last through a breaking sky. Gwynhr knelt by Justine's side, and pressed cloth upon her wounded scalp, which would not cease its bleeding. "Tend to what is before us," Justine insisted, despite herself. "You must rend the bear before the wild people arrive. We must eat some of it raw, and then flee with the rest, such as we can carry. We cannot stay, our way here is much too apparent."

"You are bleeding, dear," Gwynhr insisted.

"Their cougars shall smell us out, as hungry as the hunters. Give me bear-flesh, and quickly, there's a good dear."

Gwynhr was sweating with uncertainty, but took her meaning. He could feel his heart beat as he entered the interior of the cave and found the bear. It was crippled, but still alive. Gwynhr cut its heart out, and brought it to Justine, then went back to dismember the rest of their opponent with all due speed. First he skinned the monster, to produce sacks for the flesh, then he rent the carcass, and thereby produced a few for all the weight they could carry.

"Hurry now, good lad," Justine affirmed, "and we shall resume our flight. The enemy shall persist in its quest for food. This is the law."

By the light of morning they crawled and slipped down the other side of the ridge, with the unearthly cries of their pursuers in the distance behind them. Below was a riverbed, and the only choice was to follow it from the shielding mountains with all their vantage points, and out into the flatlands again. By the time they reached the ancient creek, which now flowed again with some little drainage (like their food some blessing against the wrath of God), they were gratified, yet also became acutely aware that their persons could now be easily perceived from above. Gwynhr was reaching the last of his fortitude, nearly dizzy and overcome with fatigue from their ordeal, but Justine urged him forward, with unswerving harsh imperatives as to the result of an end to struggle.

Even in the dark, she knew, the smell of blood would lead their pursuers on. It was only after sundown that day that she allowed them one pause to consume more bear meat and rest some little while. Gwynhr was entirely unaccustomed to such exertion.

"There are no two ways," Justine insisted. "You must find more strength. The enemy is swift and fervent with desire."

"When can we sleep again?" Gwynhr gasped. "When shall it be over?"

Justine took pity on her husband. "The way is not clear, except that there is no going back, and no relent from our adversaries. We hurry on, or we are surely doomed."

Alvin tried as best he could to consume the raw flesh, and ate as he was directed. Their loads somewhat lightened, they continued with a rising moon to follow the little creek.

Mountains came and went on either side of them, and for the night they only paused briefly to slake their thirst from the temporary gift of water. At another dawn, they were confronted by another stretching arroyo much like the one they had left, of blazing heat and dry grass, with little to eat. The waterway trickled out into the sandy earth and was absorbed. The last rains to this area had come and went, there would be no more. Behind them they could just ascertain the drifting smoke of the wild people. Gwynhr shook with fear.

Justine shielded her eyes and looked out across the desert. "It's called," she said grimly, "being between the rock and the hard place. I know this direction, it leads back the way I have come, to Salt Lake City. There are other wild people there perhaps, unless they have fed on each other now. Yet there is no other choice, our adversaries will pursue any chance of food such as ourselves, and the way is long..."

"Can we make it, Justine?" Gwynhr asked, thinking more of her survival than his.

"There are the grasses, and locusts, and beetles, and if we are very fortunate, some honeycomb. What is lacking is water. I have dug for water before with success, yet it shall not be much."

"Darling," said Gwynhr, "let me clean your scalp."

"We shall risk a brief moment here, to quench our thirst with all we can, and I shall clean off this blood, and we must take the first flowers to rub on our bodies and so cover our scent. Then we must fly like the wind, and only pause to forage as seems possible and likely. It is a hard road, and if we pause too long from exhaustion, we are caught. Equally, when we find our destination, it will be none to our liking, but there is no retreat: all behind us is now the possession of the wild people; but I know which stars shall guide us: we shall travel by night as well as day, only in so doing will we not be outpaced. Behind us are the hunters of the

Wilderland, and they are swift."

Thence they journeyed outwards into blazing heat and, at Justine's constant urging, did not pause for several days, eating bear-flesh even as they made their way over the rolling arroyos. Occasional sounds of cougar echoed across the rolling expanse to goad them forwards. At last, in one early morning, Justine had them pause.

"Here is some grass with some green in it," she said. "I will dig for water here." After more than a week's sleepless exertion, Gwynhr collapsed. He dreamed of the wild man they had seen in the forest, of knotted hair and painted with elderberry juice and mud, and he dreamed of the mans cougar, which prowled at the edge of his imagination, and finally, before waking, he dreamed of the bear, and the instinctual fight for survival that had emboldened him. When he awoke, it was as though his nightmares had not ceased. It was only then that Gwynhr began to perceive into the heart of Justine's genius, into the unrelenting nature of a fight for survival against the odds, driven by cunning and canniness and a constitution bred of many years of hard living, grief, toil, and uncertainty. Gwynhr doubted his own qualities, and thought of offering himself to her as food, but his love for her was such that even this seemed selfish, for the one thing a being truly starves from is lack of love, he realized then.

That morning they ate the last of the bear, and

refreshed themselves somewhat upon a minimum of muddy water which Justine had dug. She had not slept.

The torrid heat of the Slat Flats of Utah coursed down from an ineffable sky, unrelenting, but equally unrelenting was the chase into this vast furnace: the one certainty of the wild people was that they would not abandon the possibility of food, and so their campfires flickered behind Justine and Alvin in the night, and drove the couple onwards.

"Once," Justine spoke in a hush at night, "Salt Lake City was a swampy marsh, but those were the days of the rain. By now, all is gravel and broken glass. We can only hope there are some edible provisions left, although perishable goods must long since have become tainted. Perhaps there shall be some remaining wild things to hunt. When my father died there were still rats and hounds and such things."

Gwynhr was hardly emboldened by his success with the bear, rather he was more distressed by such necessities, and his empty belly groaned and creaked and longed for something substantial. Weeks went by with only raw insects to eat, as they could not pause to roast the few locusts and beetles they found. Twice they had discovered a lizard which Justine managed to catch, but Gwynhr insisted she have them. After some debate she gave in, although Gwynhr was steadily wasting away.

Behind them, the wild people were finally consuming their tamed cougars and renewing their own energy for the hunt.

The outskirts of Salt Lake City were as nothing Gwynhr had imagined. The ticky-tack dwellings of suburbia stretched over the broken pavement towards burned-out tenements. In the distance, the one sight most prominent to behold was the Mormon Tabernacle, which still mainly stood as a testament to a distant past enshrouded in the lost memories of people now dead long since. Gwynhr stumbled along next to his wife in a daydream, trying but failing to comprehend the lives such people must have lived. There was no sign of movement, not even a breeze.

Eventually, they came to an old AM-PM mini-market, but found the goods long-since salvaged by the desperate, not even a can of dog food remained. Scattered about the place were various skeletons of some of the competitors.

"We shall not easily find food here," Justine indicated, "but there are good tidings: the sewers must still have rats, and we can use a few insects to bait and catch. This we must accomplish with all haste, or be surrounded. With what we have caught, we shall have some glimmer of hope, of which I will show you, but before I get your hopes up, we must seek out guns that are still operable. For this, we have at most merely a few hours."

Upon finding the police station, they discovered

no guns, but they did find a phone book that was not past total decay, and they were thus able to locate gun stores. All were looted. In a growing frenzy, they searched house to house, apartment to apartment, seeking the security devices of individuals. Along the way they were able to collect some knives, and found valuable clothing to replace their own tattered robes. Justine retired her bearskin, for a pair of cotton pants and a light blouse. Gwynhr caught her making some light murmurs of respect as she discarded her well-used former appearance.

Finally, in the run-down shackle of a last survivor, hidden amongst a pile of empty food tins, they discovered their goal: a Colt revolver with leftover rounds. Justine threw her arms about Gwynhr in an unexpected embrace.

They rushed to a likely looking sewer and pried open the rusty lid, and baited some hooks with beetles, and waited. Soon, in the distance, they could hear the howls of the wild people, who were committing strange rituals upon discovering this unfamiliar territory, but Justine urged Gwynhr to be patient, for this, temporarily, was the only option available.

As foreign, cruel cries drew nearer, their first bait succeeded, and they had caught a wizened old rat that nevertheless had some flesh on it. Justine urged more tolerance, and soon another rat was caught; but the war-cries approached.

"We do not have more time," Justine stated, herself growing quite nervous. "I will show you what we do."

She took Gwynhr's hand and they raced through the ruins towards the Mormon Tabernacle, past junk-heaps and old fires of melted tires and old bones flung carelessly aside by the starving. The stained-glass windows were long since disintegrated by heat, yet most of the old church structure stood, and Justine knew where they might find temporary refuge. The altar had been looted for wood, but behind, she knew from her father's report, was a compartment for the chief priest, an adytum. This, too, was looted, bereft of all the vestments and candles, yet intact was the priests toilet-chamber. She pulled Gwynhr inside and bolted the heavy door. With a rare look of futility, Justine turned the tap on the sinks faucet. Rusty brown water trickled forth. "There is yet some reservoir!" Justine breathed with relief. Gwynhr kissed her on the cheek. "Let us roast the rats, and replenish ourselves. We must wait here as holdouts until the wild people are done looting. This is as much concealment as we shall find."

With the opportunity, they sat down and gnawed at the roasted rats, and drank as much of the water as they wished for, as they had not done in weeks. They bathed and scrubbed the sweat-soaked sand from their skin and eyes, and inspected each other's emaciation. "We're quite as thin as those rats," Gwynhr managed to joke.

"Yes, and we shall only have water indefinitely. For now we load that gun, and then we shall sleep."

Their newfound shelter received some light from a high window, and the sun's rays came and went a number of times while they were both deep in slumber. Gwynhr dreamed of a bear who became a beautiful red-haired woman, a queen of both night and day. On the fourth day, they were awakened by calls going back and forth outside the tabernacle.

Justine put her finger to her lips, and they pause as the calls continued. Gwynhr reached for their pistol, but then handed it to Justine, as she was the surer shot. They awaited for some noise upon their door, and soon there came a loud banging, but the hinges and bolt remained sturdy, and, it seemed, the wild people without had decided there was little use in the effort, for although they could readily grasp the notion of a cache of food, they did not comprehend a bolted door, or that anything of value might lie within. To them it looked like a wall. Their calls receded into the distance as they continued their own hunt for food, and for those they had pursued.

Justine breathed again. "Despite the rats in the sewers, the wild people will soon think this area is depleted of food. They might follow some byway until they meet with an Interstate freeway, and attempt to make their way to foodstuffs, but unless I miss my guess this band shall soon turn on each other in hunger and frustration. We shall stay here with our rusty water for a week until we must exit for food. At least we shall be armed with the gun."

Over the course of the week some screams of acrimony did reach their ears, as the wild people argued among themselves who was responsible for leading them on a futile pursuit. The weaker of the people were collectively sacrificed for food, and the stronger made their way further into the Desolations to hunt, yet this would prove a quest with only one end: starvation. Radioactivity and competition had by then greatly depleted nature for hundreds of miles, until the distant coastline again furnished foodstuffs. Justine knew this as well, although she did not tell Alvin.

The pair emerged and began fishing for rats, yet this, too, was a limited supply, Justine knew. Gwynhr perceived the necessity, however, and together, back at the adytum, they would take their fill sufficient for survival. Justine was waiting for Gwynhr's strength to return. After a few weeks she decided to explain the situation.

"Gwynhr, my dear heart, we cannot stay here," she revealed, and kissed him for the first time on the lips. Justine took Gwynhr's hand. "Sometimes in life there is no going back, and little means forward. Yet every lost road means to go on searching."

"I shall never forget Jack, or the abbess, or my poor abbey," Gwynhr told Justine, "but I shall always remember that I am here with you."

Justine flushed with desire for life and fear of death. "The secret word is love," she said, and then the pair remained silent awhile. The ineffable sky, at once containing life and death, turned to grey.

CHAPTER FIVE:
THE COMING OF BABYLON

Justine and her father Barnaby were in the early morning dawn, sitting about dying embers. Before the Days of No Rain, Salt Lake City was a teeming marsh. They were surrounded by the tell-tale calls of frogs and toads and crickets, but they were especially awaiting any noise from larger creatures, such as the slimy swamp-bear, or a man. Barnaby's eyebrows bristled over the wafting smoke of his deer-antler pipe. It was the last of his precious supply of tobacco.

He kept his manual harpoon at the ready, and Justine remained mindful of torches from the embers. But no extraordinary supplies met their ears. The morning sky was slowly breaking, to reveal the evidence of sight once again. The dawn was the most dangerous time, when the risk of the hunt was most likely to be applied. They themselves had stockpiled provisions such as insects, mice, and a solitary marmot. They were nearly prepared for a full retreat back to their concrete bunker in the undergrowth about a mile away.

Yet no retreat could come, as, following the wispy yet apparent smoke from their dying fire, creatures from an alien world were about to arrive. First, there came an unfamiliar slogging and sloshing from the surrounding marsh, which father and daughter could only guess at. What it was was naturally indecipherable, the sound of a few last operational mechanical vehicles, army tanks whose batteries had been shielded by lead from the Electro-Magnetic Pulses. Barnaby, as rustic as he was, still had old night terrors about terrible serpentine swamp monsters which slithered and crawled amidst the mysterious jungle. He raised his harpoon to full vigilance. What was to next meet their ears was worse than his nightmares: an ancient recorded mechanical voice delivered the last lines of a dead civilization: "You are now in the possession of the United States military."

"Run, girl, and don't stop running!" Barnaby indicated to his daughter. We are fatal outmatched. I shall act as a ruse." He handed Justine the harpoon and shoved the carcass of the marmot towards her, and collapsed back to wait. Without further diraction, the eleven-year-old Justine had to pause, remembering the brief time surviving alone which her father had shown her, remembering the nearby bunker, remembering the uncertainty in a world of survival of the fittest. She clutched the harpoon and marmot and began to run desperately. A torrent of a blizzard swept in from the North, mercifully shielding her footsteps. She did not know where she was running, but it was towards the Desolations, ironically the only place to survive. The sound of motors would sound in the distance, the haunting, alien remnants of a militarization now almost reduced to the very few bands of people who had not turned on eachother in wrath and retribution.

The marmot was soon consumed, and the harpoon useless with nothing to fire upon, as there came the Days of No Rain. Justine's imagination could not contain her plight, as barely enduring she taught herself and discovered the ways of foraging in the Desolations, in the Wilderland where hardly anything grew or lived. Shivering in the night, she would hum childrens verses to herself, and sing snatches of song, alone, the only person within a hundred miles. Sometimes, searching through culverts for water, her sounds would echo back to her lightly, gently, like from a world she had never known. Her red hair curled and flowed, but eventually all she came to know was a flight and a fight for survival, and only one person: Justine.

CHAPTER SIX:
THE WAXING GIBBOUS

Gwynhr had listened to Justine's story with horror, and inklings of his own recent terrors and deprivations. He tried to think of ways to console her.

"At least we have these two bycicles," he said, and the mere sound of his voice eased her mourning somewhat and returned her to her new-found humanity.

"One day we may find flowing streams," she sighed, halfway between optimism and despair, "yet it is my belief that the rain is caught on the other side of distant mountains. And you cannot ride a bicycle and forage for locusts at the same time."

"No, that would be difficult," Gwynhr agreed. He offered her a roasted rat, and ran some rusty water into a pail for her bath. "We are caught between serendipity and a void."

"You speak truly, for it was ever thus for humankind," replied Justine. "And here we sit as their exemplars, running low on rats, with wild people possibly roaming about, and no place to get to that we know." But she would not give up. "We must learn those bicycles."

The weather that day was 120 degrees in the shade, but they pulled their creaky, rusted, and bent bicycles, bereft of tires, out under a blazing sun, onto the cracked and broken gravel, to attempt to achieve balance. It was difficult, and required a lot of swerving. When they had strapped their meagre provisions upon the bicycles, it proved even more difficult. Gwynhr turned to Justine to see if she knew how comical they must seem, and she took the meaning of his look, although morbidity had almost overpowered lightness in recent weeks. Justine decided to let Gwynhr play, although in fact their prospects had barely improved. Gwynhr seemed to easily forget mortality, but it was one thing Justine could not forget. The other was Gwynhr.

Interstate I-80 was nearly overcome with sand, but a trail could be found to be visible. Justine knew that behind any sand dune wild people might lurk, and herself carried the gun, a fiercesome symbol of mutilation and treachery that had become perhaps the most valuable of objects.

They had begun their trek at night, with the light of the new moon to guide them. They had left behind a few surviving rats, their only known supply of water, and all the remnant trappings of what once was a teeming metropolis of people, now long since a graveyard, like so many townships down throughout the ages that had come to ruin. They took with them a supply of cooked rats, four tins of rusty water, and some small hope against the odds to keep them alive.

The wild people were lurking, although not many. Lack of food and water had reduced them once again to feeding on eachother, until only the hardiest remained, unable to carry on, but only able to lurk behind a sand dune, each one consumed by the utterly miserable frustration and suspicion that the other two thought him to be food. As a waxing gibbous moon was rising, the wild people could hear far off the sign of rusty gears creaking away, as Justine and Alvin manuevered their bent rims over crumbling gravel. The wild people knew the sounds could not be Nature, and therefore must be Man. They sharpened their sticks in the newly illuminated nighttime.

While Gwynhr labored away awkwardly, all of Justine's senses were alerted to the faintest forensic tracery, as bred by years of a hard life. In the past, the moon had been her closest friend and deadliest enemy. This night held the lightest of breezes, and so the moon was her friend, as she could just descry an unnatural flow of sand along the ground dead ahead. She gestured to Gwynhr frantically to stop, and so they abandoned their bicycles in the road and made cover in the most convenient ditch from which they could still observe the bicycles.

A pall of silence fell over the scene as the waxing gibbous rose, and the wild men nearly snarled in vexation, yet knew themselves to remain absolutely silent. It was stalemate, except that Justine and Gwynhr had taken of food and drink, whereas the wild people were threatened with encroaching starvation: they must be the ones to make the first move, and, the wild people knew, it was safer to do in the relative darkness, although

they strongly suspected their position had been given away somehow.

The wild people crept forward diagonally towards the last sound, just peering over the edge of Interstate I-80. Soon, they could make out the features of the abandoned bicycles, but they could no betray themselves and approach openly. It was stalemate again.

Gwynhr's negative anticipation was getting the better of him, after their long flight from these savage and hostile peoples, but he remained absolutely silent on account of Justine, who nudged him in his ribs. She herself was at the ready, with the Colt revolver and six shots poised upon the scene of the bicycles.

However, the three wild men slithered along the sandy ground towards the conveyances, and, moving low, did not make good targets in the moonlight. Justine was in another predicament, as was her lot: if the wild men were able to make off with the provisions, Gwynhr and her would be truly stranded, and doomed to die in the desert heat, and she did not want to pierce a cannister of water with a shot, but make them all true and find their marks.

The gibbous moon shone down. Justine could just espy a tin of water being slowly lifted. She did not know how many opponents she had, she only knew that she must be offensive, so she leapt up for greater vantage and released all six bullets towards the bicycles, as the only known target, and the voice of the gun cracked the desert air of the night.

A few snarls were emitted, and then one thrashing wild man, keen on the direction of the alien noise, came hurtling upon the pair with two pointed sticks and a javelin.

"The bullets, Gwynhr! Where are the rest of the bullets?!" It was too late. The javelin pierced Justine's right shoulder. Gwynhr was awakened as though he had been asleep, with a quickened sense of alarm that could barely contain a reaction. His instinct took hold of him, as it had done with the bear in the mountains, and he flashed sand upwards into the wild mans eyes. Throbbing in Gwynhr's heart was his love for Justine, and even as the wild man snarled with temporary blindness Gwynhr yelled as loudly and terrifyingly as he could, despite himself, and in the half-light grabbed each of the wild mans wrists, and produced his opportunity: he butted with his head to the wild mans nose, and then in the next few moments that this gave Gwynhr, he tore at the savages grasp upon the sticks, and won. The predator was now the prey, and, contrary to the genteel and pastoral life he had known, and the very ground he had walked on as a child, Gwynhr thrust forwards with both weapons until the savage lay dead on the ground.

Gwynhr stood, splattered with his opponents blood, as though looking at a mirage. No further snarls were heard, but as though from some dim twilight world Gwynhr heard Justine moan: she lay prone with the javelin clear through her shoulder. Alvin felt almost as though his own life was slipping away. Nothing in his upbringing held forth for these eventualities, yet he did what he must: he placed one hand on Justine's shoulder and grabbed the javelin with the other, and pulled. Then he tore part of his sleeve and contrived a tight bandage.

He kissed Justine's forehead, and, confused and dazed by this living nightmare, still managed to whisper, "It will be all right. I love you." Gwynhr waited by her side, but she would not awaken.

At last the gibbous moon was setting, but was replaced by a still more glaring uncertainty and doubt, the tremendous, overwhelming heat of the desert sun.

A scene of vicious carnage was revealed. Justine's six bullets had killed outright the other two mad people, which had enraged the third to an adrenalin frenzy. Yet, this one lay quite dead himself from Gwynhr's onslaught. Gwynhr held his knees together and wept with fear for Justine, and then tried to get her to accept a little water, but she barely swallowed. He covered her with a lean-to of their old blankets, protecting her from the direct sun, and tried to do as she would and think of a plan of action. At least her blood had clotted, and the javelin had missed her heart.

Gwynhr was as though alone, and the heat of the sun and the heat of his passion made him feel like he was evaporating. The only solution occured to him then: he must roast the dead wild people before they spoiled, and feed Justine back to strength. Gwynhr set flint to the tinder of another old manuscript, and went about a gruesome performance, using the knives they had foraged in Salt Lake City: he dissected all three bodies carefully, and threw them on a blaze, while suppressing his natural revulsion at the task with thoughts of Justine.

Justine seemed to be in a deep trance, and would not awake, as though possessed of a penultimate denouement, the natural realization of an ultimate truth, that the fight for survival against such unlikely odds has only one natural conclusion: defeat, a physical failing of one sort or another that resolves the matter at last. She could not be roused.

After the fourth day from the skirmish her eyes flickered, and Gwynhr, ever watchful, said, "Eat! You must eat!" and raised her slightly so that she may. After several bites and a few sips of water she moaned again, and then again passed out.

Gwynhr huddled there awaiting the worst, the arrival of more wild people and/or Justine's demise. The moon began to wane into a crescent, and slowly, ever so slowly, Justine would take in more food and drink, as though some secret indomitability of strength yet rested deep within her. Gwynhr ate and drank only enough to sustain himself.

CHAPTER SEVEN:
DREAMERS, AWAKE!

Justine was hot and feverish. A restless sleep brought with it fitful dreams. She never would dream of stores or malls or things from a civilization she had never known, but she would dream of endless vistas, winds of sand, and a long marching from nowhere into nowhere, and she would dream of water, lots of water, such as the lake in the mountains which Gwynhr and she had been forced to abandon. Sometimes she would dream of people she had never met, who lingered on the edge of imagination like a distant fog off the coast. This night in the desert furnace she dreamt of one such person, a little girl with bright cerulean eyes. The girl came to her and took her hand and said, "I want you to know something..." Then Justine awoke, and she was under a blanket lean-to looking at a thin setting crescent. A torment of pain shot from her right shoulder, and her right arm was partially paralyzed.

Gwynhr had allowed himself some sleep, despite vigilance. He dreamt of Jack the hermit, who said through his honeycomb, "Life is what happens to you and life is what you make it. It's both. The ultimate ruler depends, it depends on..." Then Gwynhr awoke.

Gwynhr would go in and out of fitful sobbing, which came and went with a sense of doom, and a heart doomed to love, and these fits could hardly exhaust themselves. He often wondered how Justine had gone on in the face of peril and uncertainty. That morning, he lifted Justine's head for her to sip water, and said, "You must eat all you can. The heat has nearly spoiled our supplies..,"

Justine could speak a little. "Go on yourself, Gwynhr. I can barely move my arm."

Gwynhr shook his head with obstinancy and finality, all of such that he owned. "I have made a sled of blankets. I will drag you to a new home."

"You are a good lad, Gwynhr. Take me home," Justine replied.

It was as if a toil once begun must be resumed anew. What then began for Gwynhr as a nightmare of physical exertion turned into a torture of hunger. He had Justine drink the last water. Far in the distance, yet, Gwynhr could begin to descry distant mountains rising into a smoky murk. Alvin knew that if he collapsed, their journey would then end. He had watched Justine persevere, and had been her companion in perseverance. His muscles ached and his eyes nearly closed, demanding sleep, but the mountains loomed nearer as a hope for life, and he wobbled onwards, awkwardly but without flagging. Yet he knew of the nearly paradoxical uncertainty: the mountains might contain only death.

Nature was forgiving, barely, once more. Even as Gwynhr was perishing, and Justine was sobbing with groans of pain and hunger, nature relented as they reached the western edge of the desert: a trickling rill from the highest ridge there faded into the savage furnace. Gwynhr first splashed Justine with water many times, to provide her refreshment and relief, if not bring her fever down, for the water was warm. Then Gwynhr filled a tin and virtually poured water down Justine's throat, and then, and only then, would he take his own fill. They both fell deeply asleep.

CHAPTER EIGHT:
NATURES DUAL WAYS

Whereas nature can be forgiving, nature can be cruel, and a human, in the end, is always fragile. Whether or not it was the end was in doubt: Justine's wounds had become infected in the desert heat on both side of her pierced right shoulder.

"Justine, wake up! There is a terrible problem, you must wake up!"

"Gwynhr, my love, where are we?"

"We are near mountains to the West. But your shoulder..."

Justine shivered despite the heat. "It can't be well."

"Justine, what do I do?! Tell me, quickly!"

"You must dig the infection out, then put dust in the wound."

"There is dust here, Justine! There are rotten old logs, and lots of dust. But, I.."

"Gwynhr, be strong, and I shall get better."

Gwynhr felt faint with horror. Yet, Justine was adamant. Gwynhr wept and trembled and could not do it.

"Gwynhr, it is that or the gun."

"I understand, Justine, but dear God!" Gwynhr had only heard of God through a few books, but it was enough to swear by. Yet, the powers that be were of no aid, only prying instruments and pointed sticks.

"What you must do, do it swiftly," Justine abjured.

"What I must do I shall do swiftly," Gwynhr assured her.

At some point amidst cries of agony and howls to her own gods, the gods of wind and water and earth and stars, and abiding superstitions of the afterlife, the Mysterious, the Ineffable, Justine collapsed into a faint from pain. Gwynhr listened nervously at her heart, and then continued his wretched task. The infection was still traceable, and after rinsing with mountain water he clotted the two holes with dust as instructed. Justine lay there and would not move.

The bicycle was useless in the new terrain. Gwynhr despaired. He had three bullets left. It crossed his mind then to end their suffering at last, but this, Gwynhr knew, was to betray the sacrosanct, and deny utterly that there was something worth living for. Gwynhr was compelled by forces that would not yield: Justine had been her helpmeet, his observer, his fortitude, his life. Her will had become his will, a product of childhood abandonment and total reliance on oneself. Gwynhr filled his stomach from the little brook, and taking the gun, left Justine's side, and ran, ran up the culvert of boulders, scrambling, striving for new territory, striving for any sustenance. He had bound Justine's wounds tightly, but his own fears would never leave him.

The way was rough and untrod for centuries. Once, when there had been more water in the bed, tourists had lunched there, children had played, transistor radios had jangled big band music from Airstream motor homes. There had been watermelon, peanut and jelly sandwiches, and Hershey's chocolate bars. Now the water was clear, but no one played, not even a water-spider in a pool.

The night was clear and warm, no clouds reached this area either, which, had he known, Gwynhr would perhaps call the Rocky Mountains. However, in only a meagre handful of months, even what he called things had been transformed, and he could not think even of the sun, moon, or stars in the same way, he was a creature of Desolations. Yet inside part of Gwynhr remained the same, so entirely timid that he had not even a quiet dignity, only reserve.

CHAPTER NINE:
WHILE HOPE REMAINS

Justine could hardly be said to have any ego, either. Part of her was the 11-year-old who had become separated from her father, and in other ways she was an ultimate adult, despite an abandonment to a cruel wilderness of dead roads, and the abiding loneliness of a seeming eternity of lack and deprivation, and the hollow laughter of nature as it continually ceased to provide. Justine had no confidence, only willfulness, and the intimations from 20 years of running that she could be yet conquer the void and the frugality of nature. She knew that she was what was hunted for, and she feared, so much that she feared herself.

She had tried to use the stars to guide her, like a mariner. Yet it was calls from the wilderness that had driven her on. Eventually she learned from familiarity with landmarks that she was journeying in wide circles When she met Gwynhr it was her deepest suspicion at the time that she had at last been found out by evil, and so she had feigned confidence in Gwynhr's story of his old abbey remaining undiscovered for generations, and that Jack the hermit lived in his forest refuge undisturbed. It was a coincidence of rare device: unbeknownst to them humanity was feeding upon each other, and they were like the proverbial island in the midst of a storm protected only by the circumnavigation of the outside peoples, like eddies in a stream.

Justine was awakened next to the stream by tickling and itching, at night under the piercing distant lamps of the stars on the flowing Milky Way: she was crawling with ants. She could not use her right arm, but with her left, filled with craving, she began picking off the ants and eating them. She found a filled canister of warm water by her side.

Gwynhr continued crawling up into the mountains. He came to an area of pathways, dotted with hermitages of piled stones yet empty: food for these people had dried out long ago, and they had trekked to the West to the other side of the mountains.

At last, following the creek he came to a small patch of meadow that was not desiccated. His weakness was temporarily overcome by his urgency and I haste, still foreign emotions, yet running truer than blood.

He found much of the grass dry, yet new seeds borne aloft by the wind had landed here. Using one of his knives he cut down anything with even a hint of green. Although he had only a modest knowledge of botany, he scrounged into the earth by some likely looking sprouts, and recovered a scarce few wild scallions and tubers. At this he felt his first release since fishing for rats in Salt Lake City, but his present decision loomed over him, for his supply was not enough. However he knew he must go on if Justine was to go on and so he chewed madly at some of his find, which somewhat delayed the mad desire of near starvation. And with this modest supply of food present he suspected some living animals, accidental strays from some richer areas, might be present. He had three shots left in the revolver, and Justine's slingshot. A solid suspicion came over him regarding any animals nearby, that they must not be diurnal, but nocturnal. He ground-up one tuber and left it upon a prominent stone, and used a trick Justine had taught him: a weak stick propping I heavy stone. Without knowing the slingshot well, especially at night, his other recourse was the gun, a remnant of man's deadly force that had proved so handy, an irony that was not lost on Gwynhr. The three remaining bullets were ever so precious.

A half-moon rose upon the scene, and Gwynhr remained motionless, and silent, although only partially concealed from sight, and, too, he suspected any wild animal to have a keen sense of smell, but hoped hunger would be his friend. Sometime before dawn a field mouse disturbed the stick, and was trapped beneath the stone. Gwynhr could hear its squeals. Yet still he waited, with baited breath, for some wilder prey to alight upon the trapped mouse.

Light was just dim in the East when an ever so soft padding reached Gwynhr's ears. He surveyed the circumstance around him to determine if he himself was the prey. However, his foreign scent alerted the starving lone wolf, who presently could be seen by the squealing mouse, its fangs dripping hungrily, the saliva glinting like dew in the light of the setting moon. Gwynhr found the head in the sites and only needed to fire once, a staccato which echoed and reverberated up the surrounding canyons.

Life head again become life, death was, at least for now, staved off by mysterious fortune, by another scant yielding of harsh nature. Gwynhr knew his trail back down the trickling rill, yet did not have the strength to carry his newfound provisions. He quickly carved out the heart and liver and brains of the foreign animal and chewed away with the breaking of the heat of the sun. He tied the rest of the carcass plus his mouse and scallions and tubers and grasses into the bundle of his warm shirt and preceded away downhill dragging his abundance, such as it was, and praying to sun and moon that Justine was still alive.

CHAPTER TEN:
NONE TOO SOON

Gwynhr found Justine the next day, alive yet passed out into a deep dreamless slumber as though on the edge of death. Making as little waste as possible, he skinned the wolf and mouse and diced the scallions and tubers and made flame with their final crumbling manuscript. He set a canister of water to the flames and in not too much time had food such as he and Justine had not known, a hardy stock for revival.

They were both near starvation. They were not quite anorexic, they could still absorb nutrition. Justine had lost her wiry strength to inactivity, but she was not yet senseless from her ordeals. Gwynhr propped her up on pillows of blankets, and hand fed her from this tin of stew until a hearty broth remained which he had her drink without delay. For himself he strapped another canister of tin upon his back. Each knew what was necessary: Gwynhr was in no condition to carry Justine over the tumbled rocks. Yet each was renewed bodily and in spirit, and they spoke in low tones together before he had to leave again.

"You must climb higher, Gwynhr, and find fishing grounds if there are such."

"I would leave you with the rest of this stew, and these final two bullets in our pistol. There may be wolves. I shall take your slingshot and some sticks. May providence will out." Gwynhr knew Justine needed much sleep, but he said, "Be on guard." They kissed for only the second time on the lips, and gave each other warm smiles of encouragement and hope, and so parted again. Gwynhr reached his meadow once more, and peered up at the approaching mountains. He attempted to deduce proper direction in the knowledge that there must be some small patch of snow on his side of the mountains to feed this rill, and he judged by the slopes and curves of the mountains where a lake might lie. High above him he saw the turkey vultures wheeling, and the redtailed hawk, but far, far out of reach. He knew, however, that there must be more mice, and so he baited his trail from the stew, complete with snares.

Out behind him Gwynhr saw the vast expanse of desert over which they had traveled, and he felt the air cool a bit, so that the weather was balmy without being burning. Gwynhr followed his watery guide higher and higher, until some peaks lay below him, and the temperature was nearly mild. Climbing over a bluff he discovered a marshy lake. He sank to his knees and thanked and thanked providence, even as he wept bitter tears over Justine's injury. As at the former mountains before their arrival in Salt Lake City, he heard at this lake frogs and toads and crickets, and to what a former man might consider so much sludge and slime was before Gwynhr the vital algae of the marsh and an abundant source of food. Across on the other side he could spy just a few marshbirds fishing in the shallows. To Gwynhr this was a paradise of relief. There were even a few pines full of cones, as at Jack's old forest, which had at times seemed like a distant dream, but was yet a memory like a child clings to like their blanket. Yet above all was the thought of his beloved, who he knew like the sky yet did not know, but whom he was determined to save: he would devise a sling of blankets and haul her up the broken trail.

He ate the last of his stew, and took great gulps of the slimy marsh water, and filled his empty canister from the algae-rich lake and proceeded not to hesitate, but clambered downwards hoping some of his snares had found prey, desperately eager to see Justine's face again. He became consumed with the desire to reach the marsh with her, and it even began to dawn on him, slowly, that there might be verdant land on the opposite side of the mountains, where rains fell.

Justine had decided to remain alert just in case, with the pistol ready with its two shots. Indeed, in a night without a moon she heard the crying of the wolf echo from somewhere. She maintained the pistol raised in her good left arm, knowing she was scented by this foreign beast. The moonless night made shadows seem to take shape as though living things. Suddenly from the gloom lept an attacker, and the two shots were fired. The body of the dead wolf slumped upon her. With some difficulties she shrugged it off and cut out it's tongue to feed upon.

Several days later Gwynhr arrived at Justine's camp and found her lying naked in the little stream. He blushed exceedingly at the blaze of red hair and diverted his eyes.

"Justine," Gwynhr stammered, "I've made it back with good news!" Yet Justine was asleep. Gwynhr stared a long time without fathoming her nudity, until he decided it was against all propriety to continue.

He discovered the body of the wolf, and set to dismembering it, along with several mice he had caught. When Justine awoke, he did not look at her dry herself in a blanket, but waited until she sat before the fire he had made from crumbled leaves, even as darkness began to fall. Justine squatted with her right arm limp and useless beside her.

"Justine," Gwynhr began again, "there is exceeding good news. I see you have triumphed over this wolf, dear. Soon we shall enjoy natures triumph. It is only several days away for me, but you are too weak, so it shall be more, but I shall carry you to a beautiful marsh where we may rest a while. And I suspect there is a land of rain not too,distant."

"You are a faithful husband, Gwynhr," Justine replied, thinking of the almond tree under which they were betrothed. "Perhaps, without going to the Great Beyond, there is yet an end to strife. I will let you carry me."

"We must still be judicious with her food," said Gwynhr, "but perhaps for a time nature shall abate in its cruelty. It is a watering hole, so we must expect the animals, but perhaps this, too, is to our benefit." Gwynhr did not mention that he had seen Justine nude, and he struggled with the dilemma of conflicting desires and portents, and he also thought of the almond tree. Justine watched his face and knew what he was thinking and smiled inwardly to herself. Yet neither would mention it.

They did not sleep, but ate most of the night away, and Gwynhr said how brave Justine was, and she in turn kissed Gwynhr on the cheek, and said he had learned and done much. In the morning, Gwynhr wrapped Justine's useless arm in a sling so it would not dangle, and created of their blankets a truss for her weight, which had dwindled even more, such that, leaning forward, Gwynhr could just manage her weight, and one canteen for water and cooking. The way would be slow, as Gwynhr had to climb forward but also avoid jostling Justine, whose wound was just beginning to heal. Justine wept a little along the way, but concealed this from Gwynhr, and would not let him know what she was thinking.

The way was slow, as Gwynhr scraped his way forward gingerly over the tumbled and strewn boulders of the little culvert, which had been left in their places since the last great time of ice, an age which would never come again. Justine frequently fell asleep, deeply, dreamlessly, as though as one in the swaddling clothes of a babe. Gwynhr was fixated upon their destination, and the next supply of food. Days passed this way, until finally they reach the bluff overlooking the marsh.

"Alvin, are you tired?" Justine asked sleepily.

"We are here," Gwynhr said softly.

"Where are we?" Justine again asked.

"We are at the lake, dear. I must set you down now."

"That is okay. I will sleep," Justine replied. Yet the day was getting late, and Alvin needed her.

"Justine, you must awaken and show me what to do!"

"I am awake. Set me down, I can see now. I know what to do."

So Justine began to show Gwynhr how to build a stony igloo of sorts, similar to the dome they had seen together when they first met a wild man. She showed him how to place stones together so that there weight would form a roof, and she showed him how one might, once within, stack stones together to conceal them in the chamber. She could not lift, but Gwynhr took to the idea and built, even allowing a cleft above for smoke to seep through. He also hollowed out a niche within and lined it with old leaves, so that he might boil water for

Justine to soak in. When he had boiled water sufficient, he left her to bait their few strings and fasten them to old sticks, and wait for a bite.

Salmon that had run upstream on the opposite of the ridge appeared plentiful. While Justine slept in her bath Gwynhr made many catches, also of frogs and toads. Other warier predators, Gwynhr could not resist. He felt an ultimate surge of delight and relief, and in the morning would awaken Justine to a veritable feast of seafood.

In the new light of day Gwynhr brought in his larder of gifts, expecting Justine to be quite asleep in the bath. However, when he ducked into the small igloo, Justine was lying quite nude by a small fire. Gwynhr had hardly had any notion of nuptial responsibility, however.

"Remember our marriage under the almond tree," Justine said softly. Alvin found himself completely at a loss, without guile or boldness of any sort. "Do not worry, it can wait," said Justine, although she seemed to prefer to lay nude as they dined upon the various delicacies of the catch.

CHAPTER ELEVEN:
FARE THEE WELL

Whereas Gwynhr had been used to it not long before, the abundance of food was a revelation to Justine, although she had often pondered how good lots of salmon might be.

The next day brought a renewed strength mutually, and a few floating wisps of clouds as a good omen and portent of further riches. They were acutely aware, however, that a food supply implied possible competition, yet, apart from a few migrant birds, no wild things encroached upon this little marshy lake high up near the crest of ridges. The air was balmy and the time to discuss matters long.

"Gwynhr, this cannot last forever," Justine revealed. "Our ultimate destination must the on the other side, where there is rain." She sat by the shore on a sandbar, chewing most excellently. "One day soon I must stay here and you must go on an exploratory expedition."

"It is not safe to leave you," Gwynhr insisted.

"My arm, Gwynhr, I cannot move my arm, although you attended and well, my love. My ability to climb is compromised, and I would slow you down. You must go for our future. Travel only by night, for the animals by night are less risky than any humans by day, as far as I understand. Until you do, though, practice with my slingshot."

"Justine, I love you. I cannot bear the uncertainty."

"We do not know everything about each other," Justine pointed out, "but my dear mama, when I was very little, said once that it is easier to get to know another than to know yourself. Gwynhr, you have proven stronger than you thought."

"I do not feel strong. It is my love for you that is strong."

"All of that is settled, for I love you too,"

"Is there a place in the world for us, Justine?"

"Ha ha," laughed Justine unexpectedly. "A pair of starcrossed lovers. There has never been a place in the world for us, Gwynhr. I read it in no a book I found somewhere."

"The world was made for us," declared Gwynhr.

"This is not a world of everlasting bread and wine and honey comb, Gwynhr."

"Without eachother we should both be dead, or slaves," Gwynhr noted. "Perhaps luck comes in flashes from someplace we cannot see."

"One does not know when one will find it, but apart from your abbey I've only known a world that is wild, and only occasionally forgives."

"I shall always remember the poor abbey," replied Gwynhr, and he shivered. "We live in a world that is hostile, indeed. Yet whereas I shall never forget the abbey, I shall always remember that I'm with you, and when we were are apart my thought shall always be to return to you."

Smoke swirled out from their campfire by the lake, for anybody to see for miles around. Yet it seemed to them that they were so far undetected at this refuge. The more improved Gwynhr became with Justine's slingshot, the more he thought of the few birds that could be seen in the opposite shallows, and the unusual geese became a part of Gwynhr's obsession. For long hours he practiced knocking little stones off of larger stones, until Justine had to laugh and applaud.

Gwynhr's world had been so circumscribed, so narrow, so habitual and small, that Justine had to show him how to pull the feathers from the bird he had finally won. His bird not only added to their strengths, it bolstered their confidence. Justine was still cautionary, however.

"Except for the lucky animal, the land is one of Dead Roads. The humans have created dead things. My poor mama passed away mysteriously when I was five. Papa had stockpiled books for many years, said it was some sort of virus, yet I still don't know what a virus is, except what is invisible may have more power than the known. We know very little." Justine continued chewing.

Gwynhr paused. "I know that I love you, and that you are loving and kind, and when you blush your little red freckles stand out about your button nose. It was when first we met, and you were in your bearskin, I thought you might be a devil. I learned early on that you were just not well. You were alone with fear and hunger a very long time, whereas, almost right next door, all I knew was that nature was pleasant and people were gentle. Now I live in your world, but at least we are together."

Justine had listened intently, and internalized every fragment. She was still compelled to say: "Now that you know this slingshot, you must be on your way, while I mind the fishing lines. We must know if we can move forward."

Gwynhr wept a few tears. "It is a hard lot not knowing what will become of you. Yet I know what I must do."

CHAPTER TWELVE :
THE WILD WOODS

After many tearful hugs and goodbyes, mixtures of love and sorrow and regret, the couple parted company, and Gwynhr, laden with two sacks made from blankets for whatever he might forage, traversed through the shore of the marsh to the inlet opposite, to continue to follow the culvert upwards. He considered the vast expanse of sky, and thought it smaller than love, and the instinctual knowing that love can bring. At some point the culvert became impassable, and by necessity Gwynhr had to climb a prominence to reach the lower passage of the cliff above. Several times he had to truly climb, often relying on his old pair of woolen shoes from the abbey. Eventually he had to pause, not only due to the steep uphill exertion, but to make better shoes from one of the blankets. He tore and shredded strips to tie about his feet and ankles.

Within a few hours he reached the lower part of the crest, and could have his vista. What he saw only made sense to him through his sense of wonder. The immediate consisted of a slope of shale with patches of snow, and the beyond was a slow marching descent of green wooded mountains. He found his stream and began running, as best he could, down the slippery slope. Greenery began to appear about him in passages, and he turned his head from side to side as he clambered down, for any of the right plants that he knew. He thought, and his mind changed, and he concentrated forward to make it to the forest eventually. Using a swift momentum downwards he came to the edge of the green wood, and with his two bags and a few other belongings began foraging, searching, making every quest he could think of from forest signs. Greedily he began taking leaves in digging up roots, climbing up trees for pine nuts and setting hopeful snares. He found sour grass and milk thistle, and then, to his further amazement, he discovered gigantic blossoms of flowers of many assortments, which had been genetically made gigantic many generations of plants ago, by the result, naturally, of the radioactive gigantism that occurs in the sensitive blooms of the flowering plants. Automatically, he then became immediately on the lookout for honeycomb

As he delved in, squirrels ran up trees away from him. Gwynhr re-found his streambed, and then immense dandelions for milk and broth. As he reached the thick of this one particular patch of woods, in the moist heat were bizarre giant insects of ferocious mein, such as moths and especially mosquitos. Gwynhr became the object of a ferocious attack as the mosquitoes gained the blood instinct of him and honed in, and he fled in all haste as he batted them away.

These are not things he could have read of in the old library at the abbey. Quite afraid and disoriented, Gwynhr tried to regain his focus on foraging, so he went to work climbing pine trees for pine nuts and setting more snares, and, to his great sense of good fortune, he found a producing patch of blackberries. It was then that he tried to calculate again the part of which season they were in, or even what month it was, and he could not.

After his initial forage he again alighted on the thought of honeycomb. There, after all, was little room for doubt. He spied giant oak trees that seemed likely, even as he spied trees he had never seen before and was inadequate to name from books he had seen ever. Then caution caught the better of him and he became aware that these might be very large indeed as well. This thought gripped him with paranoia, and he immediately sprang into action and set flint to tinder, even though the entire forest was thickly strewn with a great many dry leaves. Gwynhr let the fires spread in a balmy breeze and fled that place for the quickest foraging he could, carrying with him a smoking burning torch of a large stick. At the far side of this patch of woodland he found his mark, and, quite correctly, he had guessed true as to the size of the bees, but equally great where the resulting hives of comb, and then Gwynhr set to producing as much smoke as he could. He filled the rest of his one large sack full of honey comb as a thief with no sense of delay, and ran back to the original fire he had set. By this time the entire woods was smelling of smoke, and Gwynhr, with all the energy of a cat, nimbly avoided several patches of fire and fled to rejoin Justine. Wood crackled with flame up behind him as he ascended the slippery shale. He looked backwards twice and felt assured the forest would burn. It was not only the best cautionary measure, it would also leave many roasted foodstuffs.

As he climbed back up to the ridge top, however, overhead began to fly clouds of many types of insects. Then even as he reached the crest, whirling, circling giant birds began to overtake the insects, including turkey vultures, red tailed hawk, and fruit bats. Alvin saw one especially great bird that was a condor of some form. All the birds came and the insects in the feeding rush, and Gwynhr, brandishing a smoking brand, attempted to scale the same prominence downwards into his culvert that led to the lake. Justine had flung blankets over their stone igloo and concealed herself within, praying for Gwynhr's safety. Several hours later Gwynhr arrived with his sack of extraordinary provisions.

"Husband, I love you!" Justine cried out, weeping very much at his safe appearance.

CHAPTER THIRTEEN:
THE RIM OF THE WORLD

It took many days for the sky to subside of activity. Justine and Gwynhr hid away in near total darkness except for a small flame. Little did they know that the clear forest would bring bear and following mountain lions and even a hulking grizzly bear, which species had just survived extinction.

"We must travel a long way around on this side of the mountains,""Justine knew to say.

"But first," said Gwynhr, "I must go to these woods again that have become uncovered and purified, and fill another bag of goods."

"I understand," Justine replied, "but be very aware of wild things. This is not our land at all."

"Yes, missus," Gwynhr agreed. "It has many good things but many bad things. I will go my way with greatest alacrity."

"May your pace be strong and determined. I will take my bath now. Whatever you meet, flee, or be very careful."

Gwynhr conquered the ridge top again and slid down the shale to the smoking, and in some places still burning, patch of forest. He decided to first search grubs and pine nuts, but thought also of doomed squirrels already cooked. He also dug up a number of immense tubers, then he fled.

He found Justine minding the tackle. With their combined larders, they agreed to flee the lake as well.

Justine used her good hand to climb and Gwynhr often almost pushed her up rocky outcroppings. Soon the quaint little marshy lake was out of sight, and they saw to what path could be found that ran along the crest of the ridge. To their right were stretching mountains, to the left was the desiccated expanse of the Desolations. The couple almost gave up care a number of times, as they sat to munch sour-grass or dig into the potent honeycomb. Wisps of cloud occasionally dimmed the sun, and then evaporated into nothing over the arroyo. They were very mindful of what was on their right, and always Gwynhr kept an ember lit. In three days there skirting path connected them to the old crest trail. Temporarily, their way was barred by an overgrown marsh with many large mosquitoes. However, they were most dogged in a special determination, and warded off the mosquitoes with smoke and flame, even as they gathered stones to throw in front of them and so form a path across the marsh. The last of their food store would be a substantial amount of roasted grubs and pine nuts, and pine needle tea. They talked long, sitting around the fire one night of great heat.

"It is a matter of ratio," Justine reminded Gwynhr. "First of all, how long does the food supply in a given place last, and, what is safest? I know of an old trick: we build a secure house up in a tree, and only go out as necessary."

"Why, then," Gwynhr replied, "that might as well be right now. We will in some time require more food, and we don't want to run into more mosquitoes, or anything else for that matter, less we can trap it, and if one were above, one would have a distinct offense, as well as defensive, position."

"Then of this before us we shall build a tree house, just because it is before us and we don't get know any differently in regards foodstuffs." Justine twiddled a piece of grass in her mouth, an old habit.

Gwynhr agreed, it was obvious. "Then what we need is a tall tree with no nests, and we need to turn our blankets into rope for pulleys." They hugged eachother warmly. They walked down off the rim of the world.

CHAPTER FOURTEEN:
THE HOUSE IN THE TREE

In the warm evenings wisps of cloud turned magenta, as though heaven was opening its doors a little. Apart from the occasional giant pink or purple moth and spectacles of extraordinary butterflies, Justine and Gwynhr were free to build. They chose a perfect redwood, all of 300 feet tall, that was free of nests and had branches they could climb like ladders. Even Justine, with her lame right arm, was able to manage the passage. Having torn their remaining blankets into twisted ropes and made pulleys from pinecones, the couple were able to lift cargo up into their new dwelling space. With their knives they cut shoots off of the straighter sticks and branches and proceeded with a hasty lockstep program of construction. From giant flower petals they made quilt soft enough for a baby, and finally they dug with sticks and made a mote about the tree, for the rains they knew must come, made with particularly light old logs as their special drawbridge against animals, such as there might arrive.

Yet food was still paramount. While Justine rested, wafting in the fragrance of many flowers, Gwynhr restlessly moved about this strange new world. To his eye many of the plants were of great interest, although he kept a sharp lookout for scat. He had spied the running of many squirrels and hares, and finally discovered a brook to follow who's eddies virtually overflowed with great water lilies, and then he was led to a beaver's dam. He was able to search his memory for what type of animal might live here, and remembered an old little told story of the delicacy of beaver tail. Gwynhr placed about this magical living wood many baits and snares, and always made it home by sundown with an ample larder for the night and next morning, if of nothing else pine nuts and flower petals. He was acutely aware, however, of giant bees and wasps and mosquitoes, but mercifully found none in this particular wood. The brook he had discovered ran smooth, and so there were no mosquitoes, and Gwynhr soon discovered what became of these when he found a clump to massive bears hair. He became impatient for rain to fill their moat.

One evening a short while into their stay a gentle mist settled upon the rift of their woods. They felt a cool as they had never felt before, and marvelled at the fine silken air, which soon set the forest to dripping.

Justine's terrible wound had nearly healed over, but her right hand dangled, useless. Yet she comforted Gwynhr that this was, after all, a small price to pay for their past ordeals. A sylvan lightness entered their lives as they put on necessary weight and bathed in the stream. When he could, Gwynhr filled their moat with steaming hot water for Justine to bathe in. Love came easily to them now, and they learned how to kiss as adults do. Yet Gwynhr would never allow Justine to stray very far from their tree home and she knew the wisdom in this. To be taken unawares while crippled may prove disastrous. Rather, they took much time high aloft to share poetry put to memory as children.

A month or so into this new life and their knowing their single-tree village, the last breaking clouds of a storm from the Pacific Ocean washed over the wood. The water was warm, and dripped a little through their roof canopy of leaves and petals and fronds. Gwynhr had discovered clay, and invented some dishware, in which he made a coney stew steeped with fine herbs. Alvin thought greedily of a gift of black bear pudding stuffed with pine nuts but hadn't the courage to face wild things, then. A quieter and more genteel life was eminently desirable. Peace and calm were like magic to Justine, and Gwynhr almost felt restored to his former self. Still, a great awareness came upon them one night when a giant fruit bat alighted on the roof of their comfortable cabin: they were not yet alone in a world of possible perils, many unimagined.

After several months of quietude and rest, they heard far away the calls and responses of what was no doubt a pack of wolves. This idea of wolves was still unfamiliar to them, though they shared a mutual memory that wolves might hunt in packs. Alvin made a quick desperate forage of the dwindling resources about their home, and with their already gathered supply they had food for several weeks. Gwynhr withdrew the bridge from their moat.

Howls approached, and snuffling was heard about their tree, but then the wolves gave up in futility after several days, despite the powerful scents of the pairs provisions. However, neither Justine or Gwynhr could tell when it was safe to descend again, but kept a small fire tended in a stone pit in their tree house. Despite having to tend the fire, they slept long hours in deepest slumber in each other's arms, almost no longer caring of safety. Yet they knew that a bear could yet reach their height and kept it tightly sealed.

Rains came again in strength, breaking over the mountains and then disappearing over the desert opposite. When at last Gwynhr descended, thick groves of mushrooms had sprouted, but Justine indicated some were not safe and not to choose them. He sought about for his snares finding the wolves had picked each one clean. Gwynhr sensed something near, and quickly went about making a torch, fearing wolf and bear, and huddled in a small dell between tree roots. A rattlesnake was soon revealed slithering his way, but he was able to swiftly put embers to it, and make of himself the prize. He realized then that the rains might have brought out many creatures from hiding and went about the usual business of grubs and pine nuts. He also found one squirrel pausing, and using the slingshot he was now expert with, brought more store. As he hurried back to Justine, his mood was mixed as he remembered what she had said: survival was a matter of ratio, the ratio of hunters to possible food. On his road home he noticed many birds alight high above him and decided that by this token matters were absolutely unsafe, that the hunter could become the hunted.

When he returned at last, he laid a snake and squirrel and grubs and pine nuts down in their pantry by the fire. Gwynhr did not know how to explain what he felt, yet related the presence of predators in the air, and a different sense to the forest. Plus, he pointed out, in the intervening months he had scavenged much. Justine said, "There must be beautiful birds eggs."

"Or serpents eggs," Gwynhr replied with no mirth. "I believe, dear Justine, we must figure out our way from here, and risk mountain lions in such. I believe we are becoming surrounded."

"Yes, I see," Justine was able to admit. Then she began to weep for their beautiful and happy home.

"Or serpents eggs," Gwynhr replied with no mirth. "I believe, dear Justine, we must figure our way from here, and risk mountain lions and such. I believe we are becoming surrounded."

"Be well prepared with torch and knife and slingshot, Gwynhr." At least they had reached their strength in full, in fact such as Justine had never known. Her features had become less tout and more softened, and her figure filled into a new svelte. Gwynhr admired her frequently, which always brought a blush from Justine.

The color was in both their cheeks one early morning's dew-fall. They well remembered the place of their tree so that perhaps they could return one day. They carried initially what they could, a goodly store wrapped in sacks of woven fern fronds, but such provisions would be lightened. They reached their brook and followed its mossy embankments towards the west and soon other modest rills were joining with the way. In three days time, scrounging as they went for dandelions and rose petals and even blackberry, they was soon next to a full running river.

None too soon, for a howls and barking broke out suddenly about them in the wood. The pack of wolves had remained silent, and now Justine and Gwynhr were in the center of the hunt. "Hold onto your bag, Gwynhr, and jump in the river!" Justine urged. Gwynhr had never jumped in a river before, but in an instant he obeyed. They were taken by a swift current and slid over slimy stones, with wolves padding along on either side of the river for an opportunity but the rains had been significant and, clutching their larder like flotation devices, the couple was carried away into a different land.

CHAPTER FIFTEEN:
THE FORK IN THE RIVER

After several miles of floating speedily along, they came to a waterfall, and in an instant were rushed over, to splash down in the pool. Without knowing how to swim, they each clung to their provisions as life preservers, then emerged onto an embankment, in a land mainly of rocky outcroppings rather than trees and foliage. The river had been warmed and the day was becoming balmy. Yet they both knew that wolves travelled rapidly in the hunt, and so made a brief consultation.

"We shall use vines," Justine declared, "to connect us to each other and our sacks, and again take the river. Where it leads must be a land of plenty, unless the wars had made more Desolations." Upon this they agreed, and when they were trussed safely, hopped into the warm rainwater, and they took it slow as the river widened, passing among many verdant mountains, which now they dared not trust. They both agreed as they floated that their great good fortune at finding a friendly home might have been short-lived, and they clung to their packs with deep regrets, but nevertheless, unavoidably high hopes. However, in one pool they discovered the skeleton of one man who would drown himself with a stone tied about his neck, no doubt an ancient creature of hardship who could not go on alone, a relic of the futility of ancient lives and a foreboding of the difficult way ahead.

Still, the Green Mountains drifted past as they floated along, but they dared not again decide upon a home in the midst of a storm.

Late that day the watercourse spread out into a verdant meadow, and it was here they took their chance temporarily. They chose a sandy embankment and climbed ashore, and set to with making fire come. Their wet food tasted especially good, having been soaked and then roasted.

When replenished, they agreed to scavenge together this wet grassland. They found many little byways of water, and many manner of birds for Gwynhr's slingshot, pheasant and grouse and coots and turtledoves and even seagulls. They also found rills with winnowing trout to fish. They both thought this was a new land of plenty, even as they discovered a ground nests full of eggs. Yet Justine speculated upon the seagulls.

"These are birds of the Great Water, perhaps," she thought out loud to Gwynhr, "we are not far from there." In fact, though, they were still hundreds of miles from the Pacific Ocean.

"What would we find, Justine?"

"I believe from all my parents said and all the books I've seen that there were many cities and many people. Now, perhaps, there are still people, but of what kind I cannot guess."

"Perhaps there are people nearby… "said Gwynhr with trepidation.

"In any event," said Justine, "we should always bivouac by the river as her protection from wild things, and, there is no doubt, this very river must eventually lead to the Great Water. As it is there where food is most concentrated, this should be our ultimate destination, as more risky or less risky a choice as it might be in the end, for we cannot be forced from one habitat to another without, clearly, major risks in any event. The more there is food in these mountains the more we shall find the wild animals.

"Yes," Gwynhr agreed. "I shall find the lighter sticks and build us a raft. "

"This is as it must be," Justine concluded. They camped there only three days, over which they expended much energy towards the forage, Gwynhr with his slingshot finding many birds, especially the pheasant which could be taken unawares, and Justine with her dangling arm searched out eggs and berries and grubs, and then they would meet back at the camp by the river for a few hours of rest then they would trust their meager belongings to a light raft, and sailed away on another balmy day. The raft would serve them well, as they could just carry it where the water appeared too treacherous, Justine always taking the right side of the raft with her good left arm and hand. And also they found good fishing even as they floated forward, and so were in good stead with nature to make their progress. They camped sparingly even to the extent of eating raw fish again.A light breeze cooled of them one day. On the right side of the river they made site of attended garden surrounded by barbed wire and sticks. This set them to talking again.

"Perhaps this is where we may rest," suggested Gwynhr, "perhaps this is where we might be allowed?"

"Paddle, Gwynhr! These are no doubt a rustic peoples. They would see you as competition and I as a prize to be conquered. This is not a fit place," Justine insisted.

"I see," said Gwynhr, and set to paddling double.

They could not detect if they were cited, but nothing further came of the matter. They came to where there was a fork in the river, and there they discovered an old stone dome such as they had seen in Jack's forest. They took a stop to look inside, but it was empty except for old leaves and a few leftover bones. Justine and Gwynhr paused to consider the matter, but then turned towards what was more immediate: which bend of the river to try. Gwynhr walked along the fork in the river of good ways enough to determine which seemed which part seemed to go most rapidly downhill. It was this river they chose.

They sailed peacefully, well fed but frequently clinging to each other on the rougher parts of the rapids of the river, until they felt safer, but upon landing towards a glowing sunset one evening, they discovered an ominous sign: floating in an eddy of the river drifted a pointed spear.

"This can mean probably one of two things," Justine explained Gwynhr. "Either a fishermen lost his or her weapon attempting to make a strike on a fish, or two warring clans have fought, with the river in the middle. Either way, this river can no longer be deemed safe. We must fish a little while we can, and then seek higher ground as advantage."

CHAPTER SIXTEEN:
SAILING TO THE GREAT BEYOND

"Why, Justine, can we not go back home and take our chances in our tree home?"

"It is clear now that wild things and wild people are roaming. There is no going back, we would only live in a temporary island, like your abbey, only briefer. You must understand, Gwynhr, that there is no utopia, except perhaps if we move forward, and find a life of peace and freedom again"

"I see," Gwynhr capitulated. "I can hear what you are saying."

With just some fish to eat they moved uphill through forest, away from the river, in constant vigilance. Yet they knew that if they were caught, they would be outnumbered, and their vigilance was useless, unless they could hide somewhere. The mountain bluffs provided the greatest vantage to survey by, and the most routes of flight, as well. However, the same bluffs did not provide much food.

This journey was rocky and difficult, especially for Justine. They could not light fires, in case there were people about, and so they ate more fish raw. It only lasted several days, before their food supply in the terrain forced them downwards into the forest again.

They heard a call one night. Had they known, they would've realized it was a wild person signaling to another of nearby deer. All Justine and Gwynhr could discern was that it was a human call, and wild sounding, and it drove a stake of fear into their hearts. Still, they found some determination, if not actual resources: they had come so far through so much that it could not end here. Quietly as possible they covered each other in a drift of leaves, and lay still.

The next day brought rustling, and Gwynhr dared peek through the leaves. He saw a strong, burly man dressed in hides, wearing a helmet made from an old bowl and deer antlers. He carried a spear and slingshot.

The man had a heavy knotted beard and thick knotted hair, and smelled bad. Yet what most alerted Gwynhr then was the man's belt, which was made in many types of small skulls. Here was a skilled survivalist, and one who had negotiated the difficult psychosocial world of hostility, acrimony, and revenge that must, Gwynhr guessed correctly, exist amidst his tribe. To Alvin he resembled those seen from an old fairy tale like an ogre or troll from under a bridge, but by far Alvin's most consuming thoughts were for Justine. Gwynhr's blood began to boil, not with hatred or loathing but with outright fear and protectiveness. The burly ogre had paused in the dell where they hid, as those smelling them. Gwynhr readied his own slingshot with the heaviest stone he had carried. Justine had sunken into sleep several hours before, and was oblivious.

The target was not distant, but near, perilously close, in fact. Gwynhr could wait no longer. He leapt up from the drift of leaves and swung his slingshot with as much force as he had, and followed upon this immediately with a charge of a pointed stick, enough to penetrate the man's hides. The stone had found its mark well directly on the man's forehead, and the spear pierced his gut. Without betraying a sound he lay dying.

Justine was awake by Gwynhr's side. She grabbed his right arm with her left. "We must fly way of this, with all haste! Fly!" The two shot off, not certain of direction, downhill through these woods, with three sharpened sticks drawn, but hardly any hope of using them successfully. They ran on making much noise in the underbrush brushing aside tremendous flowers and scrambling through sprawling ferns and fronds, and heard cries, harsh and cruel, seeming to echo all about them. They guided themselves briefly to go in the direction no calls were coming from. The way downwards steepened, and Gwynhr tripped over dead logs and fallen branches. Those who knew paths were gaining upon them.

Quite suddenly, the pair came to a ledge with a fall of about 100 feet down into roiling rapids. Calls came close on their heels now. Gwynhr looked at

Justine in defeat, but Justine pushed Gwynhr over the cliff, and then jumped herself.

They landed heavily in a deep pool, and it took some time before they could orient themselves, as they were also dragged by a heavy current. They came to the surface with stones and spears falling about them and a race was on between their current in the river and the running of wild tribe members above who were skilled hunters with a far range. Justine urged "Swim!" Yet Gwynhr did not know how to swim, and could merely paddle. Justine herself, with her dangling arm, could only barely manage to stay above water. The bluff began to descend to water level as the these semi-civilized wild people began appearing along the embankment, but out of a sudden moment Justine and Gwynhr were swept over falls, and again found themselves in a roiling pool. Underwater Justine could see that Gwynhr was sinking, not having recovered from the roiling passion of his protectiveness for his wife, and Justine, with her left arm, grabbed out and pulled him upwards to the surface.

"Prepare to keep floating!" Justine cried, even as the wild calls receded behind them.

"Justine!" Gwynhr cried.

"Quiet!" she responded. "You must be very quiet!"

They were slipped by the water over massive stones and through many smaller pools, and then again over stones and downwards. Miles and miles went by without a call from behind, until suddenly they found themselves in a wide pool with barely any current, full of fish and with fishing lines adorning the banks, and to their great good fortune the lines were unattended. Swift as they could waterlogged and sapped in strength from struggling with the current, they filled the rough satchels of squirrel and beaver hide they now carried with as many fish as they could, and emerged soaked to the bones on a wide damn, then climbed down the other side to find a current again. Soon the water was propelling them further and further, they clung to one another and paddled with all their remaining strength, though they could merely float. And at last night fell, with orange and then red and then purple wisps of clouds above.

Had they known it was the end of a strange brief summer, and soon mists and rains would turn to frost and snows. As night fell they found a relatively shallow place, and crawled to the shore, utterly out of breath and exhausted, and threw themselves down on some turf.

Justine rousted Gwynhr. "Eat more fish," she demanded. "We are not in luck except for this provision. Both the hills and rivers are occupied with darksome tribes, and I fear rapine and carnage. We are back to where we were, in so far as we must follow this river, though it were our only road."

Gwynhr had enough strength to chew some fish. "We have no raft," he mused, "nor does there seem time enough to build one. Time is not on our side here. Best get back in the water by cover of darkness." Upon this they were automatically agreed.

In a short while they found a log to cling to, they would not rest for sleep then for many nights and days, as they had traveled many miles towards the Great Water. Fortunately, the river flowed well, and indeed they found many joining creeks. They chewed raw salmon and trout as they journeyed, and this seemed something of a feast, at least enough to bolster their physical fortitude. Yet even as they escaped evil fates, their spirits flagged as they wondered over what foreign land lay ahead, and possible dreadful dooms which lurked on the borders of their imaginations. They had been through too much, however, for delirium to fully overcome them, although there was no getting used to the risks most probably inherent in meeting the survivors in this strange new land. Generations had gone by since the Great Wars which had inflicted civilization with famine, blight, and disease,, and now the survivors were not as the previous humankind, unless, they thought, some lone abbey like the one they had fled still enjoyed some relative peace, or perhaps, that they could find a place of food alone together. For now, they sailed into the Great Beyond, with barely scraps of hope, and they daydreamed of their abbey and their treehouse. As the waters increased, so did their hopes and fears and dreams and nightmares, and only after two weeks of sleeplessness would past would they take to the shore again.

CHAPTER SEVENTEEN:
GROUND ZERO

The couple ate of all the giant flower petals they could find, and they made a stone pit to boil dandelion soup at night, when there smoke was least apparent. They took a few hours of restless sleep, and then took some meager store of provisions back with them to the log. The next day they spied on one embankment a prowling mountain lion, who appeared wary of them and skittish, they mutually agreed not to hunt such an animal. It was only their second confrontation with a cat, and left more scars upon the limited imaginations.

After several more weeks of floating with little sleep their downhill run smoothed out into a vast plain of meadowland where more of the giant insects preyed upon giant flowers. They had baited lines attached to their log, and would not rest upon a shore, though relied on what the river would give them. Behind them were the mountains of the Sierra California and before them lay a great delta. They began to observe half sunken towns and cities, and, one day, a miraculous tower of glass that was not cracked by heat. This shiny, reflective, and gleaming monument left them in wonder.

"This may be the possession of a great tribe with a terrible warlord," Justine supposed as possible, but no fleet of boats or ships plied the delta. On their right past the ruins of the capital city, Sacramento, and they heard dogs barking, but no other signs of animal life. Little did they know that they were forging into a Ground Zero for some of the atomic blasts that had rocked the world, the result of preemptive strikes born of deep suspicions. Justine and Gwynhr began to experience a sinking nausea, and Justine knew from her childhood that invisible forces could make for debilitating illness and disease. "Once again," she told Gwynhr, "we have gone far enough by river. The land ahead are dangerous, poisoned ruins and we must find the directions. To my understanding we must veer Northwest and hope to strike the edge of the Great Water where there is not an invisible disease."

"I do not feel so well," said Gwynhr.

"Splash water on your face," Justine told him, "and then we will crawl if we have to."

They found a sandbar to their right and abandoned their log. Here indeed they had to crawl, struggling against nausea and the difficulty of holding down food. In fact, food itself began to taste unpalatable as it became increasingly poisoned by radioactivity, by night they did not dare travel as they heard the barks and howls of wild dogs. By day Gwynhr used all his strength in hunting these same dogs with the slingshot, but they knew they were surrounded. They kept a fire constantly burning, not only against the wild dog but more swarms of immense mosquitoes, which would appear in waves upon the breeze, and, had they known, they were most fortunate in warding them off, as many carried malaria. They struggled then tremendously, not only with nausea but by forced wakefulness, and the weight they had put on was soon vanishing.

Yet finally, in a desperate sparring hunt, Gwynhr was able to bring down one of the dogs, and they ate as best they could. Then, again, they would stay huddled together over a fire at night and literally crawled forwards by day.

They traversed ever so slowly a vast delta plane in continued warm weather. Then the ridge of high pressure broke, and an arctic cold descended. This refreshed them somewhat, so that they could go for stretches walking upright and gathering plants, but soon came brutally cold rains that finally turned to snow. Their blankets had all been used for other purposes, but they had maintained a collection of a number of animal hides, mainly squirrel and beaver but also wolf. Gwynhr made sure that Justine was warm, and they built a small cabin of sticks next to a pool, and this insulated them a bit from the outside world and they huddled together by a fire. They had reached the eastern front of a stretch of coastal mountains although this they were entirely unaware. They risked the smoke of their fire here, believing somewhat that there were no people about, and that their cabin would protect them from wild animals. After the further confrontations with the baffling wild mosquitoes, however, they clung to each other in fear of wild things, and suffered many night terrors. What lurked on the edge of the imagination was no thing to confront by the light of day.

CHAPTER EIGHTEEN:
A WOMAN OF THE SNOW

They again began to hear, with further snowfall, the distant call of the wolf, and imagine other animals must appear with this alien fall of frozen water from the sky. They discussed cougar and mountain lion and lynx and the fox. Driven again by looming necessity Gwynhr left Justine behind to use the sling shot and sticks.

He wore boots of hide, and patrolled over now frozen tundra into thick redwood forests. The air was good, and for the first time Gwynhr confronted cold. His breath seemed to him a confusing dreamlike fog, as though his spirit was leaving his body, but more importantly to him he spied animals foraging, and thought of Justine. With his slingshot he went about his work, and brought down many squirrels who had dared reveal themselves. In the distance he did spy the brown fox, but it was too wary and on the hunt itself for smaller prey.

When Gwynhr returned, again triumphant, to their little hut, he found that Justine had insulated it with snow. For several days they lived in each other's arms, only stirring to eat and refresh themselves with water. The smoke drifted up from their cabin, but they were left undisturbed, until one day an event would change their little lives in the great world forever.

"Coo-ey!" came the cry of a woman's voice, as they huddled in their hut. "I come in peace! Make yourselves known! "

Justine and Gwynhr could barely think of what to do. They had not heard English from anybody since the days of the abbey. They knew they were found out, though, and after some hurried discussion decided to risk possible death, or worse. In any event, they assumed that they were trapped. They gathered their remaining food as an offering of peace, and departed the cabin.

About 60 paces off was a figure white as snow in a bearskin dress. "Show your hands and you will not be harmed!" came her command. She had a crossbow aimed upon them. They obeyed, and dropped their food and raised their hands in the bitter air, except for Justine's right arm.

The alien figure moved towards them slowly with her crossbow still directed at them. "State your intentions, and you will not be harmed!" the stately figure again commanded.

"We come from far away seeking peaceful lands," Justine cried back, her voice quivering.

"You say that you are from a distant land," cried the woman, willing to believe as much from the looks of things. "How far distant?"

"We do not know," Justine replied. "We have come this way without maps, and journeyed far by water."

"You will come with me," the woman decided. "What is that that you have dropped?"

"Our only food, as a token of goodwill," Justine said.

Gwynhr had to speak. "We are seeking peaceful lands. What is your intention?"

"Peace will be met with peace," the woman declared, but did not lower her crossbow. "Come forward with your arms raised."

"My right arm is useless from injury, and this is my husband," Justine declared. "We will submit to your power. Please have mercy on our souls."

"You may bring your food," the woman said, "and we shall walk."

Upon closer inspection, Justine and Gwynhr discovered the woman was such as a fearful ghost in the snow. Her hair and eyelids were white, her skin pale as the snow, and even her enamels barely pink-white, like coral. Her white eyes dissolved into her eyeballs. Had Justine and Gwynhr heard of an albino they perhaps would have been no less amazed. Here was a result of a unique genetic mutation.

"Are you armed?" the woman demanded.

"I have a slingshot and a stick," Alvin admitted, with nothing better to do.

The woman almost smiled, despite the pathos that was obvious to her upon inspecting them.

"You may keep your weapons," she said generously. "How far can you walk?

Justine spoke up. "We have been exceeding weak, at times for a long while. Can you take us to where there is food? We intend no harm, and only seek the company of good-natured individuals." These last words hung in the frozen air.

"You will come with me to my encampment, and from there we shall see." They followed her abjectly, not knowing their fate.

They hiked many miles up into these mountains, and there they reached a ring of redwood trees with a large burning fire pit within. Hung high in the trees away from predators were the carcasses of many manner of animals, black and brown bears, mountain lions, foxes, moles, carrion birds and other birds of prey.

To Justine and Gwynhr's great relief, the ghostly-pale figure said, "You shall sit and eat." It was the best token of goodwill the pair could receive.

Indeed the feast was plentiful, seemingly endless, a great supply of strengthening animal meat. Justine and Gwynhr said warm by the fire, and the stranger sat a little ways away and merely observed. Justine and Gwynhr ate in silence. The woman unfolded skin and constructed a tent for them with soft cougar fur for a bed. "You may sleep when you like," was all she said.

After eating ravenously for several hours, the couple did decide to lie down and sleep, fully engorged and content in their stomachs. Yet first they had to discuss this unfamiliar development.

"She is not as I ever imagined humans," Alvin began, "and seems more like a shade from the netherworld"

"She is certainly keen with her crossbow. I am no longer famished. This is great good fortune, unless we are being fattened for the kill."

"She betrays no foulness in her person, as odd as she seems," Gwynhr said. "I tend to think that fortune is with us, that we have met with a peace. Where there is one there may be many, but she has not spoken of others."

"She does not seem to deem us a threat, in any event," replied Justine, "and I do feel sleepy from our meal. Come take my hand, Gwynhr, and let us rest." This they did, until dawn's breaking light.

When they emerged from their tent, the woman was absent, but a black bear was on the fire. Another rare feast was before them, and they began to feel contented, despite a lingering trepidation.

That evening they experienced another miraculous site: the pale woman appeared riding a sleigh, which was neatly pulled by a fine white mare. The woman, without so much as a word, began to release the carcasses from their purchases in the redwoods, and place them one by one onto the sleigh. Justine and Gwynhr watched, respectfully mute. The albino's paleness seemed to fade into the snow about them.

At last the woman signaled to them. "There shall be more to eat tomorrow, and then we shall go to where the drifts of snow meat a cliff. Our bounty shall go down to the shore below, where our ship is waiting. Do not be un-calm, it is safe here for now."

"My name is Gwynhr," Gwynhr put in without much emphasis.

"And my name is Justine. We have come through Desolation and Waste, and it seems you are well provided for through some mystery alien to us, although we have taught ourselves to expect the unexpected."

"I am Eldril," the woman said quietly as though wishing to not pronounce her name too loudly. "Your survival is unlikely, but our ship is small and the seas tempestuous. Yet we shall do as we may."

Justine and Gwynhr took this to be an offer, and retired to their tent to discuss matters.

"She is not too foreign," Justine noted, despite the woman Eldril's peculiar demeanor. "As far as I see, this is a redoubtable grace, her appearance, and we must look forwards. Such risks as we may be taking cannot compare to the risks of what we as have seen, unless I miss my guess of this woman's ability to survive. She may be bringing us to a foreign place, but this I deem we must risk."

"Never have I eaten so fully and completely," Gwynhr noted for his part. "I would deem this purely altruistic on her part."

"So it seems," said Justine, "but all this talk of a ship on the water is strange talk indeed. Perhaps the ship is you only way to remain safe, and gather bounty." Justine looked at her own tattered linens and woolens, and thought of the requirements of surviving as the Old World passed away into the New World. "She does mightily well by herself with her crossbow. Never have I seen such a larder. Yet, what if she is of a cruel folk?"

"She is paler than a ghost," said Gwynhr with some fear of such a total unknown. "In the end," he continued, "the world is wide and there may be many lands across the waters, they consist of what we cannot think of. She has not killed us, although perhaps we have use for her besides this. On the other hand, she does not appear to think we are a risk to her."

"Gwynhr," Justine said warmly, "hold my hand, there is a good dear. I believe we are being taken far away from what we have known."

"I see," Gwynhr noted for her. "Then let us not look back, but look forwards."

"I agree, and if we may, let us try ingratiating ourselves with helpfulness to our benefactor,"

Justine replied. At this the married couple exited the tent and almost in supplication asked the albino if they might help in any way.

Eldril smiled, if that's what you could call it, because it was merely the faintest curlings at the sides of her mouth. She said: "We need logs for the fire. Do either of you know how to make a stick straight for the crossbow?"

Justine and Gwynhr looked at each other. "We do not," Justine replied. "You find in the two of us a pair with different backgrounds, yet each of us are simple folk."

Eldril smiled a little more, then, almost revealing sympathy. "I have enough arrows, for now. But the wolves shall be about in packs soon. Go gather the firewood, and we shall produce a ring of fire about the circle of redwoods." She paused. "Avolondiae," she said softly, mysteriously.

Justine and Gwynhr went to search out logs. "She speaks in tongues," Gwynhr commented.

"Perhaps she is from far away, or a kingdom from long ago. She certainly is deadly with the crossbow," Justine said admiringly. Her right arm dangled. "Here, Gwynhr, help me with this log." They sweated away for hours at their task with logs and also gathered many dried leaves and needles and of these they produced a wide ring around the circle of redwoods, finding Eldril missing again. She soon returned, however, and congratulated the pair after a fashion:

"For the simple, you do good work. I have found the wolves shall be approaching soon."

"We fear ye as much as the wolves," Justine admitted.

"Am I not strange? Yet if it is in my power, your days and years of fear shall be lessened."

"Thank you," said Justine, sweeping curly red locks from her eyes.

"Yes, thank you," put in Gwynhr. The token signs were improving.

Then wolf calls could soon be heard, coming at first as echoes and then approaching. The scent of Eldril's larder had spread to many wild things, and the carnivores had begun lurking. Yet this was a part of her plan, to attract more food. Both parties there crumbled leaves to dust and set forth with flints, ever so valuable flint-stones, of which Justine had kept hers for many years, since her parents had first taught her fire when she was very young.

Soon a great roaring blaze had been produced, even so that it flickered about the surrounding ring of trees. Justine and Alvin watched Eldril lay out a row of arrows, and Eldril tested the horse sinew of her crossbow for effectiveness.

Nightfall came, and with it the first of the prowling wolves. Eldril's white horse, tethered to the sleigh, which was securely bound to a large stone, began to whinny with fear. Yet the wolves could not pass the ring of fire as it blazed initially, and Eldril took her sites one by one and brought wolves down with deadly accuracy. Justine and Gwynhr took to work fueling the blaze, so that no wolves could jump over and attack. In this manner there were soon no less than twenty dead wolves about, and as many as ten more could be seen prowling at a distance. Eldril took sight of these remoter moving targets and brought a number down, until finally the denuded pack gave up, hungry yet wisely informed by this defeat. When a few hours of night had passed Eldril ordered Justine and Alvin to use stones and build a temporary bridge through the flickering embers and gather to the central hearth the dead. She then gave Justine and Gwynhr the knives for skinning, and by the wee hours many wolves had been placed upon the central pit, which Gwynhr tended neatly, rotating the bodies with sticks for an even roast.

Eldril addressed the pair, who had solemnly conducted their labors. "You have done good work. Now with the gathering dawn I should begin to pass with my sleigh by a trail I have forged, to go down to the cliffs I mentioned, and given our provisions will make several journeys today. Then by nightfall we'll journey together. All should be well until then, but do scare any carrion birds away with your slingshot until the entire larder is transported. Our dangers shall be met up on the open seas, which sometimes seethe and rage."

Justine and Gwynhr had to consult each other privately again in their tent, with hushed voices.

"It is not beyond pretense that she is leading us," Justine informed Gwynhr, "but she is a creature of few words. I take it, though, that the sea is not her primary source of supply in every way, and better foraging here is meant to supply another land. We do not necessarily have much license with her, but now is the time to put questions directly."

"I see," replied Gwynhr. "Let us go to her now."

They found her sitting on a snow drift carving out arrows with a special sickle make of some metal. At first she did not look up from her work, but then she recognized them.

"I see you have questions on your mind," said the woman Eldril, her retinas an uncanny black in her white eyes.

"We are unsure of our course, "Justine began. "You have been very kind. Yet naturally we are still feeling our peril, and would very much like to know whither we are bound."

Eldril's answer was direct. "In ancient times the Earth moved, such that a few islands lie off the nearby coast. Except for seabirds and sea lions and such, it is a private place. There are, however, marauders upon the high seas and we should be prepared to set sail. For as long as it lasts, thanks to the Great Spirit, we may find consolation and peace. I see that you are most weary of your world."

"We are, at that," Justine almost laughed."You do exceedingly well. Where do you come from?"

"I come from a little isle," Eldril revealed."My tribe was destroyed by a sudden earth movement wave that crashed upon us. I saved my horse and sleigh, and there was a ship still anchored offshore to sail. Usually I fish, but the supply here is irresistible, and I do survive well."

"Tell me," said Justine," have you heard tell of a safe land?"

"The South was over run overrun a long time ago, and is wild, the North is cold, but I have not given up entirely on my thoughts on the matter. What of you, child, what is your story?"

"I, too, lost my parents when I was young. After many years traveling in circles I found Alvin living in a peaceful place. But it was taken by the wild people. It is been many moons since but we did not give up hope."

"You are fortunate to have had another to rely on, or, clearly, you would've perished. I've seen your injured arm, and Gwynhr does not look much of a survivor."

"He has done remarkably well." Justine began to feel most jealous of Eldril's unusual beauty. Eldril guessed what she was thinking, however, and said:

"I do not come between people. May you be happy in your marriage. Yet come with me and hope to live. You shall not if you maintain your course."

"Yes," agreed Justine immediately upon hearing such fair words, "we shall join your expeditions."

"I shall give you light duty, as you are injured and most weary. So Gwynhr's endurance must be tested. Nightfall is come again, and so we sleigh to the cliff. Gather such as you have."

"Thank you," said Justine with tremendous relief, and excitedly roused the drowsy Gwynhr for a new life.

The sleigh ride was dizzying to the couple, as the white mare galloped a beaten path with no urging from Eldril. They passed through the trees and at last reached the edge of a cliff.

"Over the centuries," Eldril explained," the risen waters have beaten this shoreline in to cliffs. The entire coastline has become overrun or crumbled away since the ancient wars."

Alvin peered over the cliff and developed vertigo. Justine took his hand and pulled him back. Yet plain to see was a moored vessel with a sale and cabin. Eldril began lowering her cargo, which was carefully trussed with many vines, and into the night all the manner of beasts she had collected, from bears to wolves to birds, were lowered to a small rocky seashore 100 feet below. And she produced some real rope, and showed Justine and Gwynhr in the moonlight of a waxing crescent how to hitch to a rope and use the rock face as a vertical support. They paid proper attention to Eldril, and managed to mentally grasp the process. Gwynhr felt quite dizzy, but the cry of wolves behind them lead them all forward. Without much light Eldril's crossbow was not nearly so useful.

The three all reach the bottom of the cliff safely, and Eldril told Gwynhr to begin loading such cargo as he could lift. Small animals like foxes and marmots and moles proved possible for him, but the bears both he and Eldril had to use special hoisting maneuvers with, such that they labored for many hours against the weight. They finished just before dawn, and it was clear that an anxiety was disturbing Eldril. She gestured silently for the two to navigate onboard, and then she deftly set the sail to the breeze, and so they left California. Although Justine could not know they never would have survived long there, for these were Desolations with bounty, and still being competed for by many wild people, who generations before killed off the meek and mild and left the generations to survival of the fittest, with the result that the most savage and cunning in bloodthirsty roamed singly and in packs.

CHAPTER NINETEEN:
THE GREAT WATER

Gwynhr and Justine had heard the crash of the waves and wondered, but with the new breaking dawn perceived to directly another site nearly unfathomable to them both, although they had heard the rumors entails: A water of waves stretched to the horizon, a beautiful blue-green ocean from some fable of romance, expansive yet yielding, soft yet un-guessably mighty.

Eldril had brought pails of ice, and she packed the roasted animals with this ice. She then showed Alvin and Justine the comforts of the cabin, spacious enough for more than three, with intact windows and even a telescope, to spy out marauders with, and to guide their ship by the position of the skies.

The skies showed their dual nature is the first day of sojourn on the open seas: rain broke and came pelting down with her freezing wind, the misfortune of strife combined with the sustenance of rainwater.

Against the crashing waves, Eldril ordered Justine and Gwynhr indoors, while she manned the ropes and pulleys of the sales. The modest crafts deck became flooded more than once as winds whipped up crashing waves, but Eldril was strong and steadfast in her maneuvering, frequently avoiding the larger breakers. Justine and Gwynhr watched through a window, and we're nearly paralyzed by this fight for survival, witnessing, as it were, a pale shade or deadly elf queen of the netherworld battle elements they never fully imagined. The struggle went on for several days more, and Gwynhr and Justine saw Eldril gnaw at beast-flesh while navigating the gale, and she seemed a fearsome adversary against nature, yet at one with it.

Justine and Gwynhr then took more time, huddled in their rocking cabin. Gwynhr felt motion sickness, but Justine actually seemed to be enjoying herself.

"We are on the right road," she told Gwynhr, "And are much less likely to be despoiled. Eldril speaks of marauders on the seas, yet she has done well for years." Gwynhr kissed Justine on the cheek, and made her wild wavy red hair into a disorderly ponytail.

"We shall help this pale elf as best we can, and see what comes our way," said Gwynhr. The couple fell to speaking of the abbey, and the quiet solitude, and Jack the hermit's honeycomb and the almond tree of their betrothal. Then they discussed their flight, the dreadful hunt of the wild people, the fight with the bear Gwynhr had conquered, their small adytum in the temple of Salt Lake City, and they even discuss the cruelty of Justine's injury with its infection, and the long road by river and mountain into the nausea of the delta. They dwelt briefly upon their quiet tree house, and both thought that here, now, neither had known a better life. Despite the ruin of the abbey and the grief, they were together, and not on a run from the dangers of the land, although perhaps trading this for new terrors, and they had evidently met a one who was in command of her senses, and had a force which overpowered nature, and was of goodwill. Neither Justine nor Gwynhr knew how to be to be religious, yet they thanked the Great Spirit, they thanked fortune and shed grateful tears together. The uncertainties they endured presently were a great lessening of burdens, of the hopeless, the lugubrious, the wearisome: and they had food.

I number of days went by, and Eldril did not join them, but continually fought the winds with her sail. When she joined that at last she told a tale

"These winds are from the south, where marauders sail. I've been working with the winds against the waves to carry us away from such people, and go to the north. The Far East may be our eventual goal."

Justine and Gwynhr had only heard of such a place in the dimmest, remotest sense: a Great Land over and beyond the Great Water.

Eldril proceeded to stitch hides with fine macramé needles to form balloons which she attached to the outer hull as extra flotation devices in case of maelstroms and whirlpools. Then she took Gwynhr to the sail, and intended to learn him of the correct takes on various sorts of wind and breeze. At first Gwynhr was only granted a scant knowledge of this, but it was all that Eldril required to at last go to sleep. With Gwynhr at the steerage, Eldril said good night to Justine, evidently trusting the pair fully.

"You are a lady of good carriage," she complimented Justine, and then readily fell into deep slumber. For a few minutes Justine gazed in continued wonderment at Eldril's hair and skin, as white as the palest lily, and then Justine joined Gwynhr on the deck of the craft.

"She will not mind if we partake some more," Justine told Gwynhr. On the deck of the modest craft was spare timber and a grated grill, and soon more bear and turkey vulture were defrosting and beginning to roast, and there were also herbs to eat them with. Justine and Gwynhr knew no better then to consume freely, but conserved many portions for Eldril. The entire supply would last them for many weeks

Eldril let the stars guide them. The way was not without merriment, as Justine and Gwynhr's buried humanity began to return again. They found that Eldril greatly enjoyed their company, and would laugh with them like the fluttering of bird's wings, but her ghostly visage kept the pair wondering about fables and legends of details of the netherworld, and other places too fantastic to imagine.

"Perhaps she is from the moon," Gwynhr whispered to Justine one moonlit night. "They have the same color."

Justine paused a long time."It may be a condition not unfamiliar to people of the past. Perhaps she is just human."

"I would prefer to believe so," said Gwynhr, "for she looks like snow and ice and cold winds, except for the center of her eyes, which shows so dark against her white, that she might also be a creature of the night."

"Do not be afraid of what is different, Gwynhr, for it is not all bad, except often as we imagine it. What did you think when first you saw a lady with red hair?"

"My fascination has been endless," Gwynhr replied gently, "although I have learned many times how you are hard-bitten by experience. Take my hand and let us look upon the open ocean and the waves, and take in the air."

Eldril was at the aft of the ship, shielding her eyes against the glare of white clouds. "I see nothing," she reported, "but the southerly winds have me worried. Marauders are likely to appear eventually, from lands of the Far South, where tribes did not kill each other off my parents told me. Us and our ship would be precisely what they are looking for, apart from the sea mammals and other strange creatures and especially my island. I have myself caught many an odd assortment of animals I have no name for. Now I shall bait and tackle, and you can both help, and I have many lines. Yet should we catch something too large or too wild, we shall let the line go."

"Eldril," queried Gwynhr, "what if marauders find us?"

"Little person," Eldril replied affectionately, "then it is then better to scuttle the ship and have done with. These southerly winds are precisely what I fear. When we reach my little island, we shall take all the stores then abandon the island, and continue ourselves with the wind to go to the north northeast."

"Then there is no place for us," Gwynhr said disconsolately, and with fear.

"Not so," contradicted Eldril. "We are three. We may make safe haven at various points potentially, and have more than enough supplies besides raw seafood. Now be a good lad and feed the horse some grasses."

"I will feed the horse," said Gwynhr. Justine and Eldril set about with the fishing lines.

Eldril spent her time on deck and left the cabin to the couple. A week later, she entered and hailed them."My island is in sight! We make landing soon!"

They moored in the smallest of bays, on an island with no trees. Yet there before there was an acre of land of grasses and other modest plants, replete with huts made from driftwood.

"Within my homes," Eldril told them," is substantial store from before the wave that took my parents, and the 20 years I have journeyed to the coast I found you on. We must make no delay, yet bring every last item on board. Much usefulness is here."

Justine and Gwynhr helped set about this labor, and found the little island replete with an assortment of valuables, such as much dried fish, many lines with catches, cooking utensils, much clothing, and an unfamiliar and peculiar assortment of personal items, such as candles, jewelry, looking glasses, magnifying glasses, and even a crystal sphere. There was even octopi milk ink. Justine and Gwynhr dutifully loaded the sailing vessel with all haste, as much as Justine's crippled arm would allow. Eldril herself delicately packed a compass and an astrolabe into her personal locker on board. Justine and Gwynhr saw her kneel briefly, and then the three set sail again.

"The rising water would have washed my island away eventually," Eldril explained," but I leave behind my childhood. Yet there may be many better times ahead, now that we have met."

"We are in your debt," Justine said humbly."Your whiteness has feared our hearts, yet we take you to be the human sort."

Eldril said: "Many strange things have happened from the invisible energies of the wars, yet my parents insisted I was normal, and I do feel it in my heart."

The winds blew colder and the waves were whipped higher as the company headed for the North-Northeast. Eldril wore many furs and hides as she stayed on deck, still preferring to let the couple have their privacy. Yet a sleet of biting ice descended, and she would occasionally join them to renew her warmth. Yet mainly she had to attend to the much strengthened sail and the ore to the aft, and with her compass they were blown along swiftly into unknown seas. One sailing vessel was spotted deep to the south, but they outpaced it and it disappeared from view.

Many moons went by, and they did not reach an end to the supply of animals of the earth, as this was supplemented with a variety of fishing catches. Only once the boat was rocked by a larger catch, and a line had to be let go.

They arrived to a place where there was no passage: the sea was blocked with ice. Yet Eldril informed Justine and Gwynhr that this was a good thing, for now they could travel the icy coastline into the East. Eldril on a number of occasions had Gwynhr sweep the weight of snowfall from the deck, but they kept some to boil down over the grill which also Eldril could use for warmth against the penetrating cold. They all had little doubt that they could meet with no humans here, although to their mutual wonder the great blue whale would emerge and below water from it spout. "Much too big to catch," Eldril noted humorously.

The islands of the Bering Strait were in a deep freeze guiding them without error to a destiny shrouded beyond dreams, perhaps containing the ordinary or perhaps the extraordinary. After many cold days and colder nights they at last reached a wooded shore, its contents hidden by a thick wood of the Asian pine.

CHAPTER TWENTY:
THE MAGIC ISLE

"Remember," said Eldril, "the peoples of the lands we have known do not take to foreigners. We are worth more dead to them then the risks of letting us live. We shall anchor offshore, and I shall swim with my crossbow to the shore opposite. If I do not return by nightfall consider me lost and do not come aground, but sail on yourselves."

"If this is your will," replied Justine, "yet I beg you not to tempt the perilous. Any wild people may be hiding, waiting the next prey to come along."

"I shall remain vigilant and guarded, and only see what food there might be briefly. This ship will not last forever, battered as it has been."

Eldril returned a short while later with several wild pigs in a sack of hide."There is good news, and bad news. The good news is that the food is plentiful, but I found trodden upon leaves and broken twigs that I do not trust. I believe this coastal area has Man. We should set sail immediately."

Gwynhr got to the sail, and Eldril went aft to the ore, while Justine kept a lookout

Light bamboo catamarans began to appear upon the rocky forested shore, as if out of nowhere, paddled by stout red-faced and golden face natives, swiftly making for their mark.

Eldril had her quiver handy."You to go below deck," she commanded," for this situation is beyond you." Justine and Gwynhr took her advice and fled, and peered out a star-board portal. The catamarans were becoming numerous, and only about 100 yards distant. They witnessed Eldril already begin to take aim and fire, and could see she had eyes sharper then a hawk. She strung and re-strung arrow after arrow to her crossbow, and Justine and Gwynhr could see many of the opposing rafts drift listless in the waves offshore. Yet many more continued onwards, and Gwynhr felt compelled to exit and man the sail towards the open sea.

The opposing rowers were now crouching low, yet did not have bows to oppose with but had spears, yet had not reached within range. However, they possessed another deadly skill: hollowed bamboo shafts to blow poison darts with. Eldril and Gwynhr took cover as their small but exceptionally deadly missiles fell within their midst. Eldril took a moment to leap up and release a volley, now three arrows at once with a swift horizontal motion of the crossbow, and to Justine, watching inside, it seemed impossible, but the multiple missiles all found targets. This was the skill of years of training, as well as the unique, penetrating vision of Eldril's dilated eyes plus an innate, indecipherable talent that is granted as a gift to the very few. Soon the catamarans floated listless. Eldril rushed to take control of the ore.

"Well done," Gwynhr said quietly, with awe.

Justine joined them to carefully throw darts overboard. "That was totally in three dimensions!" she exclaimed. "Devastating!"

"Now, with this fight," Gwynhr tried to figure, "we seem to be creatures of the open sea, unless there is, possibly, a deserted island."

"Yes," agreed Eldril, "and for that we shall search. As I said, this ship shall not remain seaworthy forever. Yet, unless my parents learned wrongly, here the South has many islands, but from what we have found we can barely trust. Not to move forward, however, is to be lost at sea."

That night, once again below the stars in the open sea, a constant southeasterly breeze moved them calmly forward into balmier climes. Very small islands eventually came and went, but were hardly above sea level and therefore useless to them. They hauled in their fishing lines and grilled a feast, and had the last of the black bear, stuffed with salmon and pine nuts and oysters, and then roasted a wild pig. "My mother once said," related Eldril, "That food is God to the hungry."

Justine became quite curious, although Gwynhr seemed more occupied by the flavor of the wild pig. "Eldril," Justine asked innocently," what do you worship?"

Eldril replied, "Everything is under the sky, including the stars, for the sky reaches into the darksome night. Without the Self, the stars would be unknown, the sun and moon useless and empty and devoid. Yet the sky gave us ourselves. Therefore do I worship that which gives perception, corrects oversight, grants beauty, and partakes in life even when sometimes it may seem meaningless."

"I have not thought of it that way, though I wandered beneath the stars," Justine admitted," but I was wild and you are bread to sophistication."

"I wouldn't go that far," laughed Eldril like a bird, "But I have sat in the snow and had ample time with food to muse upon things."

In time they spied a likely looking mountain of an island, with its top in mist and a jungle canopy below. They came to a pristine reef of coral and Eldril guided them over this then leapt into the water. Justine and Gwynhr waited the better part of that day nervously, but Eldril returned as an orange red sun broke through clouds and set.

"I've reached the other side of this island!" Eldril cried joyfully," and there is a spring of fresh water and no sign of Man. We shall tomorrow hide the boat with some palm fronds and look about together more fully." They hugged each other in turn, and ate of more salmon, and they all told jokes handed down by the generations, and all three laughed like never before, even at the bad ones.

The next morning dawned with radiance silver clouds from faraway, and the threesome expectantly moored, and gathered palm fronds from the jungle. They then tracked a little way to the pool of spring water Eldril had discovered, all the while wondering at the lush jungle of giant fronds and flowers, and also banana and mango trees and coconut, and they knew this area must receive much warm rain.

They were also very much aware of the possible presence of exotic insects, of mosquitoes and spiders and scorpions, but found no living thing except the plants and trees of this island. "This is a new place, which the Earth has given up from under the Great Water," Eldril explained. We are most fortunate, indeed, at last."

They set to by the pool as the day lengthened and built huts against the rains they knew must come, remembering, however, their path back to the ship with its protected cabin. Justine chewed upon a dry piece of grass, as she was wont to do, and thought of nature as containing a friendship she had not been fully cognizant of before. Then Eldril went inside one of their new huts and let the couple play in the pool, and Justine and Gwynhr splashed about.

They fed upon fruit as never before, which bloomed so fully that they hardly had concern to conserve, as it was evidently a steady providence.

The next day, nearly covered in hide, Eldril swam out to the reefs to investigate, and there found glittering aquariums of bounty, but swam back wary of shark and such creatures as could be there. On shore, she set about weaving baskets as traps, and Justine and Gwynhr were again greatly impressed by her skills.

The three walked the next day to the misty summit, and, looking about them, could find nothing but ocean, with no other landmasses. This gave them an added sense of relief and security.

Weeks turned into months, with much cooking and bathing and mirth, but lingering regret remained, Gwynhr dwelling upon his dear old abbey and Jack the hermit, his friend, and Justine and Eldril of their long-lost parents. Yet the mutual perseverance through many hardships gave them mutual strength as, one by one, cares were diminished, and their burdens lightened.

CHAPTER TWENTY-ONE:
THE PASSING OF A DREAM

After many years of fulfilled dreams and peace and freedom, the company felt a lasting security. Yet they were not immune: at last Eldril contracted a mutated tropical pathogen, and began to waste away before Justine and Gwynhr's very eyes. With very little in the way of medical knowledge between them, they did their best to keep her comfortable, but she became increasingly feverish, and one night of heavy breaking rain passed away without last words. With overwhelming solemnity and tears, she was buried with great ceremony and overtures of peace on the tip of their small island.

Justine and Gwynhr descended the mountain without words, and quietly undressed and huddled together in one of their huts. In several days of fitful skies, the rains passed.

"We shall not be a whole," Gwynhr told his wife.

"Yes, Gwynhr," she agreed tearfully, "we shall not be whole. Gwynhr, we owe a great debt we can never repay by any friendship."

"Promise me, Justine, that if I die you will go on."

"It is a hard-pressed matter to be alone, Gwynhr. Yet, I promise. Please sing me some snatches of song, let us eat mango and just lie here. We shall find greater strength in some future time."

"I will find strength in you," Gwynhr told her.

"You are my dear husband, Gwynhr," Justine responded. "Sing a sad song, if you wish."

Life went on with many years of song, and no ailment touched the couple, nor did the outside world interfere. They developed some lines of care as they reached middle-age, yet both being young of spirit preserved them well, and they each still blushed sometimes when looking at each other.

Their pool was fed with a lightly warm and fragrant water among the blooms of great flowers. They soaked luxuriantly, yet always remembered their debts to each other. Never did an acrimony or harsh word come between them, but they always used gentle and kind thoughts as their mutual guide. In this respect, no age touch them. They frequently would lie together and let love have its way.

They noticed the continuing rise of the ocean waters, and sometimes the trees would shake with earthquakes and so sometimes they felt fear of their mortality. Yet it was not to be, and in peace and freedom they led long lives, until Gwynhr's hair had turned quite white, while Justine's remained, mysteriously, quite red.

It was indeed Gwynhr who passed from this Earth first, of natural cause and in his sleep one night. Justine kept her promise of long ago and remained into a great old age, and, too, died of natural causes.

"Gwynhr," Jack the hermit had once said, "always live for something greater than yourself."

"I shall always try to appease the Great Spirit," Gwynhr had replied. "Yet I need a guide." This was before Gwynhr had met Justine.

"Everything can be your guide," Jack had said.

Gwynhr strolled back to the abbey that evening in some perplexity, and was noticing his surroundings in a new light, the flight of bees and a few birds, the aroma of flowers, the color of the sky. No messages came, except to remain attentive and steadfast and not be misguided by disorganized thinking in fruitless endeavors. He looked up at the sky once as dusk was setting in, and longed for it to tell him something, but no answer came except the deepening gloom and Venus on their horizon. He reached the abbey with his supply of honeycomb, which everyone was eager to have distributed as part of that evenings dinner. Gwynhr just had time before darkness to thresh a little wheat.

The abbey lacked light. There were no candles or oil lamps. Yet everyone had a hearth in their chambers and Gwynhr spent that evening by the fire reading a crumbling volume entitled "The Knights of the Round Table." The book was from so long ago that Gwynhr could not tell if the stories were true or not. The abbey's library had never had a librarian, and such as it was it was rapidly becoming unreadable.

The next day Gwynhr helped dig another canal for the plots of grapevines and grasses, and they had poured dead leaves on the dry soil to fertilize.

He went to the abbess that evening. "Something is troubling me," he confessed.

"And what is that dear?" the Abbess Eliana asked kindly.

"I would like to be a real monk, like in the old stories, but I do not know how," Gwynhr replied.

"You might pray that our spring does not run dry," the abbess suggested, "or, you can take on extra work duty."

"Yes, that would be helpful," said Gwynhr, "but will it fulfill my calling?"

"If you do it with the proper sincerity, it may take care of what ails you," said the abbess. "Otherwise, you must wait upon a special fortune."

"Nothing changes here, except when I see Jack."

"We could always use more honeycomb, if you want to be of special assistance."

"That is what I will do, then. I shall bring more honeycomb."

"Gwynhr, wake up!" Justine prodded. "The sky is turning orange and it is time to gather mangos."

"Yes, wife," Gwynhr replied mildly, "I was just dreaming of you. Is it sunrise already?"

"The day is perfect," said Justine." I have been up for hours roasting bananas for you."

Eldril sat by the fire outside."I am thinking the birds are tamed today. I will make my rounds." For deep retinas were like the shadowed darkness of night in a pure white cloud, her look like palest coral. "Today is a day of special celebration," she declared, "for the Great Spirit has chosen to smile upon us. We shall not have to gather for days, but can sit here and softly sing. Earth renews itself."

"We should give thanks!" Justine cried."Even now the day is lightening our little lives as though the world lives for us."

Alvin walked about blearily to the edge of the small campground. "Hard work has been well rewarded, somehow. Ours is not to reason why," he said, "when nature was against us."

"Perhaps it was Omyranth," said Eldril. "When desire is enough to shape and mold Fate into Destiny, then the powers that be can choose between life and death."

Justine and Gwynhr paused to dwell upon this idea. "It appears to be luck," said Gwynhr finally.

Justine chuckled lightly, but did not speak, but then she said, "Hard work was with us, and overcame, even though we are small and the world is great, and it was chance, for we could have made the wrong move at any moment or fate could have intervened, and so this Omyranth must have smiled upon us. It is all a great mystery, except to say life is more powerful than death in the end and existence favors life."

"Not so for many left behind," Gwynhr commented, and Eldril nodded.

The dawn sun began to beat down upon their modest encampment. Eldril faded into the underbrush to forage, while Justine and Gwynhr watched the waves and the fishing lines. They held each other's hands, and Justine felt like weeping, but fought against it.

"What is wrong, dear?" Gwynhr asked quietly

"Your bold to save my arm," she said."There was no chance in that."

"I did what I had to," said Gwynhr. "Now your arm is useless but your life is saved, that is the important thing."

Eldril returned with all manner of bird in a truss, from grouse to pheasant to geese. "I thought the day would go well," she commented.

A particularly large swell washed up to Justine and Gwynhr's seat, and tickled their toes.

"It is almost as if," Justine began again, "this island is not supposed to be here. Where once we were lost now we are found."

"It is likely that no one shall find us," said Eldril. She began wrapping plucked birds in banana leaves."None have been here before as far as I can tell." Her pale eyes were offset by the blue of the sky. "When you bury me place me on the top of the mountain."

"What do you know?" Justine asked. "You are young yet."

"I do not feel unfit," she assured them," but my parents always said that because I am pale like a ghost or phantom that I would be called to another world before my term here. They said I was a creature of the past, so my sojourn here would be limited."

"Perhaps you're being superstitious, and were meant to grow old," said Justine. Yet she herself had doubts, for Eldril was pale as a shroud.

"Always have I had it in my heart, this belief," said Eldril, "and superstition is not always just subjectivity. We believe in many unseen things as though they were real. Without abstraction, we would hardly be human."

Gwynhr said, "Jack the hermit said once that even some animals know when they are going to die, and then they seek out some special place to lie down, and then and there they pass away. Perhaps you're more like an animal than most."

Eldril laughed at this, and the sound of her laughter drifted off into the blue sky like gulls crying.

CHAPTER TWENTY-TWO: THE ANIMALS

"Gwynhr," Jack the hermit had once said, "humans are a lot like animals, and animals are like humans in many ways. Only kill an animal when necessary, for it is wrong to take a life, this is our age-old tradition. I live on honeycomb, bread, and wine, which suits me well enough. When you are in the wild or hungry, it is another matter, yet when at peace do not tempt the Great Spirit to anger with wanton slaughter. For, after all, we, too, must live with a temporary life, and should not disrespect this by taking another. My mother used to say 'live and let live,' and gave me the vocation of beekeeper.

"My mother also gave me the story of the deer named 'Ayallah.' Of all the does in the forest, only Ayallah new instinctively each part of the woods, for she had the keenest eye, the most sensitive sense of smell, and the most acute hearing. She knew the juniper berry, and the paw print of the bear, and she knew the weather of the day by the type of morning dewfall.

"Yet once there came a hungry hunter who was set on venison for his table, and he came with special weapons to his purpose. Ayallah was the first to sense something was wrong in the forest, and directly she warned the other deer, and the deer began to warn the other animals, they warned the badger, and they warned the stoat, and they warned the weasel, and they warned the wild boar, and they warned the coney. And soon the hunter found that the entire forest was quite silent, as everyone had sought out refuge and would make no sound. Yet the hunter found a doorway into a warren of rabbits, and set about smoking them out immediately, for he was in increasing hunger. Ayallah it was who first this out, hidden in a glade of ferns. She skipped and ran back into the depths of the forest, and told her friend Erwin the bear what she knew.

"Together, Ayallah and Erwin devised their scheme. They knew that the hunter must be quite hungry to journey so far into the woods, and so they watched him smoke out the rabbits, and when he had caught just one, Erwin came out from hiding at the hunter, who did not have time to use his weapons but had to run himself, which his one coney as a catch.

"Therefore did Ayallah and Erwin consider the Spirit of the land to be appeased, knowing as they did in their hearts that the Spirit favored man, and wanted him to live. However, the other rabbits were very sad, for somebody lost their mother, somebody lost a sister, some an aunt, some a cousin, and the entire forest went into mourning, rather than being happy for the hunter. The Great Spirit itself was appeased yet also sad, for it knew that whereas life is sacred, life requires sacrifices.

At least, Erwin the bear, following Ayallah's purpose, had driven the man from the forest, and he would be too scared to return, and so would have to create his living in some other manner. Who is to say lives and who dies? No one except perhaps the giver of life also takes life, but this is probably not the case."

Gwynhr had listened attentively. "Jack, who is the Great Spirit?"

"A good question if there is one, lad," laughed Jack, "but the Great Spirit is not a who but a what. The Great Spirit is the heart of the world, which exists for all who listen closely enough to hear, like the doe Ayallah. Then the hearer can take part of the Great Spirit into their own heart, and the Great Spirit is always there to be heard."

"Does the Great Spirit listen, then?" Alvin asked, trying to sort through things.

"No, the Great Spirit does not listen," Jack replied, "although it may make sounds. Its greatest quality is in the silence wherein the listener might be be led to hear."

CHAPTER TWENTY-THREE:
STORIES AROUND THE CAMPFIRE

Eldril weaved a wreath of orchids for the doorway to the common hut the three would meet in, and upon completion gave one of her little laughs like a bird. The three had decided to hold a conference, although there were hardly pressing matters to confront. They roasted bananas and set to discussing whatever came to mind.

"We are hidden here on our island," said Eldril, "and it looks as if no marauders shall arrive. Yet we must continue to look out in the directions in case of ore or sail, and we have our boat if need be."

Just then a particularly high wave washed into their encampment, and they found water up to their shins. "This is a greater danger, this unpredictable surf," said Eldril, "and we should consider moving up the mountain towards the mouth of the spring." Eldril's pale skin was like the moonlight, and her retinas like unfathomably deep wells."Then we shall establish safety from all but the greatest of waves and vantage point to search the seas." Upon this they were all agreed and proceeded to decamp for higher ground.

This series of huts they built grew into a circular enclave, with huts for weathering storms, huts for sharing meals, huts for sleeping, and huts to go when you wanted to be alone, as well as a sauna. At the center of the circle was a great fire pit, and that evening there were pheasant and grouse to turn on the spit, and they waited patiently and thought of long ago.

Their stories were both happy and sad, for they had fond memories of places long ago that were no more.

Gwynhr's memories were more present, as he had only just left the abbey. In fact, it was not so long ago. "They were all kind and goodly souls," he lamented, "and I had a wide circle of childhood friends, who I grew up with as companions and playmates. When I was given the task of trading with my friend Jack they all felt certain resentment at the favoritism, get this was swiftly overcome by my special deliveries of honeycomb. Hardly anybody would stray far from the abbey, although Monsignor Dutton and I would take books to read out on the arroyo when it was not too hot. It was he that showed me foreign scripts from long ago, in manuscripts nearly crumbled to dust from time and heat. He showed me that there were many languages, and each one stressed special emphasis on different sorts of meanings."

"English was taught to me as a second language," revealed Eldril. "My family clan, who occupied just the one rocky island off the coast, had few words from long ago, as more and more was forgotten as time went by, and so they developed a speech of their own. But some words of English crept in. They told me to ship was an 'errant,' a fish was a 'glimmer' and my eyes were 'moon skies.' Slowly one of the elders taught me my English letters."

There came a protracted silence. Justine is fretting and picking at the hem of a cotton blouse from Salt Lake City. "My dear mama and papa passed away. I was only a young child when mama died and 11 when my father told me to flee. I do not know exactly what became of my father, except that he was prepared to meet his fate. They showed me books which I remember something of, especially 'A Child's Garden of Verses.' We lived alone in a bunker in swampland which slowly turned to dry with a few years of drought and searing heat, with the Days of No Rain. When mama died, papa told me to read as much as possible, but after I was 11 I did not see a book until I reached Gwynhr.

"The former world is a place of great complexity which ended with the Wars of long ago. My papa tried to teach me, and said that some cities contains millions of people, who all held special tasks all their own, and would mill about in vast tracts of tall buildings, and they had possessed complex sciences and religion and art, which grew and flourished. My papa said that there were also many wars, but that very few people expected their world to be destroyed, despite the fact that there were hostilities and strife for many generations and that many people seemed to be preparing for war.

The people were lulled into a false sense of security, as they say, and dismissed the idea of the Wars, and gave no thought to the coming Desolations, for this concept was very dim in the consciousness of the people. Had it been known, the people would have risen up and protested and would have attempted to seize power from the elite who created the Wars yet this was never attempted really or things might've been different. But the real power lay with the very few ultimately, and my father told me that this was very dangerous, as many secrets were held from the great masses of the people, and there was nothing that people could think or do that could change their predetermined plight. There is no one left to blame, as the elite committed a suicide and there's no one to remember their names. It is all academic, perhaps, for if not them other peoples would have destroyed the race in their place. Papa said that when there are many people and only a few occupy positions of real control and power, then the same result is always destined to be."

"I too, was told the same story," said Eldril," yet these stories are from so long ago that their lives cannot be recovered to remember by any peoples, I know of. We have only a few books and these too shall fade from time. The life I was given and the society I was raised in head little remembrance of such things so long passed, except indicated that they imbalances in nature and in the weather was the result of the Wars, and without the Wars there would be no wandering wild people terrorizing the land. What is once lost is ever so difficult to recover."

"Our time is now," said Justine, "and perhaps we have escaped the Wilderlands of adversity, so what is human yet remains."

"Who shall remember us?" Gwynhr asked them.

"Sometimes," replied Eldril, "stories are carried on the wind, when it whispers in the treetops."

"The trees shall always remain," said Justine, "yet who shall hear us?"

"Everyone who is part of the family will know something of who we are, in a way," said Eldril.

Gwynhr said, "I am not certain I believe we shall be remembered, for time is long and memory is short, and the winds blowing in many different directions."

That night the wind blew a strange sound: an old buoy beacon let out a piercing whistle. All three were awakened like cats, but they could not figure what the sound meant, they just hoped it did not forebode Man.

That morning they all gave thanks, and made the short journey to the mountaintop and spied out the water, but could see nothing but the rolling swells.

CHAPTER TWENTY-FOUR:
A New Life

Many generations passed, and, slowly, the wild people began to die off, from over-foraging, and starvation, disease, infant mortality, and the death of women in childbirth. Ever so slowly, rebellious children would escape the enclaves of the wild people, and wander into various uninhabited lands, some of them quite rustic, but others pursuing and gaining a liberation from ignorance through self-education. As the lands became steadily more peaceful, wandering hermits would meet up with each other and form unions, bred of the common consent towards mutual self-preservation, and against the deprivation of loneliness.

Eventually, the hermits would meet and form their own enclaves, personalized little townships where all participated to the common good. Primarily these people would finally settle near the shoreline as the source of relative abundance.

Nicholas had been meek and subservient as a child, and slaved away under the yoke of his villainous father. His band of people was small, and struggling against the lack of resources, for they were somewhat inland in Southern California and it was difficult to sustain livestock or even gather enough water from dying streams. He hatched a plot to run away, and, as a stable boy, he possessed a fortuitous access to the few horses on the plantation. Nicholas secretly hoarded books and a few other items of practical value beneath bales of hay, and then, one early evening under the cover of nightfall, when he was only 12, he made his escape towards the coast, hushing his horse and silently stealing one of the only carts with wheels. He spat on the ground once as he left.

He drove his cart in an uncertain direction, headed generally towards what he knew to be the West Coast. His road had been little traveled for a generation and more, yet there remained a little tract to negotiate his horse and cart. He would not miss his former township, as it was filled with mean-spirited and selfish folk, except for one young girl he had been fond of named Susan. They had shared secret meetings and private discussions, but Nicholas had decided he could not bring her with him into the unknown and uncertain. However, as he expected, his disappearance had been soon discovered, and a plot was formed by some of his townsfolk to follow and intercept him, and regain their lost resources. So he urged his pony onwards along the grassy trail, and did not hesitate.

When he reached the coastline he was forced to abandon his horse and cart, has his desire, in all the prudence as he personally followed, was to find some way to set sail. All his most valuable possessions he stored in a heavy knapsack, and he released his friend the pony to wander and graze while it yet lived. Nicholas then tied strands of seaweed tightly about some choice driftwood, set his one fishing line and hook with a locust and set out paddling over the initial waves, he knew not where to. He had very little food and there was nothing but ocean before him, although at least there was floating seaweed and algae, and perhaps a fish to catch. Freedom at any cost proved to be better than slavery under any conditions; this was his lesson, hard-learned.

Although he was only 12, he knew full well how desperate his actions were. There were no known lands to the immediate West, and only a few tins for rainwater. Yet the high seas were preferable. On his fifth day of paddling, he was hailed by a sizable fishing vessel. They dragged him aboard with cries of wonderment, and some laughter in derision. Now he had found a new life. He immediately went about performing routine tasks, and learning the sails, which the vessel had four in total.

The crew consisted of 20 men and 8 women, one of whom was the elder matriarch. The women all oohed and ahhed over him, and tousled his tawny hair and pinched. This life proved much better for now than the one he had left, and a most improbable gift.

Nicholas was outwardly bold and forthright, but inwardly nervous and timid. He had only learned to appear as strong, out of necessity. He preferred sitting with a good book, and he still had several of his own, and there were also other books on board.

He was greatly relieved as to his fortune, which had begun with such desperation. The fishermen were generally kind unless roused, and he was not beaten and abused as he had been.

The youngest of the women was nearly 13, and Nicholas took an immediate liking to her, although both of her parents lived on board and were extremely protective, as was only natural, so Nicholas and the girl, whose name was Jenny, spent only scant spare time together. Yet sometimes they would look at a picture book together, or watch the waves, and once Jenny shared some mead she had stolen from the ships hold, which was well stocked with barrels of such, from a rare trade the ship had made with land.

Jenny told Nicholas many stories that his isolated life had never really confronted, tales from her life, of weathering hurricanes, of the catch of the great marlin and the white shark, and of the courage of her mother and father. Nicholas's mother and father had been killed in an argument over salt rations, because Nicholas's village was not well-versed in collecting salt, and his parents wanted extra because they had a child.

Jenny liked Nicholas well enough, but thought him a bit simple. She had not had to labor hard in her brief life, but was given time and instruction to be book learned. So she took pity on this castaway, and when he had free time would instruct him some.

A squall appeared on the waves of the open sea, on the waters much swelled with snowmelt. Cold water sank in the oceans, and the warm water stayed on top, disrupting the natural flow or "rivers" of the seas, and causing unpredictable storms, unpredictable even to the elders of the ship. The sails were brought in, and even the masts lowered to horizontal with particular cranks. Humankind had not been entirely inactive over the generations in the renewed development of industry.

The 20 men and 8 women and Nicholas all gathered in the hold, made watertight with hides and pitches and resins, for the duration of the storm, as the vessel was rocked to and fro and washed above with tumbling waves. Within the hold were furs from trading and a brick grill for heating and cooking, and Nicholas felt a new peace, and looked after well, indeed, as he had never been so well-fed, but for the duration of the storm the rest of the crew mainly huddled against the rolling of the vessel, and some spoke unfamiliar prayers against being capsized. The captain with a stout elderly man, who was usually of a mild demeanor and gentle mien, except when pressed by work and duty, which he partook in like the rest of the crew. His position was largely symbolic and that of a figurehead, yet his presence lent a sense of confidence. He urged all present towards common security, indicating they had weathered worsen in his day.

His name was Jim, and he often showed kindness towards Nicholas, as Nicholas was the only young adult on board save Jenny. He would often give Nicholas extra rations for extra duty, and very occasionally would start with Nicholas and his letters, such that after several years Nicholas was not so ignorant, but caught up to Jenny in book learning. These were good years for Nicholas.

"Land, ho!" came a cry from a yeoman. "Starboard side!" The entire crew came to look at it this sight, and found a patch of green on the horizon. It appeared barely above sea level, evidently, as there were no trees visible. Jim instructed, therefore, the crew to make an approach. As they moved closer they were all astounded, as the patch of green kept changing its position.

"A floating island is found!" Jim exclaimed in a sense of wonder even after long experience on the waters.

It was the case. Many centuries ago unrecyclable plastic, such as plastic bottles and bags and even the loops of six-pack beverage containers had formed an extensive floating island in the South Pacific, which had gradually started its way northwards to these waters. As time had passed, seaweeds and algae had formed a bed of slimy earth amidst the plastic items which were all tangled together, and slowly dust had landed on the breeze, and blowing seeds had taken root and formed a plot of land about a mile across.

"Great good fortune!" cried Jim the captain. "We shall moor here indefinitely and set lines! Surely there is much life hidden below!"

And there was much bounty to fish, like a reef, and the crew celebrated for many weeks. Also, they had found a place that was unsinkable. For this there were many prayers of gratitude and thanks. They were all isolated from the possible cruelties of the land, and had a significant dwelling to roam, and to build upon with their supplies in driftwood, and with flotsam and jetsam, which there was often appearance of, for as land was flooded it would give up a store. They knew this floating island could easily be swamped by waves, but would always return. Therefore they tended their fishing vessel tightly to the island, and knew that they had found extra providences towards unsinkability.

The weeks of rejoicing contained many prayers of thanksgiving towards the miraculous, and indeed the almost singular nature of this serendipity against the inevitable eventual fearsomeness of the open seas. By consensus they determined to drift with the island to some remote outcropping, to dock and have done with the uncertain waters. This small group had successfully avoided the folk who competed in foraging on land, as that population grew, not as wild people but often cruel and vicious in their competition.

As they drifted Nicholas now all of 15 and Jenny 16, unsuspected danger was brewing. The greatly risen waters were applying a certain weight upon the ocean floor, and a floor quake of great magnitude occurred one night. The night shift rushed to the hold, and the hatches were battened down, as outside a tremendous whirlpool was brewing as cracks opened in the floor of the ocean, and the ship and the floating island were pulled in dwindling circles amongst crashing waves.

The weight of the islands earth mass pulled against the lightness of the plastic mass and the timber of the ship, and the entire crew was sent tumbling to the floor which was beginning to pitch headlong into the maelstrom. Waters sprayed in from the hatches and some cracks developed in the hull, which began to trickle and then rush with water. Yet the whirlpool gave up its momentum, and the plastic island pulled the ship out of the depths. Waterlogged, yet safe and with only minor injuries, the incredulous crew were able to ascend to the surface of their ship once again, and under breaking sky decided to take some refuge on the island as they watched their ship slowly sink.

They undid the moorings, and so were stranded on the revealed plastic of the island with only their fishing lines attached. Yet all thought that their fortune was better than not, and that the plastic island had been sent as a gift from the Great Spirit, by any other name.

Jenny hugged Nathaniel."We're alive where there would've been no hope! This strange surface has saved us!"

Nathaniel was a young man of few words, yet he blurted out," I love you Jenny!" Fortunately, this is not in hearing distance of Jenny's parents, Herbert and Nellie.

Everybody tried to rein in flotsam and jetsam that was now appearing from the sunken ship and Jim the captain lead six other strong men in an expedition into the roiling waters about them. They collected as much wood as they were able, but very few other objects. Yet at least one crew member had preserved a flint stone on her person, so they were guaranteed eventual fire.

This ship of un-recyclables floated along, driven by swirls and drifts and rivers of water. It was too great to make any rowing useful.

CHAPTER TWENTY-FIVE :
THE MAGIC ISLE REVISITED

In the middle of the Pacific Ocean they spied the island of Justine, Gwynhr, and Eldril. "Everybody do the backstroke," commanded Jim, and so all 29 leapt into the warm water to swim to their destination. "Land, ho!" cried Jim.

Exhausted and bedraggled, and barely having avoided the reefs, the group, like a family, all reached shore safely. They wandered in wonderment, in astonishment, hungrily consuming bananas and mangoes and coconuts, and came upon the spring of freshwater. No one had been there since Justine had passed on long ago.

The crew shouted to sea-chanteys as though never before, songs of victory and triumph over adversity. Over many months of good living in hard work, a township grew up of driftwood and palm, and apart from an occasional storm and hard pounding earthquake, always serene, and the great bounty was enjoyed.

Nicholas would wait a long time, respectfully, before asking Jenny's hand in marriage. Once, while collecting flowers in a particularly large grove of such, he found a tiny mound with a wooden placard, and written thereon, in octopi milk, was this single name Alvin.

Nicholas showed Jenny, and they sat there for a time, lingering, their imagination full of wonder at this deserted island, and what befell the person who buried this Gwynhr. No doubt, they agreed, their own lives, so narrowly bought, so dearly lived for, and were still circumscribed by the final fate. They became transformed, and cherished more than ever their little lives in an unfathomably wide world. Justine, who had buried Gwynhr, let herself die in the open, and crows and other birds arrived and carried offer remains.

"Every life has a strange ending," Jenny advised Nicholas.

Nicholas felt stubborn, as he often did. "Every life can have a new beginning," he said.

"Nicholas," Jenny soothed, "you will never know these people."

"I shall come to be as these people, the last to survive, perhaps, and with you, and everybody yearns for the same things."

It was true that as the youngest of the colony, Jenny and Nicholas were most likely to survive, unless it should be a birth, but the children would arrive stillborn. Jim the captain officialized over many deaths, and slowly the colony thinned out, until finally only Jim still lived besides Jenny and Nicholas, and had reached a great age.

Jenny and Nicholas were middle-aged when Jim finally passed away. He received his dying wish to be placed on a raft and floated out to sea. By then Jenny and Nicholas had learned they lived through hardship and tragedy, but they locked arms walking back along the beach from the reef.

Gwynhr made another notch in his log, and it was the third day, and so it was time to visit Jack again. He gestured to Justine, who was relaxing with a book in the shade of the last almond tree of the monastery.

"It is time for our walk, dear."

"Just coming. One more page and I shall be ready," said Justine.

"Ready or not, the day is getting hot," Gwynhr quoted.

Jack, as usual, was in good spirits, and stuff on honeycomb and bread. Gwynhr lay more bread on his picnic table and some more wine for them to share. Justine had one sip of wine and then went to nap on the mattress of soft lichen.

"She may have strange dreams," Jack noted. "Remember when she said that she did not have a name?"

"I remember," Gwynhr said nervously, "but everything has a name."

"No, Gwynhr. Not everything has a name," said Jack.

"I will search for names," Gwynhr vowed.

Jack was unusually speechless, but finally began. "When I was a child I saw a hummingbird, and I asked my parents what manner of bird this was and they told me it was a hummingbird. Now I know that each hummingbird has a different name. In the same way todays sky is not as yesterdays, it might look like the same color of blue, but it is changed its name. A cloud that drifts along has a new name every time it shifts and moves. So, too, it is with our own selves, that when we pause or work or think aloud we may have another name, and we participate in the great poetry of life. Most of these names are lost, for we forget how we felt, but many things that are lost can be found upon reflection. Yet when we discover a name, already events have shifted, and the very air has breathed new life into our souls."

Gwynhr said, "I do not wish to be lost. I wish to find the names, and know which cloud is mine, which sky has produced the cloud, but I shall never fly as does the hummingbird, which vibrates so swiftly that it beats many names into the air, yet as I name things I shall find some peace and understand better."

"You shall do well," said Jack," to find the name of a single flower, and as this flower blooms so may change your heart. The poets were right."

"I think I take your meaning. To grow the inner rose we must first grow the outer rose," said Gwynhr.

"Not the other way around, as some suggest," Jack said. "Gwynhr, in your time you shall do well!"

Gwynhr roused Justine from sleep. "My love, it is time we walked again."

Justine got up drowsily. "Hold my arm as we walk and we shall make it back home, you and I, and bathe in the sacred spring."

"We shall make it home, you and I, and as we walk we may speak of your past life, and what it means to be renewed."

CHAPTER TWENTY-SIX:
HOPE SPRINGS ETERNAL

Gwynhr held Justine's hand tightly as they walked back to the abbey monastery. They played a game as they went: Gwynhr would close his eyes and try to guess by sense what plants they were walking by.

"Marigold!" Gwynhr tried.

"Right you are, lad," Justine admired.

Back at the abbey they washed from a pool which was fed by a canal from a very small spring that trickled in those parts, without which the abbey could not sustain itself. And they went out to tend to the grapevines, which always needed tending, and they extended some more ditches for more grapevines to grow.

The sun was getting on for setting, but they yet had time to gather some wheat and wild oats for the supply of bread, supplemented by some of Jack's honeycomb. The evening meal preceded until all had to retire due to darkness, although there was a sleight moon to guide by. Justine and Gwynhr chose to sit on the arroyo together and watch the stars rise. They cheered and clapped when Orion's belt appeared.

They were due to be married soon, but they had not even kissed. That would have to wait, as Justine gave her self willingly only in the most slow fashion. Gwynhr did not mind at all, in fact he hardly thought about the fashions of marriage, just the union of hearts and souls, although Justine, slim and pretty with curly red hair, was the apple of his eye both figuratively and literally.

The ceremony was conducted by the abbess, with Monsignor Dutton playing some small role in officiating. The entire abbey of 192 people were in rapt attendance at this unique event. The abbess was not one to pontificate, yet gave both solemn and happy words for the occasion:

"We the congregation do hereby recognize, on this joyful occasion, two hearts that have become one. They are not one through hardship and they are not one through ease, though both they may know in good time. Rather they are one because of the Greater Guide, the Judge, who marries misfortune with fortune and guides the righteous together, in their humility and mildness and mutual goodwill. So this occasion is explained by such, that heavenly dewdrops have moistened the earth, and it is a gift to the wise. Let us now break with solemnity and drink some wine, and hear from each party varying words of equal merit," concluded the abbess. Even Jack the hermit was in attendance, paying close attention as he sipped of wine.

Gwynhr began, "When first I laid eyes upon thee, my dearest Justine, I mistook you for a bear. And something of the bear lives on inside you. Yet have you maintained, against all odds, the fragility of the human spirit that is our ultimate guiding light, that shows forth gentility and gentleness like unto cracks in a prison wall, this fragility shows the robin how to take care of their young, it shows how to spread seeds on the wind, it even shows the sky how to rest after War and make life possible. I do not assume to claim it as my own, but my love for you, Justine, has made me frail with concern, consternation, and a greater desire for lasting peace than I've ever known." The couple sat across from each other in the shade of the almond tree. "Could I give it to you without harm, I would show you how my heart breaks, for you're most fragile and have endured greater hardship. If it is within my power, never shall I deny thee, and may I approach only in tenderest supplication for one word, one gesture, one glance, for this is all I need to fill my heart."

"Gwynhr, dearest Gwynhr, I have not yet found the strength of the life of gentility, but may I never refuse thee in your supplication, but be willing heiress to your thoughts and needs and desires, for I know you to be most gentle of spirit, and this is indeed the great commonality and bond that unites all of us here today in loving kindness, that we may recognize collectively this strength that comes through fragility, and learn a little better how to love. Love is a great problem, be ye simple and quiet at heart or of the informed wise. May I vouchsafe now, against all cynicism, that I have rediscovered true love when it was most lost to me, or, rather, this love found me, quite literally. May our standard be to never belittle, but to show forth for forbearance and tolerance and patience and such like that ultimately leads to acceptance. May our humble motto be to seek tolerance, to be infinitely tolerance, except of intolerance. We enjoy now the springtime of our lives, and ask all present to participate in celebration." At this the couple was strewn with flower petals, and many garlands placed about their necks.

The abbess spoke again: "Thanks to our great good friend Jack, who has graced us with his presence on this very special occasion, there is very much honeycomb. Would you like to say a few words, Jack?"

"I would indeed, on this, one of my rare visits to this community which lies so close to my heart. And my stomach," he jested and all took merriment in his rotund features."Times of true union are scarce, we cannot overvalue them. Our dear friends Gwynhr and Justine, may you know that happiness that only love can bring. Love was never the delusion of the romanticists, but the true locomotion of our former Earth, although here it failed. Yet love between two people may last for so long as they do, and even make the plants grow stronger, and all their fragility. Whereas many roses have thorns, this union shows forth the embodiment of our highest ideals, such as you practice here in the abbey. We best learn through love, and kindness, and the simple joys two people may know among themselves only. This has stood as the grand mystery of the ages, that true love does indeed exist, and today may be consecrated to tomorrow in great joy."

Monsignor Dutton, who had recently found a marriage to Justine's friend Honica, handed Jack a flagon of wine. "Let us now set to our victuals and enjoy good spirits," said the Monsignor with a double entendre.

Nightfall was coming again, and Justine and Gwynhr decided to accompany Jack for the ten miles back to his bee haven hut, and so honeymoon there, in a place of honey.

Justine felt greatly a sense of innocence renewed, and Gwynhr, who had never lost his innocence, felt an overwhelming sense of relief that he could be Justine's helpmeet. Trotting along with Jack, who had been gifted a new robe as the abbeys especial luminary, they talked quietly together in the twilight.

"Jack," Justine began," tell us of your parents." Gwynhr had heard stories before, but Justine had not.

"Well," said Jack, "they lived where I do, alone in the wood. They were what you might call traditional folk, used to simple living, basic values, the core of things without too many trimmings, if they were also somewhat odd in their own right. They believed in bees more than anything else, except perhaps the forest. One night as a child I found them looking at the stars, and I asked them what the stars meant, and both became resentful, as though I had pried into a part of their unknowing they were protective of. You might say they value the known above the unknown."

"My dear papa," said Justine, "taught me they were like this sun, only further away. He said many places like Earth were up in the sky, as well, and before the Wars people reached up into the sky, because they were curious."

"I read stories in the abbey library," put in Gwynhr, who once had been inquisitive of such matters but then had given up," and many people were very strange. The peoples before the Wars thought many things."

Jack said, "It certainly must have been a grand time, yet so frequently do people miss the point. A simple life is given so that you can do hard thinking, and reflect a little."

"Their lives must have been complicated," said Gwynhr.

The track ended in the gloom of the dusk, with stars just winking in to say hello.

They all three brightened up when they reach Jack's log cabin. They set a roaring fire to blaze and toasted bread and melted honeycomb over it. They then set the table with wine, and enjoyed good cheer with many smiles from Justine to Gwynhr. She loved him so because he was simple and kind, and homely, and his adoration for her was one of deepest sympathy and gratitude for her existence. She had renewed his quiet spirit and made him think about the right way to treat other people, not just her.

CHAPTER TWENTY-SEVEN:
THE CITY BY THE BAY

Nancy Drake slipped a cardboard sleeve about her large paper coffee cup, folded that days copy of the San Francisco Chronicle newspaper under her elbow, and exited the café to await her commuter transit down Market Street to work. She worked in the financial district   shuffling papers mainly, papers of very little import or reality, which involved numerous cases of identity theft that had never been fully investigated, and never would be fully investigated, primarily because the victims had renewed their drivers licenses, credit cards, Social Security cards, bank account numbers, and other pieces of identifying material. Nancy Drake would put all the hardcopy related to each case in its own folder, and the folder would be placed in a separate warehouse facility, along with its own barcode.

On her one hour lunch break Nancy Drake went to another café for more coffee and a prepackaged sandwich, and opened the contents of the San Francisco Chronicle newspaper to peruse. Whatever she read would usually be forgotten by the next day, but in passing she noticed on page 12 another article upon the increased international tensions due to counterintelligence measures that were newly uncovered, a matter that had stuck finally in Nancy's brain due to repetition.

Yet it faded from her attention temporarily. That evening she had a gourmet Asian French fusion dinner with her boyfriend Nick, whom she called "Nicky." They had met online on Facebook.com, and had found they had many mutual interests, such as horror movies, tennis, and good food. If the dinner went well, Nancy knew, there might be time for intimate relations later. Unless of course Nicky had work-related obligations. Nicky, as it happened, also worked in the Financial District, as a bank teller, so probably this evening he would be free. Only sometimes did he have work to take home.

Whether or not they might go back to his place or hers was always a matter of some discussion and sometimes disagreement. Nancy lived in a prime apartment on Nob hill, whereas Nick lived in Hayes Valley in a Victorian style house up in the attic room. Apartments were at a premium in San Francisco, making it as expensive as New York City.

Nancy took a taxi cab home at two thirty a.m.

Nancy and Nicky were exposed to a significant amount of media information on the one hand, more than a medieval man was exposed to it in an entire lifetime, yet on the other hand lived dualistic lives, and were creatures of simple habit. It ultimately drove them into intractable disagreement, and with argument overwhelming them both, they mutually decided not to see each other again. Both went back to scouting on Facebook.com for potential partners.

Their story went unrecorded, although it was true to say there was a lot of recording going on. The San Francisco Chronicle reported that there were 10,000 CIA agent and 4,000 KGB agents in the San Francisco Bay Area, primarily due to the local nuclear industry, the local computer industry, and the local biotech engineering industry. Yet news like this gained only passing interest in some people's minds, people who also went unrecorded ultimately, as electronic surveillance was doing to go the way of the dinosaur, with the massive War it caused. In the end, very little that was recorded lasted for the record, and the facts of lives in political movements and clandestine operations were brought to nought.

Yet for a time, information gathering and counterintelligence created an underground "Cold War," which, on the surface, was nearly unrecognizable, and the diplomatic relations between sovereign territories was mainly accepted as the political truth, despite the published facts and the outstanding military-industrial complexes, regarded as necessary for "defense." As Albert Einstein said, "You cannot simultaneously prevent and prepare for war."

It is a hard truth, but agreements, once reached, can and do fade away with time, and there was no "cumulative benefit" politically as the generations passed, rather a tendency towards increased tension, like the road Nancy and Nicky traveled in there somewhere prefabricated relationship.

Humanity hung in the delicate balance of the very few people at the very top of the so-called "chain of command," who were not trusty stewards. Nancy was about to drop another case in a file in her office and Nicky was about to hand out another roll of 20's at his bank, when sweeping blasts reaped their deadly harvest from the San Francisco to Rio de Janeiro, from London to Paris to Rome, from Nairobi to Hong Kong to Tokyo, without so much as even the emergency broadcast system alert on television and radio. For some unlucky survivors was a boiling blindness from the flashes of nuclear lightning, and fatal nausea. A swiftly spreading malaise swept across the continents.

No one would ever be able to say what the ultimate causes was or who the first perpetrator was in this holocaust, only that it was probably the result of power breeding corruption, as the generations had shown so many times as the repetitive truth of humanity. Some blamed the military; some blamed the economic elites, and some, also, and blamed society at large for allowing it to happen. It was all the same to Nancy and Nicky, who were unceremoniously atomized at a Ground Zero blast; even the South Pole and North Poles were struck, ensuring howling storms of rising water over all the oceans. Inland, and away from major centers of population, was, of course, the most likely place to survive, except certain metropolises like Salt Lake City that were spared the doom. Nobody seemed concerned with bombing the Mormons.

CHAPTER TWENTY-EIGHT:
THE TALE OF AN INFANT

The ecosystem would never be the same. Freak storms of thunder and lightning flared, sudden hurricanes and monsoons rose up from the boiling waters. Blizzards and sandstorms swept over hills and plains, and humanity was reduced to the desperate few, apart from those masses who must die from radioactive poisoning slowly, ever so slowly.

What became of humankind was a slim margin for survival. Rogue desperados were outmatched by clans, and clans did war upon one another and betrayed each other. Yet some escaped to wander the vast expanses of nature, learning a little but forgetting much about what came before, as a struggle for survival dominated. Fewer and fewer children were born, love was nearly conquered in a world of strife, hostility, and uncaring. The race was nearing a point of dying out completely.

Yet then something happened that gave meager hope. Small families hiding deep within mountains and out in the High Plains began to emerge and congregate, ever so slowly. They brought with them the seeds of humanity, a love for life, a desire for the company of others, I desire for the quiet and simple pleasures of the hearth and home. Many could not survive the wildly shifting climates, and many were massacred for food. Yet some of those who wandered the expanses went unnoticed by others.

Homer Stack and his wife Demetria were two of these. Their horse pulled a large part of belongings as they wandered out from the Black Hills of South Dakota, having survived from the one place they had looted amidst the food riots: I camping store with freeze dried goods. This along with rainwater and the wild Idaho potato had sustained them, and the Black Hills had shielded them in isolation. Now supplies were running thin, and they had set their horse and cart on the march, sometimes walking beside for exercise, sometimes sitting on top of their belongings smoking tobacco. They had seen the violence and escaped it, and now years had passed since the fourth generation after the war. At first they had been truly desperate, of generations of Amish farmers use to simplicity, yet, fortunately hard work as well.

Their discussions were modest and convivial as they made their way slowly west, without encountering a living soul. Yet to either side of them, North and South, a few hunter-gatherers made a meagre living from the land.

One day, perhaps in spring or summer, but in any event a sunny and hot day, they heard distant cries up ahead. They listened briefly and determined these were certainly not the cries of a wild animal or wild person, but that of an infant child.

They move forward together, Homer and Demetria Stack, with all due expectancy. Rounding a rocky outcropping they found a small baby in swaddling clothes, with a note written on a scrap of paper next to her that read, "Please feed my baby, or bury her if you find her deceased. I cannot bring a girl child into my tribe. Her name is Justine". This was to be a distant ancestor of Alvin's Justine.

The Stack's reasoned this tribe might be quite nearby and the infant newly abandoned, but not starving. They immediately decided to assume parenthood, and fed the child some of their dwindling supply of water in a sauce of baked sweet potato from a store of these, but they could not wait long for their fear of this nearby tribe, so went out into a dusty desert with such provisions as they had, enough to last several weeks at most. They gave no thought to competition for food and water, only that this precious little life be saved and maintained, and that love might enter the world anew.

The arroyo contained, providentially, small trickling springs that the cracked earth had given up, and there were additionally tubers and scallions and wild grasses to harvest. Bird and beast were few here, but Homer possessed a working Browning rifle which he had never used, but had saved it as a logical contingency measure. On first meeting a beast, a wandering, hungry cougar, he brought it down with one clear shot.

This supplied the couple well for a while, and they ground some of the flesh for the teething little infant.

Demetria rocked their new daughter, and gave her sips of water in between her crying. "There is a good darling child," she comforted, and cooed the infant to sleep

One pleasantly warm night, with only a few drifts of clouds to block the rays of the brilliant starry sky, they heard the distant, muffled speech of other humans. They were forced to muzzle the horse that pulled their cart of provisions, and then they sat down together to wait what fate might befall, but the voices receded into the distance in the South. It was clear from this noise that these people did not expect to meet anyone besides their own kind.

Homer and Demetria Stack had a deep discussion that night. "It is evident," Homer began, "that there is some society to the South. Forwards is only more of this same desert arroyo. We have a distinct choice: if we move forward into hardship there is no telling what we might find, and her food is running low."

"These sounds," said Demetria, "I did not make out to be wild, and they must have merely taken a short journey, if I guess rightly. Somewhere directly south must be a place of Providence. I vote we head in that direction, and discover these people, and if they are wild it is to our great misfortune, if they are civilized the child will survive."

"It is risky," Homer agreed, "but my vote is with you." Consensus had been achieved, except for the poor infant who could not speak, who could not know, who occupied the preconscious of a life named Justine, whom Barnaby generations hence, would name his own daughter after.

The morning came bright and breezy, and the child was fed, and the horse received dry grasses.

They can do where they spied an old forest in the distance. This in and of itself was good news, but their hearts had misgivings about the occupants. Homer Stack contemplated his rifle, but then thought better of it, for they were almost surely outnumbered. When they arrived at the outskirts of the woods, they were met with a hail: "Hail and well met! exclamation point friend or foe?"

"Seekers after peace!" cried Demetria with as much seeming baldness and she could muster.

"You are welcome!" came the unexpected reply, and two warriors in white robes armed with bow and arrow emerged.

"We ascertain," said one," that you are a humble folk." the two approached and spied the infant. You are indeed in great need, with your suckling babe, caught in the desert. Let us be your guide to a fair dell in these woods where matters might better be discussed of such destiny as has brought you here."

"We are up of a disposition to follow you," said Homer.

The two warriors led the horse and carriage along a track of laid stone, yet occasionally made rough by extending tree roots. What seemed most peculiar to the Stacks were, interspersed along the way, wood and stone carvings of odd figures, people gesturing with fist or fingers, people as though frozen in the midst of time, as sorcerers and enchantress and children and warriors, all finely wrought by the hands of skilled craftsmen, not rough hewn at all. Here were miracles of rare device, to be marveled at and wondered at and loved for their elegance and great beauty.

Soon, surrounding them up in the air, were many tree houses with people in them, people evidently going about a domestic life, chattering away and cooking and fixing and cleaning and making objects of art.

Eventually they came to a hillock some way into the forest, which was occupied by a dome skillfully made of rock, seamlessly put into place by master masons. At a hail from one of those accompanying the Stack's, a lone figure exited the dome. She had brown skin, and, lo and behold, nothing less than spectacles perched upon her nose. She, too, wore white robes, which offset her deep brown eyes.

"Dr. Radakrishnan," one of the warriors explained to the astronomer, "these are vagrants yet not vagabonds. See how they have survived, with horse and carriage versus the Desolations of the wild, and they bring an infant."

"Hello," said Dr. Radakrishnan, and she extended her hand, and shook Homer's and then Demetria's in turn. She then inspected the little child named Justine.

"She appears in health!" the Doctor of Astronomy exclaimed."All is well, for now, and we shall devote special care to the nurturing of this infant, who knows not what to make of the world except comfort versus hardship. We will make you a gift of our most spacious extra treehouse, and see that you are provided for. I noticed that your carriage has many varieties of working implements, and, if you do not mind, in exchange for daily provision, please allow our craftsmen access to your tools. Your weapon, two, if we may borrow it, shall come to good use in supplying our community.

"I see that you are elderly, yet not entirely infirm. Although we are only one island of humanity, we have sat here hidden for generations since the wars, when a group of scientific people banded together to establish as socialized a community as possible. Some may choose to barter, others make candles of beeswax, others simply objects of art to beautify our little lives with. We ask for nothing if you accept the caring for the infant."

"Dr. Radakrishnan," Homer began, his heart swelling with tears, "we might easily have passed you by on our trek across the desert. Thank you for your kindnesses. All three of us require rest and recuperation, yet already my wife Demetria here and myself, Homer Stack, have found a sense of security and what is clearly the stability of generations here. We gladly accept your offer, and shall labor on behalf of the child in this, our old age."

"So be it, then," declared Dr. Radakrishnan, "you will have your quarters appointed post haste and food brought so you may rest. I hope you enjoy coney stew."

"Coney stew!" cried Homer. "My favorite!" All seemed well.

The infant Justine stayed with Homer and Demetria Stack for many years. At first they kept her confined to their tree house, one of relative luxury, with cougar skins to softly wrap the child in, and a grill for the colder nights. Eventually, when the infant Justine was about two years old, they let her down from the treetops to familiarize her initially with a remarkable community, where they yet had musical instruments to sing along with, a great supply of craftsman tools, and a population given to good humor and cheer in the midst of an unhappy age.

Yet Justine always clung to her parents, seeking comfort and consolation, as though she were lost. The entire population there was less than 300, but fed well by crafty hunter gatherers who journeyed increasingly far afield.

When Justine was barely 10 years old she was placed in a special school for children and young adults of all ages, and Dr. Radakrishnan became one of her mentors. The dome made of stone was a favorite place for the children to congregate, and peer through a telescopic lens at the night sky, whose brilliance sparked in the imagination and made many dream of fables of distant lands and the heroes of the ages. The night sky provided much inspiration for the artisans of the woods, and new statues and figurines were produced as a craft which was handed down to the generations of the future, representing the gods and monsters and battles inherent in the sky.

Very few foreigners entered into the woods, for this forest was isolated in the great expanse of desert, and few braved the Desolations, and fewer still survived. Yet lives outside were short lived in any event, as the cruel fates of competition for decreasing sustenance ruled most places.

When Justine was 11 years old Demetria passed away in her 70's. Homer was already reaching 80 years old, and he sought out new parentage for the maturing child.

First he brought an idea to Dr. Radakrishnan. "For added security against roaming bands who may yet prowl these very woods, I believe we should establish a sister community. There are some few springs out on the arroyo to be found, and so land might be cultivated. I believe it is time to divide ourselves for added security." This wisdom Doctor Radakrishnan could hardly gainsay.

She said, "We shall send a party to search out such a likely place as there might be water and earth, and when found we will send our finest masons to build." Thus, many generations before his own life, Alvin's abbey was founded. A portion of the population in the woods were inspired with the adventurous dreams for the future, and buildings sprang up on the arroyo and rare clippings of grapevines planted, and white grasses cultivated on some earthy plots. Rains would still come to this area, and so the abbey at last was deemed a success.

Homer took Justine to live not far from the abbey, still in the woods but nearby the new community, in a log cabin his friends helped him build. He busied himself as a gardener and beekeeper, as well as collecting books from the general supply and his own personal collection for Justine. Yet Homer at last expired, and a friendly young couple occupied his cabin and looked after

Justine, but when Justine came of age they sent her to the monastery for greater community.

Justine was friends with everyone, and labored hard on extending canals from their little spring, and planting and harvesting and threshing grain, and stomping on grapes to produce the very popular wine. Yet without her parents she felt the loneliness, and, in time, being too proud to accept a suitor, although she had many admirers, she thought of leaving the abbey. They all knew that to the west one came eventually to Salt Lake City, and the people of the small community strongly advise Justine against attempts in that direction. Yet did Justine have a restless spirit, and desired to find a different folk as might contain her husband. She was seeking beyond the genteel life, and desired someone of another stock, and someone who had known the rigors of the humanity outside her enclosed life, that she might teach and save and take care of him. It became an obsession, and she knew that one day she must leave the abbey and search towards the West.

Dr. Radakrishnan was the acting abbess, and urged Justine not to go. "It is a fool-hardy quest. You leave safety, comfort, and quietude for ultimate dangers of cruelty, lustful abandon, hardship, and strife. If you must go, we shall send our finest warriors with you."

Justine said, "I cannot lead others down the road of folly, and I am not of your world originally, and as I was saved, I feel someone else must be saved."

"We do not abide easily your decision. Yet I can see that where your life is dear to us, someone else's life might be dear to you. And there are no ultimate rules concerning such things: we come and go as we see fit!"

The starry sky was Justine's guide as she, like a mariner, headed in the direction of Salt Lake City. Although she had brought all the good food she could carry, the way across the desert was longer and more arduous than even she suspected. Springs were few, and she finally was reduced to eating grasses. Yet in all, she could not regret her decision, but she felt that destiny lay ahead.

One day, after a gradually sloping arroyo had been partly descended, she saw the spires of the city in the distance. She began to hear toads and frogs and crickets, and indeed, as she as she descended some more, was presented with a spanning marshland which stretched onwards into the city proper. It was, she surmised, although she had never seen one, much too treacherous to cross on foot. After much searching about on the parameter, she discovered a dry log which might be a hollowed into a kayak. She had become a slave to circumstance, yet her spirit was driven, she had to move forward to find her freedom, which was, after all, dedicated and motivated towards finding her love. She knew that many unfamiliar folk might live in this unfamiliar environment, but in her hollowed kayak she dared the marsh and paddled with old branches to a labyrinth of the ruined suburbia on the outskirts.

She was halted in her tracks by wild calls and emitting from before and behind her, and she began to perceive figures hunting the marsh ahead of her, and other figures on the shore behind. She, despite a certain hardiness of spirit, was immediately frozen in fear. Yet one small hope remained in view: it was a concrete bunker which she recognized as perhaps containing safety for a while. She paddled in this direction, beginning to despair.

The bunker door was made of solid steel. Justine pounded upon it with both fists, and rapped with a stone, praying to the stars that a peaceful folk may let her enter. "I am a woman!" she cried. "I come in peace! I beg you let me enter!" The door slid open noiselessly, and a middle-aged woman confronted her.

"Where have you gained your freedom from, child?! You must hurry in!" The woman told Justine.

Justine nearly leapt through the door, which slid shut noiselessly behind her. She was confronted by a concrete and steel interior that stretched into a number of corridors and rooms, with many tins and cans of perishables and freeze-dried stores stacked high all around, and handful of gaunt and grey denizens confronted her with trepidation, yet extending hands of invitation.

"Do not fear," Justine said immediately," I intend no harm."

Among these pale phantoms Justine would eventually choose a husband after many years of searching out their souls. He was an awkward and unlikely fellow, barely bred for survival, yet conversation between them always turned to the philosophic, towards thoughts of an abstract world which had nearly no basis in the actual. Sometimes their speech lead to thoughts of fable and fairytale.

Justine was trapped within this little world that she could not leave for the dangers without. She'd traded her freedoms for one singular love. So it was that many generations later, when the food and population within the bunker was running out, another child was born named Justine in remembrance of survival and hope,

CHAPTER TWENTY-NINE:
THE DISAPPEARANCE OF SAMUEL HOLDSWORTH

Gwynhr turned six years old, and was taken under the wing of Monsignor Dutton as a child who took to books. At that time in the monastery there were more than one almond tree, and every year there was held a celebration where everyone enjoyed a few almonds each.

Gwynhr was of the kind that was very shy and timid. He never played with the other 10 boys and girls, but he sat reading, swept hallways, and walked out on the arroyo. When he was eight, the abbess personally showed Gwynhr the way to Jack the hermit, who had grown too tired to deliver the honeycomb to the abbey. It would be Gwynhr's duty to bring him bread and wine exchange for great slices of honeycomb. The arrangement, everybody thought, was mutually beneficial. Gwynhr was not so timid that he would not occasionally sneak just a few sips of wine.

Gwynhr enjoyed much bread with honeycomb. Being given the privilege of making the delivery to Jack was considered an honor indeed, and many were envious. Yet it took Alvin hard work to go the ten miles there and ten miles back every three days.

"So you are this Gwynhr I've heard of," said the rotund Jack at their first meeting."You don't look like much, but I suppose this is how Mother Nature plans important things. I look forward to your visits. Before I settle into my wine, why don't I show you the bees?"

In the backyard of Jack's cabin were boxes and barrels and crates all with drawers in them. An immense number of bees were swarming, flying on missions deep into the blooming forest and out into the open meadowland, producing an enormous quantity of honeycomb.

"The beehives have been added to for generations," Jack explained, "to my parents from their parents from their parents and so on. You could never tell what time will do with enough time." Jack laughed a little."It is been a fine inheritance, and this peaceful forest. Yet my joints are getting creaky, and I simply get shagged out marching all the way to the abbey loaded with honeycomb, and then back again with bread and wine. So, what interests you, Gwynhr?"

"I like stories of cats and dogs," said Gwynhr shyly.

"There is a fine thing, cats and dogs. Man's best friends, I believe it was often said."

"Have you ever seen one?" Gwynhr inquired with wonder.

"Well, no," Jack admitted, "but they are a fine thing to imagine: small and tame and caring about their owners. You just don't see that in the few animals these days."

"What animals have you seen?" pressed Gwynhr.

"Well, I once saw two deer, a buck and a doe. They were not too far from here, but became skittish and ran off. Still a very fine sight to see, and one that I shall always remember."

"All the books I read," said Gwynhr, "were written before the Wars. Most are crumbling and dirty, but some have pictures. I've been hearing quite a bit about cities. What do you think of them?"

"No doubt too large for their own good," Jack suggested. "I think that one from above would look very much like an ant hill that's been stepped upon, people coming and going and not really working together. It would be a shame to get mixed up in one, and always be driven from one place to another. I think that people require a life that is simpler to remain themselves, otherwise the mind gets distracted and cluttered and one can't quite think freely. No doubt, some people considered them quite necessary, always having a place to go to next, but it doesn't make sense, really."

Gwynhr considered this a while, and then said," I brought a few almonds as a gift."

"Really!" exclaimed Jack."I haven't had any since last year. Thank you, lad" Jack immediately began relishing the small handful of almonds."Just like I remembered them: delicious! Now for some toasted bread and honeycomb!"

"Only briefly," said Gwynhr. "The days getting on and I must make my stroll home."

"Yes, of course, lad. A pleasure meeting you. I'm sure we shall enjoy each other's company. See you in three days time!

"See you then!" So Gwynhr departed Jack the hermit's log cabin, thinking himself very fortunate indeed.

Nick winked at Nancy over lunchtime coffee in the financial district of downtown San Francisco where they both worked. "Perhaps one day we'll get promoted, eh?" he almost quipped "It's impossible to move up to assistant manager, there is too much competition."

"You could try to stand out more," Nancy noted cruelly.

"I do everything extra I'm asked, but others have more experience, or are better liked for their past personalities by the management."

"Poor Nicky," Nancy replied. "Always a third wheel."

"I'm thinking of becoming a bartender," Nicky said.

"Someday never comes," Nancy said with irony, not knowing that governments everywhere were hostile to her existence."I'm late!" she cried. "Got to keep the filing up!"

"Will I see you after work?" queried Nicky wearily.

"We'll see," said Nancy.

Samuel Holdsworth had once worked for the Office of National Intelligence, the bureau that oversaw all other information gathering, intelligence, and counterintelligence organizations in America and her territories, from the Marines, Air Force, Army, Navy, to the FBI, CIA, National Security Agency, National Security Council, and several dozen others, mostly highly discreet. Through hard work and dedication the overqualified Samuel Holdsworth climbed the mountain into the realms of highest security clearance, above which were only shadowy industrialists who were never voted in or appointed, except by birthright perhaps. For many years Samuel Holdsworth labored, fully aware of the clandestine nature of the fourth branch of government, which made the executive, judicial, and legislative branches pale by comparison in terms of actual practical work put forward in their respective fields. The fourth branch did more man hours of work, spent more money, and dealt with more information than the other three branches combined.

Samuel Holdsworth was one of the rare few: a cog in the integral segment of government who had an over-weaning conscience. He knew, in full possession of his patriotism, that what he was doing was wrong. Yet having achieved higher clearance you almost couldn't change careers, for he had been exposed to privy information, and therefore was something like an indentured servant. However, that was about to change.

One early morning, at dawns breaking light, Samuel Holdsworth cut his beard and mustache into a ragged roughness, applied some bleach carefully here and there to look older, and dressed in ragged and soiled clothing he had found in the street. He took the back elevator in his expensive apartment building, the Trump Towers Philadelphia, and retrieved from near the dustbins a shopping cart full of recyclables. He then slipped out with his cargo into an alleyway, and proceeded from his posh neighborhood as, to appearances, a homeless man, destitute and miserable and doing recycling for extra money. His route, however, led him away from the city central and out into the parkland where, months previously, he had hidden a bicycle in the underbrush. He was in a hurry, and determined to make it to the Sierra California in time for the fireworks display he knew was coming.

He was embarked on the least likely course of action, and yet the most prudent considering all that he knew: complete disappearance from society. He had stuck with his governmental positions tirelessly, a man respected for devotion, allegiance, and hard work. Now his retirement would be utter, only to confront other humans on the Pacific Crest Trail, where he would perform equally hard work: the life of a hermit fisherman gatherer. He possessed no doubts about his ability to do so, and was as determined or perform work as he had ever been before.

His disguise worked as he bicycled across the country, and at the end of his journey he spent wisely on all manners of camping equipment and the necessary supplies of an existence in the wilderness, including a light canoe which he actually carried for 10 miles despite his middle-age up into the mountains. He made several trips similarly laden with goods, and established a front by a likely lake. His meetings with other mountaineers would be occasional yet, but it was not so long until disaster would overtake civilization, as he knew full well it would. The information he had been exposed to left no doubt as to this, and he had rejected the notion of participation in fallout shelters for greater freedom, freedom desired by many but attained by only the few.

Samuel Holdsworth was a good man, despite his means of former employment: he was good-natured, affable, yet had been disposed by the conditioning of his work to wear a demeanor of sternness. This sternness was only truly realized about three weeks into his stay in the Sierras, when one dusty, dusky evening tremendous mushroom plumes arose on either side of his mountains both in California and Nevada. He swallowed some anti-nausea medication just in case the winds were unfavorable and did not sleep that night or the next, but rather continued to search out a means of hiding that was nevertheless close to a plentiful source of fishing, for as long as a supply might last there. Then he would make several more trips and carry his canoe and other valuables to another likely spot. He practiced self-concealment, despite his compassion for any travelers who were caught off-guard in the mountains with limited supplies. His own supply of food was limited. Yet he had memorized over the years a good number of means of surviving in the wild, and had good advantage. He had a special preference for wild asparagus, steamed.

"I found you at last!" a gasping breath came Samuel's way. It was his old spy David Lester Brinkley. "Once you disappeared, we followed old satellite imagery of an old homeless man exiting your building, and tracked your bicycle journey to these mountains. I've been wandering about for weeks. "Hello, Lester," Samuel Holdsworth nearly sighed, although he was patient. "You look hungry."

"Famished, really. Anything about?"

"Fish, of course."

"Be a good man and share, Samuel. I nearly avoided hellfire. I see that must have been your plan. It was a Hatfield's versus the McCoy's once again, eh?"

Samuel thought upon his own patients. "Nobody knows how it began, or who finished it. I imagine it was a simultaneous preemptory strike."

"So how did you figure it out? Without you leaving and headquarters sending me to follow, I never would've made it."

"It's a long story, Lester. The trail had been growing for years."

"But your timing, Holdsworth! Spectacular!"

"I was privy to certain papers. Plans were in the works for decades, it wasn't much deduction to figure when everything would explode."

"In a manner of speaking," said Lester Brinkley."What do we do now, old chum? Sit on a heap of rocks?"

"I have a few good books," said Holdsworth. "Basically, though, we're waiting for anybody who likes to fish, to hunt, or to gather."

"Spectacular, old man." Lester was good at none of these, except he knew how to use a gun.

They would arrive in a steady trickle, campers stranded on the Pacific Crest Trail by the massive detonations, many of them running out of supplies, destitute and with nowhere to go, no planned destinations left, unless one descended from the Sierra to places of doubt and strife, the beginnings of the Desolations, places of competition, food riots, and brutality.

Samuel was ready to run a clinic of sorts, to teach and train survivors towards the science and art of surviving in the wild. All comers were innocents, trapped, yet enjoying a relative good fortune. To join a small community, many were willing to share freeze-dried goods, rice, lentils, and the like. Yet soon Samuel had showed a growing number of people what plants to look for, how to harvest pine nuts, and likely places to fish and set snares. Some were already fishers.

Tents grew into a tiny colony, and soon cabins were being built. Newcomers were always welcome, for there were none of ill will, and most were ready and able to become useful. Samuel himself partook in much of the labor, and was soon sitting in a position of respect and honor as the best informed and most industrious.

Yet they were soon buffeted by tremendous winds from both sides of the mountains, and expeditions for food ran into the difficulty of blinding rainstorms and then blizzards. Yet it was only a short-lived sort of winter, and its spring came unexpectedly balmy and mild.

As he was a modest man it could be forgiven Samuel that eventually he would seek a wife. The entire Pacific Crest colony came together most peacefully, as all were peaceful people gathering in the spirit of goodwill towards each other, despite being of varied background. It helped immensely that there was a doctor among them, Miss Mary Newsom, and she naturally became the object of Samuel Holdsworth's enduring affection, as she, too, was a creature of modesty, and kind and of patient endurance.

At first the struggle of the colony was great, as producing enough food for a growing number of people proved most difficult. Yet with shared means, a plan was produced to penetrate the surrounding area with scouts, on the lookout for all manner of edibles. Soon, however, it proved that the colony would have to be mobile, just to find enough food for fifty plus people every day. Everybody was respectful of Samuel and Mary and their services, and he occasionally enjoyed the wild asparagus, steamed. Everybody had an opportunity to dine on dear, beaver, and fish, and while the work was hard, generally they evolved systems of efficiency to lighten the hardship. However it soon became apparent that were they meant to survive, they must break up into groups to do their foraging. On this part there was heated debate, as everybody naturally desired to be with their friends and favorite people. Married couples, it went without saying, could remain part of the same group.

Lester Brinkley was the thorn in Samuel's side. He insisted they be part of the same group, and Samuel could only suspect that, despite all circumstances to the contrary, Lester maintained a devotion to the government, or, rather, what would have been the government, which was now virtually annihilated. Samuel also suspected secretly that Lester's wished to drive a wedge between himself and Mary, by way of feeble Machiavellian motives left over from Lester's days as a counterintelligence agent.

The group decided to draw straws. Everybody wished to be with Samuel and Mary, the most successful and invaluable of the band, as Samuel was an expert gatherer and Mary the doctor. They would split into groups of 10 and head in separate directions, another matter of heated contention, as everyone had an idea as to which direction was most desirable. Lester was obstinate that he stay with Samuel, and, alternately, the group of about 50 gave into his insistence, mainly because they didn't want him along with them.

They attempted to divide the goods between them, and so tents, fishing rods, the few rifles, and means for making fire were distributed. There were lonely goodbyes and brief expressions of endearment as the groups split.

There was no question about approaching civilization: the survivors were sitting on limited foodstuffs, and food riots had broken out immediately among those not too ill. Samuel and Mary and eight others, four men and four women, bundled in down coats and parkas, made their way to a distant lake to try their luck. Fish responded, and so there was some hope.

Samuel and Mary had immediately known each other, as if they had before, and they were the best educated of all of these survivors, who by chance or luck had ended up in a remote area at the right time. Only Samuel had planned his escape, and he explained to Mary the inevitability of atomic disaster.

"There were those who thought they owned the world, yet were opposed by others of equal leanings, even as though the world could be divided up like a pie, but there were too many guests for dinner," said Samuel. "For a long year as I had planned in secret, learning more and more each individual's positions and power. The elite had plotted against each other until nothing was left except the final solution. Those who hunger most for power are those who hunger most for ultimate disaster. Those who rose by appointment or vote did so on the basis of money, not morality. Thus it went."

"Samuel," Mary addressed her husband, whom she had known only a few months, yet trusted implicitly, "I am not bred to meditation, and these lonely hills leave little else. We must take solemn bows not to leave each other even briefly, but follow the path of intimacy that is now largely gone from the world. The pockets of those who have survived shall only truly lived through love, and those who fail in this shall fail to live, as sure as to love is to live. Let us be our assurance of survival, and the way towards a long life of healthful living in joy."

"I've been a man of sorrow," said Samuel, "but you have completed my dreams."

The sky turned dark splintered by magenta fire beams. "Has the catch been good today?" Lester inquired of Samuel.

"You will get your share, Lester, but tomorrow you still have that extra fishing duty."

"I would rather gather pine nuts," Lester returned.

"Those who had extra fishing duty today, due to your lack, are those who go gathering tomorrow. Or, if you prefer, you may take a fishing rod and make out on your own somewhere."

Lester hesitated as though contemplating a crime, which in fact he was. "I will stay with the group," he responded."What is a little extra fishing duty, after all?" Lester was jealous of Samuel and Mary, and had very little moral compunction. He was a model creature of the worst of his age.

Samuel was rightly guarded, as he knew Lester somewhat, and trusted him less, and he was protective of his new wife, whose inner beauty shone without with a bedside manner of caring and compassion.

One day Lester was missing, and so was their only rifle. The remaining nine, including Samuel and Mary, conferenced in the gravest of tones at this development.

"Perhaps he is going to do the tour of hunting," one suggested.

"Or, perhaps, he has gone to commit suicide," another put in.

"He may be insane," said Mary, "criminally insane. He ever delivers signs of stress and lack of confidence in us. If he is hiding in wait, then we are indeed in jeopardy. He may be lurking behind any rock, thinking to take us unawares and possess what little we have."

"I know Lester a little," Samuel advised, "no immorality is beyond his inculcation into the higher levels of government. We should consider him dangerous, otherwise he would have notified us of his intent."

Yet Lester returned at the end of the day with a young buck strapped over his shoulders. "I hope this makes up for any previous lack," he told the little enclave. The rest nodded their assent, some with relief and some with trepidation. It was clear Lester was handy with a rifle.

Samuel wisely stepped in. "You've done exceeding well, Lester. Now Jonas here shall take the rifle for his turn tomorrow."

"Why, yes, of course," said Lester, and handed over the rifle.

The band was building huts about their tents for added protection from the elements. A number of freak storms came and went, with torrential downpour and blistering winds, as the outside world was rocked with the invoked fury of Mother Nature. Spring, summer, autumn, and winter were all interchangeable suddenly and none could predict the weather. Samuel and Mary huddled about the last fuel for their cooking stove, boiling trout with herbs. Mary had a great many questions about the government she had lived under, this societal machine she had played such a successful role in, as a model doctor, but worst of all she wanted to know Samuel. Samuel was at turns dour with consternation, and then less stern and rather warm to the point of elation. His life had been of a solitary creature, but that had changed in recent weeks, and he began to display a joviality of spirit, even in the face of their disaster. Mary began to depend upon Samuel more and more, while in the background, lurking was the figure of Lester Brinkley, a shrewd and calculating creature of the machine who behaved much more simply than he really lived, yet was nearly betrayed to the rest of the group as a potential danger. The issue of the rifle and Swiss Army knives, of down feathers sleeping bags and a few canisters of lighting fluid, dwelt in the minds of them all, in their distrust.

And it was true. Samuel, ever a light sleeper, was aroused one stormy-wracked night by rustling and shuffling, and getting up to investigate found Lester gone, along with significant supplies, including the rifle. A council was held that morning.

"Is he going to make his own way?"

"Do we try to follow him?"

"How can we know we are safe?"

These were some of the questions asked. It was Samuel that answers them. "We cannot assume that once betrayed he will not betray us again. To follow him would be to invite danger and yet it would also be true that to do nothing invites danger. In any event it is my opinion that he shall return, and that a distinct danger haunts us all. I recommend we devise a defensive hut for the women, and allow the men to go out sparingly. It shall diminish our harvest yet reduce potential risks."

In private with his new wife Mary, Samuel was more practical. "It would seem to me that I am his primary target. Therefore, the same might be said for you. I consider it prudent to dissolve this colony, and go our separate ways before circumstance get worse."

"Samuel, we depend upon each other," Mary resisted, but Samuel replied:

"It is on an exercise in futility to remain as sitting ducks for a madman. Lester was born and bred into a career of subterfuge. That our civilization is gone has not reversed this, if anything it has reinforced it. Do take my point as informed of experience, and go pack your bags while I alert the others."

"I admit it is better than uncertainty. I will pack."

The other seven members of the colony were dismayed, yet Samuel told them, "Perhaps you can catch up with some of the others, our find success by yourselves, yet I deem it increasingly unsafe to remain here under a possible threat from a lurking unknown."

Jonas spoke up."We will heed your advice, Samuel. Lester is an unknown factor, and this alone is intolerable." The members of the colony proceeded to de-camp. Samuel told them of his own plans.

"Mary and I shall head in the direction of the Carson River. Therefore, decide among you the best choice for your own paths, knowing that mine is the one most of most potential danger." In the end the seven decided to stick together and follow the opposite direction.

Samuel and Mary crept along cautiously, but it wasn't before long that they were betrayed.

"Samuel, I can see you!" Lester cried from behind an outcropping of boulders. Samuel and Mary immediately ducked low."Samuel, you're a traitor!" barked Lester."You may be the best traitor ever, but you're still a traitor!

"Be reasonable, if you know how," called Samuel."What I did saved your life."

Lester didn't hesitate."Our renewed planet was supposed to rise from bunkers, not the wild," came his response.

"It would never work," cried Samuel."The world they created is too wild for a few to tame. Come out, Lester, and let's talk."

Shots rang directly overhead. Samuel and Mary hid behind rocks as best they could, but they could not discern which direction Lester might come from.

"Should I give myself up as a ruse?" Samuel asked Mary with grave doubt and fear.

"He'll kill you," said Mary," it's me he wants."

"I have this camping stove," indicated Samuel."Light it, quick!"

The stove was lit. Samuel could just make out a rifle staff looking over a boulder about 20 feet off only. He aimed as best he could with the lit stove, and heaved it into the air. There was a flare for a moment, and Lester Brinkley screamed in agony. Samuel leapt up to disarm him, and found Lester rolling on the ground to put out the fire on his face and body.

Mary approached."Nice aim," she said, "Now what do we do with him? He needs medical attention."

Samuel picked up the rifle."It sounds cruel, I know, but we must run from this place. We only bring more evil upon ourselves if we help him."

They strapped the knapsacks tightly, reviewed their compass, and ran, so that Lester might never know what direction to follow. They always tried to work the higher ground so as to detect others first, and avoid the storm of hungry survivors from the food riots. Samuel and Mary sought out the most remote, the most hidden territory. Rarely did they ever exchange words with others, as they always moved on at sight of strangers. In so doing, they could never be betrayed again.

Their daughter they named "Oakleaf." It was an unusual choice, to be sure, yet Samuel and Mary had settled into a remote area where fishing game were abundant, and had themselves become increasingly creatures of nature. It was inevitable, for as the metropolis breeds creatures of an information paradigm, a world of propaganda, so, too, wilds might engender the gentle qualities, if nature proves not to hostile. Samuel and Mary raised their daughter to be self determinative, confident, strong of heart and will.

The nighttime campfire was always a source of good cheer and good humor, so Samuel and Mary shared the most comedic anecdotes of their lost world and only revealed the barbarity later. Oakleaf grew up a child who enjoyed walks in the woods, sitting by their stream, and collecting the little treasures of nature, like pinecones and birds nest and sap to season their tea. She grew up strong, yet without pride, except a certain sense of honor towards her own humanity, which recognizes itself as the most valuable thing in life, except for the humanity of others. She grew up strong, yet sensitive to every last expression of eye and mouth, and every articulation of speech and what it implied. In the end, though, there was no one to share this secret knowledge with, as first her mother and then her father passed away. Oakleaf felt the deep sadness of destitution, yet sang songs to herself as her parents had taught her to.

CHAPTER THIRTY:
THE TALE OF THE OAKLEAF

When Oakleaf was about to turn 60, and the chill winds were blowing for an unseasonal autumn, an older man appeared, thin and bent over and using a walking stick. Oakleaf had only seen her parents before, among all humans.

"Would you like some fish?" Oakleaf asked politely.

"Yes, please, if it is not too much trouble," the elderly man said. "My name is Zacharias. If I do not presume too much, we are of approximately the same age. Those that remember the time of the Great Wars are growing few indeed."

"I will remember my parents, "Oakleaf responded immediately.

"Mine were goodly souls, as well," said the old man Zacharias. "It is always best to keep what is useful and discard what is not."

"I like to sing," Oakleaf said.

"That is very nice. I'm afraid my own voice is grown a bit hoarse."

Oakleaf's wrinkled face smiled at him. "There is always room for another voice with singing."

"You shall scoff," said Zacharias.

"I'm sure I will not," said Oakleaf.

The tale of Oakleaf from Zacharias would have none to tell it, for neither would meet another human for as long as they lived. Both were charmed with an exceeding lifespan and spent many a day enjoying each other's company, wandering through the woods by a flowing brook, watching the sunrise and set, and reciting such lore as had been handed down to them. They developed a particular joy in taming wild animals, and soon had developed a crowd of devoted squirrels which they fed pine nuts to, and each received special names, such as "Drowsy", "Elfin", and "Doolittle" after their special qualities. At last, using tidbits of miner's lettuce, they tamed a rabbit they named, "Polkadot." The animals would wander about the camp and not mind Oakleaf and Zacharias at all. No wild animals ever approached the camp, and Oakleaf and Zacharias were left in peace and quietude, as were the animals for Oakleaf and Zacharias had made a pact never to take a life. It consigned them and to a marginal diet yet one that was sufficient.

One day a pair of deer entered their little dell, and ate some miner's lettuce. Deer were not uncommon sites yet rarely entered the compound. The rabbit "Polkadot" was especially jealous of his food supply, whereas the appearance of the deer's seemed to make "Drowsy" the squirrel especially sleepy."Elfin" pricked up his ears at them munching, and "Doolittle" became quite still and would not move until the deer were gone.

The elderly couple delighted in this, and distributed pine nuts and miners lettuce to their little family. The sky was growing dark with clouds that evening, and so they dugout trenches about the camping tent left Oakleaf by her parents Samuel and Mary, and they gathered their animals into a special corner allotted them in times of poor weather. Polkadot the rabbit was the one who became especially nervous during thunderstorms, whereas Drowsy and Doolittle slept easily, and Elfin seemed to contemplate every raindrop sound about the tent, as though listening to music. That night the thunder and lightning broke heavy from a sky rent and torn by the wake of the Wars, and Polkadot had to be extra to finally calm down. She curled up in a fat ball with the squirrels about her.

Oakleaf and Zacharias were among the first generation since the Wars. What they oft suspected and discussed was the chaos and madness of the outside world, and they deeply hoped it would never encroach upon their lives. Yet they seemed to have nothing to fear, as year after year went by with barely any indication of an outside world. Once, a jet black plane passed overhead slightly to the north, but Oakleaf observed to Zacharias that this plane was what was called a "drone," and was unmanned. It was still taking magnetic resonance imaging pictures while running on hydrogen cell batteries. Eventually it would come to earth, not at its prescribed destination, and the videos it captured would never be seen. If they had been seen, they would reveal" hotspots" of high radioactivity areas with carnage below, and other areas of desperately wandering folk who would survive the expiration dates of tinned goods and raided one another for supplies of pastas and grains and other foodstuffs that still existed as a meager viable resource, entirely insufficient to support the population. The population had been nearly sabotaged completely by the savage nuclear blasts of the hoarded arsenals of many nations, and the first failing of the generation that survived was cannibalism. Nuclear war and cannibalism were the two singular inevitables which long had preoccupied the mind of Samuel Holdsworth, and Oakleaf and Zacharias kept and studied as their Bible a guidebook entitled "Hiking the Pacific Crest Trail," just in case necessity drove them. Although many individuals pressed on into the Wilderlands, Oakleaf and Zacharias remained providentially remote from any searchings. As their good fortune extended itself through the years, they mutually agreed not to worry but simply to live, although Oakleaf did assemble an alter of branches and pinecones and stones to pray and meditate by for mercy and grace and benedictions to sustain themselves against the odds.

Snow and ice were melting away into water and Oakleaf and Zacharias enjoyed their modest brook amongst the trees, and a meadow of flowers that the brook spread out into forming warm pools, but this was as far as they would wander. They had the option of the cold brook or the warm pools for bathing, and dipped and bathed and played like children, although they were already quite senior, when they had first met. The great good fortune of extended years would be theirs, as they knew nothing of, nor could quite imagine, the stresses and cares of the former Earth, the Earth now passed away. The lifestyle of nature perpetuated the lasting peace of years.

Nevertheless, Zacharias, when they had first met, already was walking with a cane due to a bad knee, and as time went by and they both lived into their 80's and 90's, the frailty of advanced years set in, asserting delicacy that younger people never fully imagine the likes of. Whereas they did, out of love, contemplate a mutual suicide so that neither would be left alone, they came to vow that, come what may of illness and frailty and loneliness, they would choose life over death, and go on even after the other had expired.

Zacharias it was who first noticed feeling "funny." By then Polkadot the rabbit was quite tame, as well as the squirrels, and Zacharias would sit with the animals curled up comfortably on his lap. Oakleaf guessed her husband's state, and they discussed what preparations could be made, as they dined on roasted grubs wrapped in miner's lettuce. There was little to do, except for Oakleaf to remember the good times and avoid sorrow. She also asked Zacharias to write her poetry to remember him by. They said their final goodbyes many times over, until, one bright and sunny day, Oakleaf buried Zacharias in the woods, and placed on his burial mound many pinecones.

CHAPTER THIRTY-ONE :
A CIRCLE IN TIME

Justine buried Gwynhr in a little mound among hanging giant orchids, with a single placard reading "Gwynhr," and she went back to her favorite spot to weep.

Justine was still strong. She possessed her old wiry strength and determined disposition. She did not weep in despair, but for Gwynhr's lost life, and for a new life alone which must now begin, not in despair but in renewed inner powers that only the few possess, and that she largely learned from Gwynhr during their life on the magical island together, and in their struggles before that. She learned because Gwynhr was simple and kind and homely.

Justine's curly red hair was turning gray and white, which, had there been anyone to see, would've given the impression of a fierce wildness undaunted by age. Yet Justine was daunted, despite inner reserves of strength, because to be alone is the greatest burden a gentle soul can bear, except for losing one's dearest love. Both had happened to Justine, as well as the many bitter cruelties of a life in the wild.

Now she walked on the beach every day and gathered shells. Sometimes she would knit daisy chains. Other times snatches of song would come to her, but her voice would fade to silence before the song was done.

Birds flocked ashore to the island, growing in numbers, but never a ship came for the duration of her life. When she had to lend to her such premonition as often precedes death, she lay on a flat stone and quietly went to sleep. She offered no goodbyes to the passing breeze, no words harsh or kind to life, no remnants of her heart to gift up to the heavens, all she thought was "Goodbye."

"Alvin, my boy," Jack the hermit said once, "The world is not flat or round, like people want to make-believe, it is oblong. It is the same with people: they're not always symmetrical, and can't always be known easily." Justine was asleep on the liken mattress in Jack's cabin.

"You've thought about people a long time, Jack," said Gwynhr, "so what is Justine really like?"

"Give it time," advised Jack. "She is inscrutable in some parts, but chinks in her armor let light through. She is happy, sad, curious, angry, tired, and ultimately loving, but there is something deep beyond our usual manner of discussing things: she was one with nature, Gwynhr, and now that is changed. Your betrothal has changed her heart, she no longer feels as wild. Be very careful, Alvin, and gentle. Answers will come in good time."

"I await on her every breath, in case she might speak."

"You are most devoted, that is good."

"She has renewed my belief in beauty, although she is hard-bitten somehow. When she relaxes, her face shows tremendous warmth."

Jack's sighed. "Time will show you what a gentle creatures she is. Be patient."

"I will," Alvin answered. "I will be very patient. I will wait forever to get a few simple answers."

"She will be more willing than that," Jack answered with a chortle." You certainly have a full platter on your hands."

"She came into my life is a wild thing. I almost mistook her for a bear. And when she was shown my sympathy was immediate. The long years of trauma were revealed."

"Alvin, are you talking about me again?" Justine spoke drowsily from her mattress. "And is there wine left?"

"We saved you plenty," said Jack. "And Gwynhr here wants to know everything about you."

"A little wine would loosen my tongue," Justine laughed.

"Things come at a price," Jack noted to Gwynhr cheerily.

"I followed the hill trail of a mole once," Justine began around the fire, "but wherever I dug the mole had moved from. I dug and dug, and finally caught it. It'd been so perseverant I had not the heart to have it for my dinner, even as hungry as I was. I made a little tie from my sleeve and kept the mole. I named it Rodney the mole, and it proved a very good companion for a number of years. I could not always feed it like I would prefer, but it would help me smell out food. Saving the mole instead of eating it brought me more food in the end. After several years of hardship, Rodney passed away. His death was mysterious, I think due to a virus, so I would not eat his flesh, but laid snares with it for a few carrion birds I'd seen recently. The snares worked, and I was not hungry for days. Rodney was a decent mole."

The group became silent for a while, and outside could be heard the buzzing of thousands of bees.

"It has gotten late," Jack noted. "You will have to stay here for the night. I've feasted so well I shall just have some parsley and pine broth to fill in the corners, and I leave the rest of the wine to you."

Justine and Gwynhr lay at silent peace with each other all night, huddled close together but not saying a word. When dawn came they took their leave of Jack and followed the old trail back to the abbey. The abbess had been waiting to distribute the honeycomb, which was rationed among the 192 residents by rotation. The abbess also had selected a number of old crumbling volumes for Justine to read. "A book a day keeps the doctor away," the abbess told Justine, and Justine lay beneath the almond tree and read the rest of the morning away, until it became too hot and she returned to her new quarters which she shared with Gwynhr. They filled a wooden tub with warm spring water and took their baths. Gwynhr would always avert his eyes for modesty's sake. Justine wanted to flirt, but knew Gwynhr was too modest.

Justine tried to explain something to Gwynhr. "This abbey is calm in the midst of the storm, Gwynhr." Gwynhr did not really understand, for the abbey had lain there peacefully for generations. "Gwynhr, take my hand, and we shall walk a ways along the stream, and I will explain how nothing good lasts forever."

"Forever is a long time," Gwynhr was able to agree.

"There are wild things roaming about, all about us even now. Were I able, I would convince the abbey to disband and become solitary creatures, to advance their chances of surviving individually. Yet content breeds apathy. I have a good mind to scout in the woods for another territory."

So it was that Justine and Gwynhr went on their expedition, and found a mysterious stone observatory of another time. Had they known the generations before, they might have known a solitary scientist, Dr. Radakrishnan, who looked out peacefully at the night sky, recounted and measured and remembered, such that mysteries began to unfold, and stories began to be shown of the fate of Man. What Justine and Gwynhr found there after looking through the telescope was the wild man painted in mud and elderberry juice, who owned a tame cougar to hunt with.

Jack had been overly optimistic. "I shall move to the abbey to be safe," said he," and a few bulwarks and boiling water shall be enough to drive these unfamiliars away. "Yet Justine knew better and secretly made plans to escape with Alvin. The abbey as a whole would never survive together wandering the wilds as a troupe.

They escaped together that one night, with wild calls about them, and headed into the mountains, to find a lake to fish, Justine knowing all the while they would be followed.

Gwynhr peered at his reflection in the lake, more of a mirror then the old bronze mirrors at the abbey, and, trapped in the wild indefinitely, began to truly wonder who he was. He remembered that it is easier to get to know another then to know oneself, and, sometimes, to get to know another is to know oneself. He was yet fraught with nervousness and uncertainty, but he had Justine to devote himself to, one thing that would save his life. Always, he remembered, live for something greater than yourself.

Justine shook his shoulder. "Gwynhr, do not fade, but takes strength. We shall help each other."

They looked at their reflection together in the lake with the mountains and the ineffable sky."We will go together, you and I," Gwynhr replied. "What shall we find?"

Justine hesitated. "The road is not an easy one, and we do not know what we shall find, yet finding things out together is always better than finding them alone. Should we be parted we must always remember each other, and reach out with our hearts. Should Fate allow us peace and togetherness, and the sky be kind then we shall not fear nor want. Right now we are pursued into the Desolations, but somewhere, over many hills and desert sands and waters, there is yet safety, and so there is hope, which we must cling to as a wellspring of motivation. Tomorrow might not be forgiving, yet so far has mercy shown upon us in many ways."

Gwynhr began shedding slow, heavy tears. "My friends are all gone to a fearsome end, the abbess and Monsignor Dutton and his wife Honica who befriended you, all gone, gone into cruelty and barbarism. Where in the sky was it written?"

Justine took Gwynhr's hand. "Weep if you must, for the loss is deep. It was written in the sky long ago, that some men brought strife to earth, and we are not our brother's keepers. Since then the strife has become a scourge, and men betray men and hardly any escape. You may be glad that Jack died peacefully, before the scourge, and never knew other than his freedom in the woods, and the drone of bees, and good wine to warm the heart. So, too, the abbey sat untouched for many generations, as some men do not know the difference between what has been given them and what might be. Our only consolation is that should the burden be light we would not know the meaning of freedom, and should we be alone we would not know the meaning of peace."

Gwynhr took some consolation. "You speak as though one who has lived many years, yet you are young. I would not expect such wisdom to come out of the wilderness as it has with you, for long years often daunt the spirit rather than feed it." Gwynhr brushed back Justine's curly red locks and looked into her hazel eyes. "The woman I first met in bear skin concealed many wisdoms in her loneliness over the years. I pray I can be of good service."

"You are good lad, Gwynhr. Already that serves us well, and where there is meekness there is often strength." Wild calls were brought on the air from behind them. "We must run, lad, and little shall be our rest, unless great providence is on our side."

"I do not believe one way or another," said Gwynhr, "only that I love you."

CHAPTER THIRTY-TWO: THE SEARCH FOR EL DORADO

While migrations of people tended to be south to north, nevertheless the south bloomed with mysterious cultures, while most of Earth surrendered to chaos. It was upon these rumors that a few lone sojourners made long voyages south hoping to find peace and abundance, and such there was in the south, only hidden away, whereas most of the south was populated by successful marauders by land and sea, slowly conquering the north, although wild folk.

One lone traveler dared risk the hostile marauders and travel the coastline to South America to find a legendary El Dorado. He had been named Gideon, and had already survived the hardships of toil and work the chaos made of the lonely tribes in the North. Now he was a young man, who had decided upon the greatest risk for the potential of ultimate success and glory in a remote sanctuary somewhere, the rumors of which had turned into legend.

His way by sea, following the eastern coast, was perilous indeed. He kept constant vigilance for pirates, and fortuitously, in his small craft, alluded being captured. When finally land loomed directly before him in the South, he knew he had reached the southern continent. He docked warily, and assembled his possessions for a long trek inland, he knew not whither exactly, he only knew he must penetrate the densest jungle before he could reach the People of the Mountain, and allusive, hidden, and occult society rumored to be inland.

Gideon was not as any other man of his day. He was refined and sanguine, determined and willful, questioning and inquisitive, uncanny in deductive reasoning and analysis. His visage was wise and disarming, with penetrating eyes which shown, the dark shine of a polished ebony stone glinting in the light, never restless, always in control and in possession of all the faculties of a complete man, integrated in whole, yet still sensitive and touchable. Yet he had decided to travel alone, for he loved solitude, and had never been a part of his society, except that many of his tribe sought out his wisdom and guidance, and he left behind more than one yearning young woman, but he was seeking his destiny far beyond the familiar.

The major point Gideon was divided upon was that he was agnostic. He did not believe in God, yet was open to possibility. He thought that his journeys may give him the answers to a higher power.

The jungles he confronted, he knew, held preposterous risks and tests of will. What flourished there was of the deadliest: anaconda snakes and scorpions and many unknown dangers. He traveled beating the jungle floor with a stick until he found a stream, and then he knew part of the way to the mountain sanctuaries he thought might exist. Yet the stream twisted and curled through the jungle and the going was slow, but such was his determination, however, that he did not grow tired but ever more willful.

It was too risky to sleep, or stay in one place for very long, so Gideon drove himself onward, ever carrying a burning torch against the wild. On one occasion, he witnessed the jaguar prowling, and snakes slithered, and spiders hung poised in the air. This territory was nothing like the North he was accustomed to, but he steeled his will and would not sleep nor hesitate until weeks had gone by, and he finally collapsed, yet slept lightly in his vigilance. In this journey, no terror touched him, only scientific curiosity, which was one of his primary characteristics, a singular scientific fascination that was nearly unique in his era. What he didn't know was the sciences that would confront him, for, high in the mountains, lived the Elders of the Gentle Race, who had remained hidden for generations.

Gideon sought out the most remote areas, wandering sometimes, and at other times following instinct derived from the shape of a particular mountain or valley. For many years Gideon wandered the Andes Mountains, yet he maintained his unique constitution. He successfully dodged what were clearly wild peoples, and moved on his way as though a phantom that could not be caught.

As he dodged he foraged, and he never wanted for food, such was his skill and cunning.

One day he chose a mountain to climb to gain a better vista for renewed effort. What he discovered from a ridge was precisely what he was looking for: a small city of stone, wood, and mortar, with buttresses and domes and minarets defying the state of his age. This was the place of the Elders of the Gentle Race, he would find. Yet for the time being he had to consider and contemplate whether these were in fact peaceful people, or masters of the martial arts.

Gideon crept closer down from the ridge towards this place that, despite his scientific leanings, seems like a place of magic, improbable, and anachronistic. Gideon had to use all of his imagination as he attempted to penetrate this great secret enclave. He wished to see you as well, without being seen. To his fortune he was a master of stealth, as though a phantom.

Gideon peered over a boulder not far from a dome. To his great surprise, even knowing to expect the unexpected, he noticed a Caucasian looking woman walking upstairs into the dome. She was certainly not a native of the continent, Gideon immediately reasoned, from a store of knowledge he had been hoarding since early childhood.

He experienced a haunting trepidation. These people seemed untouched by the chaos dominating most of the world. What then would be the results of interacting with them: was it unfair to introduce any part of the outside world into their culture? Now that he had found his destination, he was overcome with doubt. Yet this sort of paradise was precisely what he had wanted and searched for so long.

He decided he must move forward, and removed himself from behind the boulder, to approach a gate in a wall. There sat a well-kept individual reading a book. Gideon felt self-conscious of his unkempt beard and jaguar skin. And then, he wondered if this person understood English. He tried an introduction.

"I come in peace, and in hopes of wisdom and learning," Gideon pronounced.

"Fancy that," said the man, "I doubt my senses. You're a rare sight indeed. Are you educated somewhat?"

"After a fashion," said Gideon. "I come from a distant land where information is difficult to retrieve from an ancient devastation."

"We've heard of that, certainly," said the man. "That's why we're in hiding. We thought no one would discover us, and you're the very first."

Gideon could not wait to ask the question. "Who are you?"

"Well, that's probably the funniest part of our story. We are the descendents of a blimp that was blown off course. Our ancestors were going to set sail for a place once called the New Zealand, but sudden torrents in the air forced them to ground here, and they decided it seemed safe and decided to stay. Our generations have been very fortunate, and our little community has room for another. You almost don't seem peculiar, if you don't mind me putting it that way."

Gideon always wished to be honest, and said, "I am mainly self-educated, from sparse resources. My intellectual life craves greater learning, plus I have journeyed far and need rest."

"Of course," said the man, "but first I believe you should have audience with the Chamberlain. He shall wish to know more specifics of your lifestyle and intents."

Gideon was led down cobblestone streets, amidst the stares of an innocent populace, who stopped what they were doing at the sight of such a hawk-like visage with the radiant ebony eyes, embodiment of acute intelligence and steadfast constitution. Gideon nodded politely.

The antechamber of the Chamberlain contained a few symbolic baubles and items of art work. The Chamberlain himself sat behind a desk quite asleep, and was clearly quite elderly, with flowing white hair and long white beard.

When prodded, he awoke with surprise, and exclaimed, "A stranger! Goodness, and I thought business was slow today, but clearly not! Right, down to business: what is your name?"

"Gideon, sir."

"Right. And what is your calling?"

"I possess a number of skills, but require my ignorance to be cured."

"Fair enough, fair enough," replied the Chamberlain. "And do you have anything on your conscience?"

Gideon paused. "I killed a man once in self-defense, but I have not sinned."

"That's fine, then, that is honest and must be accepted. Bear with me, young man, but are you at all at licentious?"

"I have always avoided relations, but I am only human."

"Fair enough, fair enough. You seem like a reasonable gentlemen, sorry to keep you, you must need your rest. You will be guided to such quarters as we can provide. Nothing fancy, mind you, like before the Wars, but enough to call home."

"Thank you, Chamberlain," said Gideon, and he bowed in respect.

The man from the gate led Gideon down more cobblestones and past the tallest of the minarets, where a young woman carrying a basket of fruit cried out, "Stranger! Come to my home, and I will teach you!"

The man from the gate paused. "The option is yours," he told Gideon.

"I seek a mentor immediately," Gideon replied. "I do not know the customs here, yet I feel in my heart to accept this offer."

"Then I will let you go your way," the man said," and I wish you every fortune. Perhaps as we might enlighten you may teach us in turn. So may it be, and I hope to see you soon."

"Thank you very kindly for your aid," Gideon replied, and went following the woman, who made an unfamiliar gesticulation of greeting.

"My home is your home," she said.

Gideon of a sudden thought of a wife, quite uncharacteristically for him. This woman was slight and attractive, with pale skin and pale blonde hair, with wide chocolate brown eyes ringed by grey. She was dressed in an unusually soft mesh of some sort unfamiliar to Gideon, but her smile was most outstanding, the smile of one knew and relished great secrets Gideon could only guess that. The entire effect was almost dreamlike, Gideon thought, deep in wonderment and attempts at deduction.

"What name is yours?" the smiling young woman queried of him.

"My parents called me Gideon, from an old book," said Gideon. "Perhaps it should be changed, as I've often thought, but the names of things are a delicate matter."

"Indeed," the woman replied, as they made their way up a little hill amidst the city, "the most delicate matter. I shall teach you, stranger named Gideon, of what may be and what certainly is, and may our discussion turn to your experiences in the wild world. We only have a few books here. And by the way I was named Min."

Gideon was uncertain entirely of the nature of this sylvan waif, yet was convinced entirely that he had discovered his legendary goal, and nothing could be more fortunate. A life of deprivations and fierce some risks had been transformed into providence and luxury, and his adrenalin surged despite himself at the thought of a quiet and undisturbed life of study among gentle folk used to peace and freedom. At long last his destiny was fulfilled, inexplicably, as though there was a God or higher power as his guide, Gideon thought, but he was a man of science, and could differentiate philosophy from established fact. However Gideon had to wonder if his new community could, or if they lived in a dreamlike fantasy. Gideon had always lived the life of the survivalist, but these people that, against all odds, he had discovered, maybe living in the midst of ease and lack of worry, entirely removed from the nature of his former life. He had misgiving, as he knew he would, that he was intruding, bringing the world to little lives.

"Here is my cabin on the hill," Min indicated. "Let us gather fruit from my little garden, then we may rest in peace and chat some about our lives."

"As you wish," Gideon agreed. "I am highly curious, after all, and your township has clearly existed in isolation, and so you might like to know of the wide world outside." Gideon regretted that he had said this, yet he knew all were doomed to make choices.

Min labored briefly in the garden, and soon there were plentiful fruits and vegetables as fair. Sitting at a little table, they paused briefly just to look into each other's eyes. Gideon felt all the curiosity of his scientific fascination in his new partners brown orbs ringed with grey, and the young woman smiled as though looking at the dawn.

"To make it this far," Min spoke, "you must be a man of ultimate constitution. While we expected to be discovered eventually, it has taken several generations. Before I begin, tell me somewhat of your story."

Gideon began with all modesty, although it was a long and extraordinary tale. "I toiled as a boy, yet began hearing rumors of a legendary little land that might exist to the South, and so my toil in grew in meaning. I fled my home while still young, and sojourned for many years. I do not know how, but here I have found my destination, as though it were meant to be. However, I do not know the true nature of this place, nor do I know my place among you."

"Yes," said Min, "you have arrived at a juncture most meaningful, when many of adventuresome in spirit would seek out new lands, and they require a guide. Yet much teaching is necessary before any might leave to face the unknown. Your survival will give them many strange hopes and dreams, and, too, others who do not wish for separation you will bring misgiving."

It was as Gideon expected. "I would not separate kin," Gideon vouchsafed, "nor lead the innocent down an uncertain path. There are many trackless wilds, and folk of a barbaric nature roam about."

"This we know, Gideon," said Min, "yet many here are restless despite established good fortune. It seems to be a part of the spirit of man."

"Man was ever contentious," Gideon replied.

"With you as our guide," said Min, "we have an opportunity before us. I myself have long for the Wide Waters and lands of the North. But you must be weary. May I bathe you?"

This offer disarmed Gideon at first, but then he realized this young woman's intention."I am not accustomed to intimacy," he replied, "but if such be thy will you may bathe me."

So it was a meeting of the minds occurred, and so it was that a relationship was swiftly forged that would last many years. Min was forthright and forthcoming, and sang a foreign tune as she bathed Gideon.

Many would be their conversation deep into the night, when I slow mist would just descend upon the small community, and Min was jealous and would rarely let Gideon out of her sight. She herself would nevertheless reveal the secrets of the Outside in conference with her cohorts, and slowly a movement preceded as to the destiny of this folk. Some of them wished fervently that Gideon had never arrived to bring about such schism, yet others yearned for the open road in the lands beyond. After several years of slow debate, Gideon could see he had developed a responsibility towards enlightening some of the quiet folk, despite hardships and toil and uncertainty. He himself often thought that this mountain enclave lived in a sort of fool's paradise, as it might be ensnared by the outside wildness at any time. Yet his fondness for his wife Min held him back from the perilous journeying, until finally it was she who virtually insisted."

"We enjoy a genteel life here," Min said one day, "but this cannot content all hearts. Gideon, dear, let us make to depart, despite this seeming foolhardiness of the venture."

"We are not impervious here," Gideon replied, "yet might still enjoy many years of comfort. Journeying is a calculated risk. Still if it is my appointment by desire of some of our peoples, I shall go."

"And I shall go with you," said Min. "This life is simple, and they say simple is best, yet it cannot content all hearts. Many there are who would take great risks to discover the true nature of the world."

Gideon could not help but understand this from his own experience, yet had come to know something of a simple peace with his wife and their little lives. And the schism his presence had caused was precisely what he had regretted before he ever reached this mountain haven. Yet did he feel obligation of a sort, despite the discord he had sown, and he knew the unhappiness that even a quiet existence might bring. It was not fully his wish, but he consented, so a party of the desirous was congregated and plans laid to journey to the East, and come to the Wide Waters that might lead up the western coast which Gideon knew not of yet could still navigate, perhaps.

Even after these numbers of years had passed, Min was an object of curiosity for Gideon. He could not quite penetrate her disarming smile, I smile as though the good things of this Earth would abide, and that the spiritual destiny might be met with. Their life together had been one of contentment, and so the party of adventurers set forward with a sense of confidence in the stability of their leaders, although perhaps unfounded, as stresses would grow and doubts set in on the long road. Apart from Gideon and Min the travelers were 22 in number, and as they moved forward into the unknown they sang many songs, and so called themselves the "terrible troubadours." The mountain valley faded behind them in the mist, and they wandered through jungle highlands down into a western desert, and they uneventfully reached the sea. Here they had to pause for long preparation for the ocean journey.

Gideon was a consummate mariner, and showed the band the skills of a shipwright, and how to sail. Slowly a ship was built, and one day of fair winds they set sail for the North. All were light of spirit, despite having left caution behind. Gideon warned them of the danger of pirates, yet their ship was fast and able to outrun, and so the songs continued on the open waters. They kept the western coast on there right and journeyed by night and day, and fished successfully as they went. A likely party name Tom became established as first mate.

One night, a storm was brewing to the West, yet the stars still shone bright. The mysterious Min held Gideon's hand. "We shall not be passed over by destiny," she comforted. "Be at ease in your mind that you have made the correct choice."

Gideon said, "I have left the land I sought for so long. If it were not for your wish I would not of gone this way. Destiny is strange."

Mexico came and went, and the little band discovered no pirates. Gideon reasoned that many voyagers had already reached the North or had sunk, and he told his troops that the shoreline must be avoided indefinitely, until they might reach a likely island.

One day, a solitary rocky outcropping offered itself to these journeyers, not far from the Northern Californian coast, and Gideon instructed them that this was as safe as they might be, however temporarily. The groups did not fully comprehend, nor could they ever had imagined the jungle, desert, and ocean that they have had seen, yet were entirely willing to make do.

There was that they built their unique little land, mainly as fishermen, living in driftwood huts, yet not entirely unsophisticated, as they had provisions from their previous culture to sustain them intellectually. Some would go ashore occasionally to forage.

No one of the party thought it an unfair exchange for their previous haven, yet took the bracing air, and sung the strange songs of love and high mountains, and invented new songs of the sea.

Min was with child. When the moon was full, the girl was born unto herself and Gideon

"We shall name her 'Edril,'" pronounced Min, and the child was as pale as the full moon. All the band rejoiced with song of this unique discovery, a girl child of pure white eyes and skin and hair like white smoke. That she resembled a ghost or phantom disturbed them not, for she was considered miraculous.

Over the years on the island, Eldril grew into an imperious and stately young woman, and yet had a laugh like seabirds crying, and she became the most expert forager of the group.

While she was out upon an excursion on the coast, a tremendous wave took her island by storm. Thus it was that her parents perished, and all her little family, so that she was left alone. Yet she knew many crafts, and did not despair, for she had the wild and the civilized harmonized in her heart.

It was many years later that she would discover Justine and Gwynhr living pathetically in the snow.

Justine and Gwynhr had followed her abjectly at first, not knowing their fate. Yet as it proved it was Eldril who was their savior, and after many adventures they discovered their magical island home, isolated from all evils and provided with abundance, far away in the South Pacific.

"One life," Jack a hermit had once told Gwynhr, "grows into another life, and no one is as isolated as they might feel, and no one can see all ends."

Eldril had hunted alone for years, her company a beautiful white mare her party had brought from South America, a land that had not known of horses until the Conquistadors. Eldril was expert with the crossbow, and hunted well. Yet ever was she wary of other folk, until she met Justine and Gwynhr.

Once she had stood on the top of the mountain where she had discovered Justine and Gwynhr, and looked about at the world, and the wasteland that was once San Francisco. Deep in her heart she held the regret, deep in her solitude she knew the misfortune, of long years and lives disappeared into the dark night, the irretrievable lives once lived in relative comfort and happiness and now reduced to nought. Until she had met Justine and Gwynhr she had born these feelings alone. Always in her hardship she lived for the day she might meet other lovers of peace and harmony, yet knowing that this rare gift might never be found. When she had met Justine and Gwynhr she was brightly gladdened, and her long years alone were shed, with many tears of joy.

Eldril had guided Justine and Gwynhr to their isolated magical island. She looked on without envy at the married couple, who had endured such hardship and deprivation, only to meet with fortuitous salvation.

When a mysterious mutated pathogen finally struck at Eldril's mortality, the ancient Wars of the human kind found a new revenge on the innocent, and for a time Justine and Gwynhr were faced with an irreducible misery. Yet Eldril said, "In your hearts be glad, and for our enduring friendship, which has known such providence, and carry me in your memories with your usual tenderness."

Justine and Gwynhr descended that one day from the tip of the mountain where they had buried Eldril, through teaming groves of mango and banana. As they cooked their evening meal, the sun set an unusual dark red color, like the embers of their fire.

"Comfort me, Gwynhr," said Justine, "for nightfall tonight is not as other nights."

"Come hold my hand, dear," Gwynhr responded, "and we shall hum one of your favorite tunes."

"Long before we get mad," Eldril once told Justine and Gwynhr, "I found a little boy wandering in my woods. Immediately I rejoiced for I thought that here was one I could call family. Like so many others the boy was a runaway from his kin, who had treated him poorly. He seemed to be walking in a dreamlike daze. I soon discovered he was malnourished, in fact it was what the ancients termed anorexia. Try as I might, I could not nurse him back to health, and he wasted before my eyes. He never spoke a word. So many times we have life in the palm of our hands, and then it slips through our fingers. Alack, this much is the truth.

"Now that I have found you, and we are no longer strangers, life is returned to my little corner of the world, and i deem myself blessed.

"However, as was predicted long ago, because I seem like a phantom from the netherworld, my time shall be cut short. What you do with your time should be measured by love."

Justine said, "Without you, Eldril, we should not be saved, and though the measure of love may be beyond us, we shall take your words and try. If you leave us, it will be too soon, yet we have your words to remember."

CHAPTER THIRTY-THREE:
THE STORY OF CLEA

The centuries would spread out to thousands of years, years of blistering freezes, high summers, and brief autumns and springs. For a long time, few children were born, and fewer still survived. Wild tribes of wandering folk would subsist for a while, in perpetual distrust of each other, and sometimes, though rarely, family clans would develop in isolated areas, and then fall prey to malnutrition and disease with the shifting climates. A few remote islands supported lasting civilization, such as where Justine and Gwynhr, and then Nicholas and Jenny, had lived in peace and tranquility.

The small crew of Nicholas and Jenny's sailing vessel lived happily for some time, with bearing trees and the bounty of sea life supporting them, and cousins marrying cousins. Yet the waters raged, and even as the island had risen from the ocean floor in an earthquake, so it was finally brought low by a massive tsunami tidal wave which made its tenuous foundation sink once more to the ocean floor, except for the exceeding height, where the grave of Eldril lay, yet surviving just above sea level.

The wild people of the world also would sink of their own weight, as their untamedness produced the futility of unfortunate stormy passions at odds with one another, until finally only solitary roamers drifted the land, with no knowledge of the past, no inherited remembrances, no crumbling volumes to preserve history by. On the other hand wildlife increased, so as to provide for the most cautious solitary wanderers.

One of these was named Clea. She had abandoned the rough hearth of her childhood home when only six years old, leaving a clan of a handful of hundreds, as she was driven away by overwork, feuds, and hostilities, to use her early-gained knowledge of survival to seek out the relative peace and freedom of a solitary existence, avoiding at all costs interaction with other humans, for all their usury and selfishness.

She wandered high in the Sierras, and discovered the ancient encampments of people who would just survived the now-forgotten Wars. She lived by a sharp innate wit, unerringly guessing at birds' nests to rob, rabbit warrens to smoke out and trap, and using all her knowledge to dig in the earth and harvest plants.

What Clea most lacked was skill at language, as she by six years old had been taught very little, but she became a namer of things, and eventually developed a vocabulary all her own, to match the color of a cloud or an unfamiliar bird.

She at first departure from her clan decided to wander many hundreds of miles, for fear of retribution, along the Pacific Crest Trail. She narrowly avoided the preying beasts of the wild by regularly tending a precious fire, until finally she settled by one of the most likely lakes to fish, where once Samuel Holdsworth and Mary Newsom, time out of mind, had made their home.

For many years Clea lived consummately alone. She had no knowledge of mature adulthood, nor could she guess at it, nor did she meet another person, for many long years. Sometimes when rains came she would go out and dance in them, sometimes a rare magenta sunset would make her laugh, and other times she would sit miserably by her fire, beneath the hanging boulder and hum to herself fragments of song which passed through her mind. Much of her spare time, when the fish were not biting, she would wander in the shallows and search out minnows and toads and frogs and sometimes this would be all she had to eat for a day or two.

Her strawberry blond hair was matched oddly by electric blue eyes, eyes which reflected the sky. She grew into adulthood years as nimble as a elf, and as sharp-sighted as an eagle, always able to the spy where birds had made their nests, and then she would scamper up trees like just an elf, and eat well again.

Life by the lake was usually pleasantly warm, and eventually, her old garments long since tattered and worn away, she forgot about wearing clothes, and depended upon the warmth of her fire if necessary against the occasional cold. The water of the lake was also warm, and Clea taught herself how to swim to the opposite shore from her dwelling, and thereby expanded the range of her foraging, eating eggs, and entrapping the abundant field mouse.

Using bait, she became expert at trapping mice and lizards and birds, and when successful she had a favorite song to hum, which in her murky sense of attribution had something to do with victory, providence, redemption, and hope. The crow became her favorite animal, as they would often show her where other food might be found, and then she would articulate odd singsong whistles.

By the time she turned 19 she had the beauty of some lost doe. She still remembered her former life, when she was beaten and abused for not doing chores, and given food sparingly, but she had grown up in the wild, and only barely resembled a child of any civilization. She was unto herself.

Her greatest wisdom was in patience, but not so much in caution. So, when she was 20 and saw drifting smoke on the horizon, she decided to investigate, rather than have whomever it was investigate her own fire. All the local pathways and byways she knew, but the quickest way to get his foreigner, she knew, was simply to follow the meandering stream that exited her lake. She nimbly hopped over boulder and bluff, and then caution did set in and she hid and spied.

There was nobody at home by the fire, yet there laid next to it the body of a mountain lion. Clea's thieving instincts began to set in, and her caution waned. Then, however, she thought that whomever had the abilities to kill mountain lions would be a formidable adversary, and then the thought of a man gave her a sense of distaste. So she continued to hide and wait, and chew on some roasted frog legs.

It was not a man's fire, however. Soon, revealing herself from the underbrush came a woman, dressed in a variety of animal furs. To Clea the woman's face seemed exceedingly old with lines of care, and it held her interest rapt as the first site of a human in so many years. She thought of many names she had made up for various types of animals, but could not settle upon an appropriate one for this woman. She thought of "zing," which meant "crow," and "lully," which meant "hedgehog," but she could not decide which this was. She decided that, however, this was not a dangerous creature, despite clearly being an expert hunter who must have weapons. Clea was about to dismiss the matter and go back to her cave, but hunger was getting the better of her. She tried to remember her proper English.

"Could I have a little, please?" she managed to say.

"Why, yes, of course, dear," said the old woman. "Let me just skin the beast first." This reply pleased Clea no end.

"You are friendly, then?" Clea tried haltingly.

"We shall soon have a feast, you and I," the old woman said without looking up, and began to expertly skin the mountain lion, and then disembowel it. "Do you like heart or liver best?"

Clea didn't know these two words, so she hesitated. "I like whatever is tastier," she replied.

"Then come out of hiding, dear, but first he must recover your modesty. I have a beaver skin dress for you." Clea found nothing averse to this speech, and so she stood up and came forward.

"I have been watching you for days," said the woman. "You're the strangest animal I've ever seen," and she laughed. "Here is your skin."

Clea immediately felt glorified by her new raiment. "My name is Clea," she remembered to say

"My name is Thornberry," said the old woman. "Pleased to meet you, Clea. For a slip of a thing you have done well to survive." The woman placed the mountain lion upon the logs of the fire. "We shall let this roast, and meanwhile you can tell me how you came to live here all alone."

"I live here all alone," Clea repeated.

"Yes, dear, but what is your story?"

"I have many interesting stories," Clea replied. "I see bear sometimes, and very large birds. My favorite bird is the crow."

The old woman Thornberry decided to overlook Clea's ignorance, and try again."How did you come here?" she asked.

"I walked. Sometimes I wish I could fly." Clea's own voice sounded unusual to her, she was so unused to hearing it.

"You were driven away by bad people," The woman asked, "or were you abandoned?"

"Oh, I see," said Clea. "Driven away."

"How many years ago?" continued the lady.

"Oh, I don't know, more than my fingers, I suppose. How soon until we eat?"

"All good things in all good time," the woman quoted. "Once it is roasted, we shall eat."

"I have not seen anyone," Clea said. "You must come from very far away."

"Yes, dear, very far. My people all died out from a dreadful disease, except for me. I come from the land of the Far North."

"You have hidden very well. I have stayed here where no one comes."

"I have my stories I could tell,""Thornberry said. "At first it was quite dangerous, but over the years there were fewer and fewer people to avoid. I doubt very much that your people yet survive. There are evil diseases about in the land."

"My mother died when I was young," Clea said, "but nobody could say why. I am very hungry."

"Be a good child, and grind us parsley. We require a proper garnish."

"Garnish," Clea repeated. "Parsley," she said.

"We really must teach you your letters, dear. There's no getting on without useful words."

Clea ground the parsley between two rocks, imbibing the heavenly aroma of the roasting mountain lion combined with the parsley. "You can have the heart and liver," the old woman said kindly. "There is plenty for us both."

Clea laughed in joy at this, and got up and did a little twirling dance. Thornberry just ignored her, and turn the animal on the fire.

Clea enjoyed more food than she ever had in her entire 20 years. She could barely recall when she had enjoyed good meat. Both the heart and liver she found delicious, and of the flesh she asked for seconds and thirds.

"I will tell you a story," Thornberry said around the campfire as it grew dark. "Long, long ago many wild people roamed the lands. Nobody knew where they came from, but they were unyielding of warfare, and many peaceful people were destroyed, and many more went into hiding. Yet the wild people ultimately began destroying each other, and the better of the folk learned to survive alone, and slowly again grew in numbers. Yet there were so many uncouth tribes, such as the one you escaped from, who had no means to possess civility and decency, but were hostile towards one another, many divided up and lost their way in the wild. Finally, the land was nearly barren of people, and they had to meet up again for the generations to perpetuate themselves.

"Nobody quite knows why, except perhaps there was great war and calamity that had divided a mighty people. Who they were is lost in mystery. Now we are very few. The wild people are nearly gone from report and hostile clans no longer able to support themselves."

"Once I thought something like this, ages ago," said Clea." Why could people not agree?"

"Food is God to the hungry," Thornberry replied. "This leads to much selflessness and competition, especially among uneducated folk."

"What is 'God?" Clea asked.

"Never mind that now, dear," replied Thornberry. "The important thing to remember is cooperation. I make bows and arrows and javelins and can track wild animals, but only when I feel weak do I do this. Usually I fish like you do. Still it isn't everything for an empty stomach."

"No,"siad Clea, "I am quite full, fuller than I have been before. I do not have much to offer in return, but these," and she produced two roasted frog legs.

"We will share," said Thornberry, "one for you and one for me. This way if one of us falls ill, there is still enough."

"You will stay, then?" Clea asked eagerly, feeling like she had found a friend at last, although she had never felt so before.

"There must be an end to running. Out there is nothing but hiking and hunting and roaming and mosquitoes. As you say, no one comes this way. If you don't mind it, I will stay."

"I have a whole dry cave against the wind and rain and snow," Clea obliged. "And there are lots of field mice."

"We shall make a team, you and I," said Thornberry. "We will divide up the labors and know a simpler life. When I hunt, I shall mark my way with stones, even as the ancients did, so you can follow if I am late, and see what has befallen, but no wild animal has bettered me yet."

"I shall widen my area of search," replied Clea, "and find many delicious things to eat. Perhaps not as delicious as this cat…"

"Here, I have some more," Thornberry offered, catching the drift immediately. "It's particularly succulent."

"Succulent," Clea repeated.

So began a long, fruitful partnership to defy the odds. The two survivors both played their roles: Thornberry would trek the surrounding mountains with her bow and javelin, and Clea would bait and snare and fish. Thornberry built for Clea a raft so that Clea could fish from the middle of the lake (something Clea had never thought of), and Clea's gleanings would act as bait for Thornberry, who had the risky business of dealing with the large carnivores. However, Thornberry had many years of experience bringing down cats and even the occasional wolverine, with a steady hand and a sure aim. When she returned to their lake with a sled of capturings, Clea would always rejoice with whistlings and there would be much mutual celebration.

Thornberry showed Clea how to make many useful things. She built a steam bath hut which Clea had never imagined before, and Clea would sit by the hot rocks in joyful glee as she sweated. Thornberry also built a hut for smoking meats. Mostly, though, Thornberry taught Clea her letters, so that every day Clea memorized 10 new words, and their conversations could expand to include Clea's personal observations, which had formerly been known to herself in her own tongue, such as why the crow flew that way one afternoon, or what the sky was feeling one sunset, or how fish exist without air, or what the face really did when making a certain expression. Thornberry listened most attentively to these stories, as though nature herself were revealing her secrets. Yet Clea was at last maturing beyond her instinctual and innate bond with the natural world, as Thornberry's presence and teachings gave her pause to reflect and consider herself separate from her surroundings and feelings, and develop an existential awareness. Previously the closest Clea had come to this was the profound need for more food that had followed her all her life.

Clea developed a restraint of sorts, and ceased to be as playful as she had been, but more considerate and slow, even ponderous. At the same time, her loneliness was largely cured, so that she did not curl up and weep as often, even when a blizzard descended.

And winter would come, yet be mercifully brief, if extremely cold. The high-pressure ridge over California gave way for a few storms, sending with them an arctic blast of freeze. In their hut of stone Clea and Thornberry took refuge by a roaring fire, and heated rocks for the steam room.

"The lake will not be warm for a while," Clea lamented, as she enjoyed swimming a great deal.

"It is better than the land running dry," Thornberry commented. "It is my understanding that the heat and cold have brought desertification about us. We should be grateful."

"I fear the desert," Clea responded. "Where nothing grows nothing can live, except beetles and scorpions and other creatures of craft of that sort. If our rain and snow cease we shall be forced to travel."

"We may be forced anyhow, for we are not alone in this world." And then, indeed, when the clouds had cleared somewhat and they came out of their cave, a plume of smoke was visible to the North. Clea was now 25 years old, and had spent five years with Thornberry, undetected. "We must both go and investigate together," Thornberry advised." I will take my bow, and we shall be stealthy. The campfire might be used as a ruse, so we might circle around the perimeter to see what might lurk."

They padded about the long way and saw no one, but detected by the plume that someone was tending the fire. They approached closer, silent as the most distant star, and saw their possible nemesis, but found a modest looking fishermen dressed in a coat of leaves, carefully turning a stick of minnows on the slow fire. He appeared disheveled and unkempt, even his hat was made of leaves, and his hair and beard were untended and long, and so he appeared unassuming and harmless. Yet Clea and Thornberry could not help having suspicions, as this creature might have some type of harm in him despite appearances. Clea and Thornberry withdrew without making contact, and slipped back to the lake. Yet they knew this fellow was moving upstream in their direction, and they considered a flight to the South. This precaution was overturned, however, when an even greater plume of smoke revealed itself amongst the clouds to the South.

"These may be the wild people of the Far South," Thornberry advised Clea." Diseases to the North, and desert to the East. Therefore our option for flight is to the West, unless we seek shelter on the mountain before us. Our encampment here by the lake will be obvious, however."

"I cannot abide," said Clea." This is my home..."

"That fellow downstream is surely making off upon seeing this dreadful plume to the South. If we stay we shall almost surely be overrun by an entire tribe of peoples, against which we are more or less defenseless, despite my bow. We are confronted by an urgency, Clea."

"We may be outnumbered, but they surely have no weapon more sophisticated than the bow, and, if we climb our bluff, we might rain down a hail of stones, or even create a fierce rockslide. They shall have no vantage unless they divide up and circle around us, yet by then they may be discouraged."

"Your plan is bold, yet too bold. We do not know their number, but they're almost assuredly following the trail due North. Pack all your bags, Clea, let us flee before they come any closer."

"We shall flee, then," Clea agreed. She had hardly any belongings to pack, only skins and a few lucky owl feathers and a favorite pinecone, and an assortment of dead insects for baiting. Soon they were ready to flee, even as nightfall was approaching, and the waxing gibbous moon was on the rise.

At first they followed the stream downwards to the North but then broke off to the left and headed West even as the plume of dark smoke overtook them on the wind. The night was spent climbing over unfamiliar boulders down a steep ravine lightly covered in snow. "We are leaving footprints here," noted Thornberry," we must hurry."

Clea had not traveled far since she was six, and had run away from home. She soon became confused and disoriented by the idea of flight in unfamiliarity, but Thornberry urged her on. Down in a culvert they found the man dressed in leaves washing his face from a pool.

"Friend or foe?" Thornberry demanded.

The man looked up blearily. "My name is Ivan," said the man.

Clea could not help but laugh. "This is no wild person," she observed, "He is clearly homely. He is clearly an easy friend to make."

"We are not of the tribe that follows," said Thornberry, "but rather flee them also. Come along with us and we shall all enjoy an advantage."

"I'm sorry," Ivan stammered. "I have not seen others for years. Disease has taken the North. If you say you're a peaceful sort, I will believe you."

"Here is a peace offering," said Clea, and held out some roasted frogs legs.

"Thank you," Ivan said mildly, "but we must hurry. The South shall take these lands, as the old stories say. The safest place is the distant coast, however far it is. Only there is there bounty as yet undisturbed." Ivan adjusted his hat made of leaves. "I know of the river with enough water for rafting. All is not lost, but you must follow me."

"Do not all the hungry seek the coast?" Thornberry queried.

"The lands have become desolate of people, as mysterious diseases ravish young and old alike, they say plagues from ancient times. Only the South is populated by cultures."

"We shall travel West as it is best," Thornberry quoted.

The trio entered a vast overgrown forest on their way to the river, so old that they literally had to wade through leaves and brambles and fallen sticks. Eventually, though, before them was Ivan's river. They set to making a sturdy raft with what was at hand, and the three of them, after several hours' labor, had constructed a fine craft of light, dry branches and logs all fitted together with vines of some strength.

"We can do no better," advised Ivan," in the amount of time we might have. It was rumored once that the people of the Far South could run a long way without abating. Even now they might be making time on us, as they spread out in different directions."

Without further hesitation the three hopped aboard their raft and began paddling under the stars.

For a while there way was lined with trees, but as they eventually reached the low lands there was only marsh and thickets on either side, and they drifted more slowly towards the coast. Soon, the way was desertified except for patches of green grass along the river banks, but there was enough water that they still moved in a goodly pace. Once they encountered a great water snake, but this slithered away from them into hiding.

It was only after several days journey that the river opened out into a delta of sorts, and before them were a series of islands which once had been hills, and upon which tremendous, burdensome waves surged and crashed, and then separated and spread out into the bay.

"If this area is populated," Thornberry noted, "We are here most definitely revealed as obvious." Yet no sign of life was seen on either shore, except for a great variety of birds, such as gulls and geese and ducks and coots and even flamingos.

This sign was obvious. "This is good fishing territory," Wilbur noticed with the other two. "Yet we shouldn't remain obvious. Clearly any denizens of this Lost Coast would travel by the lee, therefore I elect we search out a likely island not far from land to take up position." Thornberry and Clea agreed.

We waited for a period between waves, and then paddled with all their combined strengths, narrowly avoiding a curler and making it over the top. Here one could see that islands were multifarious, and one was indeed a mountain. This pleased the trio as the correct choice, as its peek could bear the brunt of a tidal wave, and one could still safely fish at low tide.

Their raft was rudely thrown upon the rocks, and they disembarked. It was a great relief them all, especially Clea. Immediately there was a bounty to be had: a tremendous supply of shellfish, mainly muscles, blanketed the shoreline, and a forest of pine stretched upward to the mountain peak above. Otherwise, no living things revealed themselves, except the birds.

Had they known of civilization, they might have known they were directly north of the old city of San Francisco, now completely inundated and washed away by the rising floods.

They made camp in a likely looking glade, and set about building habitation and creating fire with their flint-stones. They dared to let plumes of smoke drift skyward, and over the next few months this proved innocent enough, as it attracted no uninvited guests. They had to assume that the people of the Far South would arrive, and their only option by foot was the North, where they knew disease to be rampant. They soon decided to light fires only rarely, and hope to be overlooked by any marauders by land or sea.

Clea took a liking to Ivan, and Ivan liked Clea, but was too disconcerted by her flirting to do other than make awkward gestures of friendship in return, such as one day giving her a pine cone. Thornberry watched their exchanges with deep amusement, and teased Clea endlessly concerning her infatuation.

This went on for many months, until one day Clea took Ivan's hand and led him into a tiny inlet where they could bathe. He hadn't the wits to catch onto what was up, until Clea gestured for him to take off his garment of leaves, even as she pulled down her dress of beaver skin, to reveal her slight, pale body.

When Clea told Thornberry of this, Thornberry laughed out loud for several minutes straight. The married life suited Clea, and she would often make high whistling sounds as she roamed through the forest collecting the abundant pine nuts. Ivan had never quite grasped the notion before, and was astounded by his good fortune.

In their spare time good three of them slowly began assembling a ship, by designing a rough frame from fallen logs and coating them with resins, then skins, for they knew that those from the south were making their way by land and sea. The main problem was that the three could not produce a mast and sail, but would have to rely upon such ores as they could create. Essentially they would end up adrift at sea, but at least then there chances of being spotted would be lessened. Still, they knew that the sea itself could be a cruel fate, and so they delayed and postponed their eventual departure, until prudence dictated finally that they must go or soon be a potential risk of capture. It was a hard lot, for they were trading luxury for hardship and danger, not even knowing if they might glean sufficient rainwater, yet to play hide and seek on land against what might prove to be hoards of wild people was almost certain doom.

They filled many flasks made of skins from local pools of rainwater, loaded them upon their ship which they had nicknamed "The Hardship," and many other provisions besides: scores of smoked birds, roasted grubs and pine nuts, smoked fish and turtles, and even several deer. After a squall one night, the sea became calm, and they rolled their craft on beams to the waiting surf, and climbed aboard with much negative anticipation.

They were swiftly swept out to sea, and they all looked back with regret at the receding land. Swells took them up and down, and clashing currents drove them in circles. For a while they tried their strength at their ores, but this soon became an obviously futile act, as progress to the East was met with competing ocean rivers of unpredictable directions, and in any event as they lost sight of land they soon could not determine their direction.

The risen water from the melted Poles produced ever rising waves and winds. On the very first day out they were nearly capsized, and no report from the horizon showed any improvement. Leaks formed in their vessel, and had to be attended to regularly with more pitch.

They were not to be as fortunate as Nicholas and Jenny and discover a floating island of plastic to save them. On a number of occasions they asserted the ores to barely avoid whirlpools that threatened to send them to a watery grave. They all thought better about their venture, and were going to seek the West Coast again, but it had disappeared from sight and the ability to navigate to. In fact, no land was sighted in any direction, and as far as they knew the general current was circular in motion. Not to mention, the constant rocking upset there gyroscopic equilibrium and none of the three felt well.

At least, Ivan could sight by the stars. "We are drifting east," he said, hopefully. Yet the Pacific Ocean was wide, and even all of Hawai'i had succumbed to tidal waves and earthquakes and had sunk beneath the water.

Their water they soon found a running out, along with the supply of food. They fished in deep earnest, and found some bounty, yet every time waves would beset them and interrupt their fishing and force them to the hold.

Clea was the most delicate of the three, and she protested tearfully. Her tears were met by a crash of thunder as a sudden squall battered them. They just managed to fix their skins to the high points at either end of their vessel to collect rainwater, before a driving wind nearly turned the vessel on its side.

Down below they patched the leaks, and then huddled in furs, and prayed to the Great Spirit that they would survive. The vessel was shaken angrily, as though some great fault had been committed, although all there were innocent.

What the trio did not lack was a supply of pine nuts, which they were soon reduced to. Yet they hardly had the heart to eat, so wretched was their predicament. What they did take comfort in was each other, and the number three was a good number for company.

They all recounted stories of the Pacific Crest Trail, now a virtual highway for the Southerners leading North, but little did those from the South know the mysterious viruses that plagued the North, and would spread inevitably through their population with no auto-immune adaptation to prevent it from happening.

For Clea, Thornberry, and Ivan there was little opportunity to fish, for they were reduced to continually bailing water from the hull with their rough skins. When they could they harvested seaweeds, which they roasted over their small fire pit below. Their rainwater ran out, and soon thirst began to set in, when one particularly stormy night they ran aground on rocks with a battering crunch, knocking a great hole in the side of the vessel. They all grabbed their satchels and leapt overboard into the surf. They had found land at last, and little did they know they had been driven all the way to Japan.

"Swim!" cried Ivan from the teeming waters. "Beware of the rocks!" Rain pelted down in the darkness as the threesome made land.

They crawled upwards out upon the rocks and up into some woods of unfamiliar trees.

"The Great Spirit did not desert us," Thornberry exclaimed in the pouring rain and whipping wind. With the breaking of the dawn came a break in the storm, and once again was revealed the wealth of shellfish to harvest. Clea hummed a tune of victory and hope, and made several high whistling noises.

"Where are we?" she asked Ivan.

"When the stars are again revealed I shall judge," said Ivan, "but my guess is the Far East. We have reached the land only dimmest mythology tells of, and here there is no telling what we shall discover."

After taking their fill of shellfish, they skirted the coast and found a bay to fish from, surrounded by forest. There was no sign as yet of any human habitation, and so they foraged in peace. The forest contained many giant blooming flowers and tremendous mushrooms, and scampering squirrels amidst the Asian pines, and so they were well fed again, defying the rough fates of nature herself, and finding again a bountiful harvest.

"I will go hunting with my bow, and also spy out the rounding lands," Thornberry told Clea and Ivan. "Perhaps I shall find abundance and perhaps I shall spy danger to be wary of."

In the meanwhile the forest dried in the bright sun, and Clea and Ivan could make a fire, and roasted shellfish and mushrooms, which they wrapped in flower petals and consumed greedily. After several days of uncertainty, Thornberry returned with a young doe on her back, and reported no sightings of other humans, or indeed any signs of former habitation. Signs of civilization had long ago weathered away. After several weeks they felt confident enough to make a more complete survey of the outlying territory. It was in another bay not too far distant that they discovered something extraordinary. Beached on the sand was a long, sleek metal craft, rusted and worn yet with the appellation "U.S.S. Nemo" clearly visible on the hull. None of the three knew of metal well nor had imagined a submarine, but this was what was before them. It was Ivan who cautiously climbed the vessel and approached to the hatch, and timidly inquired if anyone was at home. No one answered from the relic. The three voted to continue, and proceeded to gather to enter. There they saw what defied their collective imaginings, as there were ancient rusted electronic consoles and bunks with disintegrated mattresses, and instruction manuals crumbling nearly to dust.

"This is not from our world," Thornberry vouchsafed, "but from a land of long ago." They struggled with the evidence of their senses and tried to put together the pieces of the puzzle. However, they could not corroborate all the necessary factors that could lead to such a phenomenon. Of the stores they found on board the submarine they could just grasp the usefulness of the supply of air-gun harpoons, and intact swimming goggles, but failed to ascertain the craft as a whole as anything but totally alien to their experience. "Once Earth was entirely foreign," Thornberry stated safely. "A great peoples came to be no more." Indeed, the crew of the submarine had drifted to land long before, and, being all of the male gender and with no one to intermarry with, the crew had rapidly faded away.

"Perhaps they were terrible monsters," Clea wondered.

"No," said Ivan, "they were united in a complex society, which industries thrived for a long time. This ship contains a story of many years of cooperation and applied intelligence. The Earth must have known many people who produced many great works, not just this ship. Some great tragedy ruined them however, even as they achieved the pinnacle of development. There is no other explanation."

"I agree," Thornberry interjected, "and so this ship intimates no possible threats to us. It is purely a relic."

"What if there are monsters still about?" queried Clea.

"No, child," Thornberry comforted, "there are no monsters about. Rather we should fear other humans and wild animals, as usual. This land is not so different as the one we have left."

Even as they were leaving the spot, howls broke out in the woods.

"Monsters!" Clea cried.

"No," said Ivan, "those are the calls of a wolf pack."

"Into the water!" said Thornberry. "They cannot follow us so easily there." The three all leapt into the surf and paddled, even as white wolves began to appear on the shore. The swollen waves crashed about them, and Thornberry had no means to utilize her bow. "Swim beyond the waves," she indicated," and find a swath of sand to adhere to."

They struggled out into the bay and were able to locate a submerged bar of sand. The wolves prowled about the surf but would not go in.

"We shall out-wait them," indicated Ivan. "They shall give up before we do."

The wolves were keen on the hunt, and hour upon hour prowled the shore. Nightfall descended, and still the threesome had to wait. Fortunately the water was not frigid but warm. By the breaking of daylight the wolf pack began to yield, and one by one slipped into the forest. Thornberry waded forward and was pushed towards land by the waves. With her bow she brought down the last of the stragglers.

Clea had never seen a wolf before, and was convinced there were monsters, and was hysterical.

"They are just wild dogs," Ivan soothed.

"What are dogs?" she asked him.

"Man's best friend," quoted Ivan. "I knew them as a child, but these ones are not so tame."

"We shall be rent apart and savaged," Clea mourned.

"No," contradicted Thornberry. "I shall build a series of buttresses to shield me and hunt from."

"And in the meanwhile," Ivan noted, "we can live in the foreign craft. That'll keep us insulated from the wild." He took Clea's hand and led her from the water, Thornberry went first with her bow, but no further challenges came.

"We do not know where we are," said Thornberry, but the providence of the Great Spirit has not failed us, against all odds. Even the raging sea has been our friend, and guided us hither. Let us fish for a time and consecrate our catch to that which provides."

The U.S.S. Nemo was now their home. Thornberry over time constructed a series of outlying buttresses, little huts of stone that might be fired from but not easily penetrated. Thus the threesome had a defense against many sorts of wild things.

The wolves they knew would return, and over time perhaps bear and cats would appear. Thornberry told a tale of a legendary white bear, that, she said, may live in these parts. For a while there lives were undisturbed, but what they could not know was that the series of mutated viruses from the radioactivity of War would haunt them, even as Death had the final word.

"You cannot fully destroy evil," Jack the hermit had once said to Gwynhr. "Even when evil is destroyed, its effects linger on, for that which penetrates the secrets of nature is part of the great continuity, and brings about a lasting wasting. We can know little of this now, except that this story is told in the sky, and sometimes does descend in the lives of men and women."

Thornberry contracted one of the deadly viruses, and began to waste with a fever. She would not except Clea or Wilbur's consoling, but only would say on the matter that she had lived a full term of life, and that death was nothing to fear.

"We cannot go on without you," Clea mourned. "You have been my helpmeet and companion and mentor."

"You have your Ivan, dear," replied Thornberry, "I know you will not be alone, and so I can die contented. Before I die, though, I will teach you the bow and arrow, that will keep you safe from the monsters." Clea still called the wolf a monster.

With the rain pelting down from a dark grey sky, Thornberry was laid to rest on top of the hill above their bay, and flowers planted upon her grave.

"Jack," Gwynhr had queried long ago, "what happens when we die?"

"Gwynhr, when we die," said the old hermit, "we go into a long, deep sleep that perhaps nothing will awaken us from, unless we sleep long enough to reach the Beyond, which is a very long time from now. Otherwise we fade away into a sort of void or oblivion that takes all manner of human and animal, and there is no awakening from this."

"What manner of person sleeps long enough to reach the Beyond?" Gwynhr asked logically.

"Only those that the Beyond already exists in somewhat," said Jack, "and this is something one can never know about another person. And now for some more honeycomb!"

Clea and Ivan waded in the shallows gathering shells for their collection. The interior of the U.S.S. Nemo had become a museum of special shells and stones and pinecones and dried flowers. The crew of the submarine, who had died out from lack of women, would never have guessed that there craft would become such a place.

Clea and Ivan said their vows beneath a particularly resplendent Asian pine tree.

"I vow," Ivan began, "to be earnest in all my ways, and keep your eyes and face my reminder of what love is, a spirit that survives beyond the mortal coil, and I vow to help you when you are sad, and to participate when you're happy, and to remind you of that which is most important to me, my love for you."

"And I," Clea said, "vow to take this bow and arrow and protect you from all manner of monsters which might be on the land, so that you are free to remind me of your love, as my husband and cherished friend, and to always create time for us to explore our ways, always remembering that you are most dear to my heart. And when we feel apart, or must be separated, I vow to return in the spirit of love, so that what we swear to today might always be renewed." Clea plucked a dried leaf from Ivan's clothing, and stowed it in a pocket of her beaver skin dress. "I shall place this leaf in our collection at home, as a token whereby these vows might be located in our hearts upon sight."

Clea's crystal blue eyes sparkled that evening in the sunset, and she made pigtails of her strawberry blond hair which she did up with vine strings. Ivan took a knife they had found aboard the USS Nemo and trimmed his unruly beard and mustache, and trimmed back his unkempt hair. His hazel eyes rested with admiration upon Clea, and so she skipped out of her beaver skins.

A sudden storm interrupted their lovemaking on the beach, and so they scampered, laughing and hand-in-hand, back to their submarine home, and lit a fire from flint stone and tinder by the hatch. The sun set beneath the Western hills, and even as they settled down to abalone from the reefs, they heard the cry of wolves.

The couple hurried out without delay to the nearest of the small fortresses Thornberry had constructed, and barricaded themselves in. The hungry wolves were on the scent, and a number padded about the barricades snarling restlessly, but a wholly at a disadvantage, as there were sites in the barricades for a Clea to fire arrows through.

The white pelts of the wolves shone dimly in the forest under a crescent moon. They were evidently quite hungry. They pawed at the barricades and made easy targets. They were not dissuaded until the entire pack was nearly denuded. However the blood sent was so strong that, even as Clea and Ivan were about to remove themselves from hiding, a great crashing came through the woods, and there was revealed the legendary giant white bear, which without hesitation began to rip and gnaw at a fallen wolf. Clea let loose all of her remaining arrows at this wholly foreign creature, and brought it down. At last it was safe to exhume themselves, and without delay Ivan took his knife towards dismembering this bounty, while Clea retrieved the arrows, all the while making high whistling sounds. The very dangers nature was fraught with yet provided.

That morning on the beach of their bay they constructed a great bonfire to roast all the meat, even as they watched the dark stratospheric cumulous clouds gather overhead.

The bounty had arrived in a most timely fashion. Even as the couple was completing the storage of their meals in lockers aboard the Nemo, the thunderheads broke with freezing rain, and tremendous gales of sleet and hail. They battened down the hatch and put out the fire, and made their home more comfortable with the soft furs of their catch. Through two round portals they witnessed ocean swells crash about their home, until, at the height of the storm, tidal waves completely overcame the beached submarine, yet it would not budge from its mooring. Clea and Ivan stayed within for many days for the duration of the storm, until it finally relented. They found the beach of sand entirely swept away, leaving the stone underneath, and many of the nearby trees had been felled by the onslaught. Yet their home had endured. It was shown that they had a safe haven, despite nature's fury, which ruled so much of the Earth.

They risked no expeditions inland, but preferred their relative security. With every storm they would seek their refuge, and come out again with new breaking light to fish and forage. They hunted and gathered in the forest, and harvested the abundance of the reefs, and collected many shellfish.

One day a stranger appeared, a squat Mongol dressed in a wolf skin and bearing a bow and arrow. They met him on the beach, and he looked at them closely and then at the submarine, and said something unintelligible, and then walked off. Apart from this, they had no other human contact.

Much of the time the sun beat down with a fierce heat, and Clea and Ivan would play in the shallows. When the tide was at low ebb and the sea calm, Clea would swim about the bay and dive for abalone. They always remember the hard times of the past, however, and their narrow escape across the ocean, and were thankful for the smallest gifts granted by nature.

Wilbur developed lines of care, but Clea seemed remarkably untouched as they aged, as if preserved by her original childlike spirit.

"Gwynhr," Jack had said, "do be a good lad and pour me some more wine, and I will tell you a story." Gwynhr did as he was bidden, and also poured a little more for himself, to hear the tale by. "When my parents were alive, my father insisted on minding the bees, while my mother would go and gather herbs from the forest and check the rabbit-snares. It was never forgotten that there should be a division of labor, and each preferred their own. As I was raised into adulthood they read to me from our small library, and I heard many peculiar tales of sprawling enclaves of people fed by cars and buggies that needed no horse to pull, but burned a sort of pitch to turn their wheels. And so the air became fouler and fouler, until many agreed that something more sophisticated must be produced for conveyance. This they managed to do, until their carriages required only water for the wheels to turn.

"Yet it was at that time that, among those in power, that a secret distrust was steadily growing, and eventually the big townships were laid to waste by fantastic weapons such as you cannot imagine which would produce tremendous, rampant fires. Since then, no one can guess what had happened, and all their many technologies were lost.

"One of the few survivors was a man who worked at a carnival, which was a sort of big party that anyone might join in, with an odd variety of contraptions as amusements. This man's position was to convey people up in the sky with a sort of bubble filled with hot air to make it rise. When the War came, he was high in the air, and mighty winds blew them far off course."

Gwynhr was rapt with attention. "That is a very unusual story. What does it mean?"

"It means that providence comes in all shapes and sizes, and that for every disaster that looms there is the accompaniment of hope. Were this not so humankind would not continue."

"I see," said Gwynhr. "We are creatures born of hopes and fears, dreams and despairs, and contain our own destruction and salvation."

"Yes, lad! You understand!" Jack exclaimed. "And around us is the play of the providential nature, which might thwart on the one hand, and provide mysterious aid on the other. This is enough to know, for to question it would be futile."

Clea and Ivan lived for many, many years in the U.S.S. Nemo, sometimes hunting the wild things, sometimes hiding from them. They developed many games that they played, such as riddles and rhymes other wordplay. They both lived beyond the expectation of years, but finally Wilbur told Clea he was growing ready for his time. One night the two of them went to sleep in each other's arms and did not wake up they were left there undisturbed, and no one ever again discovered the U.S.S. Nemo.

CHAPTER THIRTY-FOUR:
BRIGHT WAS THE MORNING DEW

Gwynhr dragged Eldril's lifeless body on a rough sled towards the mountains height, through mango and banana groves, as Justine followed along, disconsolate, with her right arm, which Gwynhr had narrowly saved from infection, dangling uselessly beside her. Eldril's lifeless body was the same white in death as it had been in life. Justine hailed Gwynhr halfway up the hill.

"A great mystery is passing, little-known in this lifetime," she commented to her faithful husband. "Nor do we know the manner of her passing..." Eldril had been a touchstone of strength and knowledge, from one of the last superior civilizations, unknown people from a mere outcropping of rock amidst the sea. With her passing disappeared many knowledge's, and stories of long ago.

"We yet maintain her memory," said Gwynhr wearily. "Do not despair, wife. I am with you."

"We shall go on together, you and I," Justine replied.

When they attained the height, Gwynhr dug with a stick into the soft turf, and after an hour closed the earth over Eldril. The couple lovingly placed flowers over the grave.

As they proceeded down from the style sacred site, they used the same sled to gather mangos and bananas.

"I will take you out for a swim," Gwynhr suggested. "It may prove therapeutic."

"I will go along, then," said Justine wisely. "And then perhaps it will be in our hearts to celebrate some."

"I will roast bananas in their skins for your dessert," Gwynhr comforted.

That afternoon there was a slight cooling breeze. Gwynhr assisted Justine in floating on her back. Gwynhr said, "We shall carve a log in her memory, and set it up as a totem."

"That is a nice idea, Gwynhr," Justine replied. She wanted to burst into tears, but spared her husband. At last she allowed the warmth of the floating to calm her, and some of her old wiry strength returned to her body. "Roasted bananas, you don't say?"

"But I do. And then for some song from your childhood, one I haven't heard before." Justine set about trying to remember a song.

"Gwynhr," Jack had once said, "once you truly realize that life will end, and love is the highest ideal we can attain to, you will not live the same way again."

Eldril had passed away from a mysterious virus, and Gwynhr had followed of natural causes. Now

Justine sat tending a fire with her one good arm, echoes of her past filling her heart and disturbing her mind. Isolation encroached upon her as she thought of her lost loved ones, of long walks through the banana and mango groves, and discussions late into the night by the fireside.

She missed her husband Gwynhr especially, although she dwelt deeply upon Eldril's existence, a mysterious albino who had endured steadfastly for her brief life, leaving behind the mystery of her strength and endurance as an exemplar of unusual courage and reckoning with hardship, who had saved Justine and Gwynhr from a most certain doom, appearing like a phantom of snow-like brilliance and passing away into the netherworld from which he had perhaps been sent from.

Gwynhr, however, had been Justine's closest love, who had originally aided in their flight from the Desolations to newfound humanity, a guiding beacon of reserve, patience, and devotion. He had been homely and unassuming, and for all these qualities Justine had loved him well. After Eldril's passing they had lived a long life together, deep into old age, always minding and caring for the other, never tiring of their companionship.

Old age became Justine well. She was sound of mind and body, except for her useless right arm, and the stripes of grey in her wavy red hair resembled the admixture of milk and blood. Her wiry strength, born of the years of desperate survival and determination, had not left her, and her mind had not ceased from its canniness and unique insight, betrayed by squinty crow's feet about the eyes, which seemed to peer even at a rock or tree as though penetrating its nature. Although sound of mind, she was betrayed by thoughts of her lost loved ones as she went about the affairs of the day. Gwynhr had built her a special ladder, with which she might crawl up the fruit trees for the bearing abundance, and with her good left arm harvest the never-ending supply of fruit. She went successfully digging the earth, and there was still a thriving garden they had established long ago.

Justine missed Gwynhr with all her emotions. She knew the one thing most irreplaceable was love, this was what binds life to life, and so she remembered always, and sometimes, in deepest loneliness she would write poetry of the past and even speak out loud as though the others were present, the better to hear herself think and remember them by.

Bitter tears were shed in loneliness. Lost love haunted her night and day, despite her self-prepossession and independence. It was a bitter brew to have only memories, and solitude lengthened the years as she dwelt upon her loved ones, but her hardiness would sustain her for many years after Gwynhr's death, although there was no one present to love.

Her magic isle gave her all the physical sustenance she required, as she subsisted well on mangos and bananas and coconuts and the occasional fish her lines caught for her. It was a tropical paradise, except there was no one to share it with. Sometimes Justine would cry out in wail in her loneliness, solitude few humans ever bear, being bereft of their loved ones, and utterly alone without human comfort. No wandering ships would ever discover her.

She would squirm at night with Gwynhr's absence, and dream deep nightmares of mythical creatures that had carried him to a distant land. Upon awakening, she would go for long walks, for the day searching for answers and relief, and she would frequently visit Gwynhr's flowering grave, nearby where the islands freshwater spring trickled forth to give her life. When she had the energy, she would hike to the islands peak, and wonder at the strange silver flowers that grew on Eldril's grave, the silver star, or, edelweiss. Any portents of her own mortal doom, such as the cry of seagulls which would meet her year, gave her no fear or sorrow, but some abstracted hope and deepest wish to be joined to her loved ones again. Still, in this she could not believe, having fought for so many years against the futility of the final end. And she would go on with all her fighting spirit despite her yearning, where others might have given up years before.

She wrote in the dirt with a stick, clumsily, left-handed:

"Bright was the morning on the dew,
Where nighttime frosts turned to water anew,
And were it the most solemn day,
Of the High One's grief,
I should look away,
And find no relief.

Yet the powers that be have satisfaction
In every last tree of the recollection,
Under which I stray,
Turning every leaf to find a lay
Of natures strength, or death's toll grey,
A contradiction, or so they say.

Gwynhr my dear is not gone,
For by the fire I hear his song
Which once I taught him long ago,
Or perhaps it wasn't so long
For his memory lingers, ever and anon,
And love continues to grow,
Ever expansive, like the sea's awesome flow.

I will not take sides:

In nature, with love and death, all abides,

And gentle was he to the end

Like the branch that does not break, but bend,

With the gusty gale which on the current rides,

So for a while my heart will mend

And Gwynhr soothe the flowing tides,

From night-time 'til dawn.

I hear his murmurs, he is not gone.

For every dawn that lingers,

Is like a new-born song."

There were no seasons on the island, but the air became increasingly hot, and sometimes strange warm rain would break with peals of lightning and thunder, and the poems of the earth would be washed away. Justine would dance in the rain, and then go to a stone covered pool Gwynhr had made for her, and she would soak to your heart's content, where all grief and wandering would find a solace, and she would find herself newborn, and the cares of the countless years would subside into a new content with life, although a life lived alone. She slowly began to learn that nothing was wrong, and her old independence in spirit would reassert itself, despite her missing loves. Justine was not one to wither away from sorrow, but even in solitude would find strength newborn, almost as though she were a child again. The moment of her passing was not far away, and yet she had learned that death did not hold an ultimate sway, but rather the renewal inherent in nature would last beyond her years, for others to discover if they could. Often she would lie on her back and peer up at the ineffable sky, I know that those who would come after would have their own plights to suffer and perhaps overcome, strifes that could not be judged by anyone else, but only the dictates of their own conscience. She finally began to accept her solitude, and even rejoice in it, for she had the secrets of the heart which should not be exposed except to those who were penultimately ready, those who had faced death and won, and those who accepted nature in all its forms, those who could be intimately alone with themselves and still rejoice.

"All things must pass," Justine breathed to herself, and she went to a rock, where the birds could pick her bones clean, and she lay down and did not wake up.

"The only thing more illogical than death," Jack the hermit had once told Gwynhr, "is being born. This sets the whole ball in motion, as it were, which ends with an uncertain climax. The most we can know is that life is ultimately good, and to be free of vain regrets. If you do not reach the Great Beyond, this hopefully will be in the last thing that you know."

"I shall die yearning," Gwynhr complained.

"Then you shall die learning," Jack replied with a laugh.

Clea was not laughing. She was waiting for a frog to bite her baited line, and relieve her hunger. She was only eight. Heavy rain began to pour, and still she sat beside her lake. She began to whistle, but this soon faded. She reached for a pointed stick, and went wading in the shallows. As swift as a hummingbird she darted forward and found her catch, a sizable salmon. She began her high-pitched whistle again, in earnest at the bounty. She could not wait to roast due to extreme hunger, and so began to chew while still waist deep. When no good part had been left she crawled back beneath her overhanging rock where she lived, and tried to go to sleep. She slept on bark and covered herself in bark while sleeping, but the night was especially humid with tropical air, and so she made her lithe, tired body hunt again for breakfast, even though it was raining.

I strangled howl came from a far distance to her ears. It was a lone wild person casting himself from a precipice to appease wild gods. Clea heard no more about it, only that she thought it might be a hungry animal, and so she barricaded herself into her boulder with a wall of stones.

Clea knew very few words for wild animals, although she had seen a brown bear once, and named it a "snarfle." In her imagination there were very many types of wild animal, yet very few of these were actual. She had learned very little under the cruel mistreatment of her parents, and had run away years previously, to live in solitude until she was an adult, and had met Thornberry and Ivan. For this time she was a creature of the imagination, living as she did in the isolation of her mind and her lake.

The first time she spider water-snake she decided to kill it just in case, as it intruded into her precious lake, and was deemed hideous, but it was too quick for her and swiftly disappeared.

In the intervening years before Clea became an adult, her life was one of routine. She fished, she whistled, she swam, she dreamed of other worlds and people, yet her life when uninterrupted. Her childlike beauty would endure to the end of her life, like a deeply enshrouded mystery only the very wise might apprehend. No age touched her, no wear of hardship, no line of care, no defect was inflicted upon her nature.

Until the arrival of Thornberry and Ivan, Clea had only a few immediate facts to grasp: her lake was an omnipresent reality, and her returning hunger haunted her, and then there were the occasional shifts in weather.

"You are very fetching," Ivan had said to her after their nuptial evening.

"To be nice is to be naughty," replied Clea, inventing a phrase that she would later tell Thornberry.

"The glow about you two," Thornberry had said that night, "is positively disgusting."

"We've come to an agreement," said Clea.

"So I see," Thornberry said.

Ivan blushed a deep-red hue. He had had no knowledge of such things, and considered his good fortune astounding. There ensued a long pause between the three of them. "My mother had always told me," Wilbur said at last, "that marriage only happens to demons at night, and other such spirits as prowl the edges of our reality, like succubi. I found it very amusing."

Thornberry laughed out loud, and Clea made a long, shrill whistling. "Ivan," Thornberry said directly, "if only all men could be like you. Now that you are learned, I am sure you will be very good for Clea."

"I already considered it my duty," said Ivan with all humility, "I just didn't realize all the benefits. I will take this new learning and ponder."

"There is a good fellow," said Clea.

"As a young monk, you would not understand," Jack had told Gwynhr.

"I assisted a midwife once," Gwynhr said mildly, "but I didn't know the causal relationship at the time. To me it seemed that the Great Spirit had bestowed a miracle."

"No matter how long you live," Jack the hermit indicated, "no matter what knowledge you gain, this is something that you will never fully understand. Only women come to that knowledge. My own father told me this."

"I see," Gwynhr replied good-naturedly. "I will be very delicate, if I can, but you only let on somewhat. Surely there is more you know."

"It is like flowing honey," Jack said, "when the comb has reached its peak. It is like the rain we dance in. It is like laughing for no reason. It is like the first time you smell a rose. It is like holding hands when there is nothing to complain about. The Great Spirit made it so that we should remain humble in the face of the Mysteries."

"If I find a wife," Gwynhr vowed, "I shall treat her with all the respect one can treat the Mysteries. Yet, surely, part of me will go unsatisfied."

"Not if you are truly married by the Spirit."

"How will I know?" Gwynhr asked.

"Of this much," said Jack, "there is absolute certitude of the heart."

"What a relief!" exclaimed Gwynhr.

Justine left strewn flowers, colorful and bright androsy, upon Gwynhr's grave. "Gwynhr, I love you!" she wailed, futilely imploring the fates to intervene, but all that followed was a murmur through the fronds. The sudden loss of her husband would leave the deepest regret, like a thirst that could not be quenched, more than Justine had ever known crossing the driest desert.

She began to fervently wish and pray for a Great Beyond where they might be reunited, as she knelt beside the grave, and at the same time she knew to give thanks, from the bottom of a torn and bleeding heart, that she had actually known her one true love, and so the fates were kind, and had shown the gift of love, a love that could yet sustain her for many years. For now, the tears were bitter with words unspoken, hugs not shared, and sunsets never viewed together. She left the grave, simply marked "Gwynhr." The rest of Justine's life would be a more complete eulogy, alone amidst the greenery and abundance she now shared with no one.

That day she made a circuit to the opposite side of the island from her encampment to gather as yet unharvested shellfish. Gwynhr had told her to remain active. She also collected algae for her soup, and she went to a cove which she might dangle her delicate toes in mild surf. The tears finally ceased, and she look forward, not back, and all she could perceive was herself, as though she had been thrown into that Wilderland Gwynhr had saved her from, destitute yet resolute, drained of emotion except the will to survive, to fulfill Gwynhr's wish.

CHAPTER THIRTY-FIVE:
THE DREAMCATCHERS

Justine fell asleep uneasily in the shade of a banana tree. Gwynhr was approaching from the high surf, arising from the waves as a phantom of the past, the now distant intimacies, conversations, pleasure great and small, a life of consistencies now gone. "Gwynhr!" Justine cried in her dream as Gwynhr arose to land. "Tell me, tell me what is wrong?

"Life is too short to tell all," Gwynhr had replied, "this is what is wrong."

"Tell me how I might help," Justine wept.

"I wish we could have grown up together as children," the ghost of Gwynhr replied, "I wish I could've known every part of you, but life is too short."

"Gwynhr," Said Justine," you loved me as well as you could."

So it came to pass that many loves knew their full term, despite the rages of nature, and the overthrows of a lost humanity, and many more knew the ravages of such a savage Earth. Poised between life and death was the albino Eldril.

CHAPTER THIRTY-SIX:
THE CLAN OF THE WHITE WOLF

Eldril sat within a ring of fire, with a spilt pool of bears blood in the center. Snowflakes landed on her white eyelashes and her dilated pupils were like dark wells amongst milky white, where there was no discrimination between iris and eyeball.

She waited with utmost patience for the nearest wolf-pack to be on the scent of the blood, and confront the ring of fire. Her cross bows and arrows lay by her side, prepared for deadly work. Eldril quietly prayed to Omyranth, the spirit who determined life or death. Eldril's methods were sure, she had never failed in the hunt, be it of beast or man. Yet this early morning something began to disquiet her patience. A crow landed on a nearby redwood branch. The life of a crow she never took, for they were symbolic of Omyranth. All her senses were piqued.

The first wolf to enter her glade that frosty morning was white. This was enough for Eldril's finely attuned senses. In a heartbeat, she gathered her crossbow and arrows and a canteen of water and fled with all swiftness through the ring of fire towards her special trail, for she knew then that to stay was wrong, and certain death. She glanced back just once to spy a band of berserkers enter her glade of frozen meats from the South. They wore the skins of the white wolf.

Eldril slipped and slid down the side of a culvert, her trail marked only to herself in the snow by a few standing stones. Shouts came loud behind her. Eldril was not afraid or desperate, for these things were not part of her nature, yet she was poised to face the worst, as she left the trail of her passage.

Down the culvert she slid, and then to a rocky climb, her chosen ascent towards the pinnacle of Mount Tamalpais, "The Mother Goddess," for the greatest vantage.

Yet the berserkers were strong with beast flesh, and had perceived their nemesis, the spirit of snow and ice. With bow and pickax and javelins and daggers they pursued Eldril in great number, leaping from boulders as she made her way up the most certain path. Their cries were for a consummate vengeance upon this alien phantom they perceived, who dwelt as one with cruel nature and single-handedly survived the elements.

Upon one rocky outcropping above the trees Eldril paused once, to catch her breath and unleash a volley. Her breath came forth like the mist of a graveyard as she dared use arrows with her most deadly volley: three arrows loaded and loosed at once, with a sweeping motion even as she fired. Three of the berserkers were disabled, the rest, as now she could see many dozen, were infuriated with this act of magic and renewed in their vengeful wrath.

Up the mountain Eldril skipped and, and behind her the berserkers, muscular yet heavy-shod, found the going more slow, and soon Eldril had faded into the woods like steam into snowflakes. Orders were barked from below, and a team, now more than 100 strong, spread out to the forest to surround the pinnacle. The snow began falling heavier, and the wind blew chill, but this deterred them not. They advanced in a great semi circle to cordon off their prey, full of wild fantasies of war with nature, of despoiling this demi-urge of snow and ice, of conquering the epitome of the elements.

Upwards climbed Eldril. She cleared another swath of redwoods and took another vantage with her crossbow, spying out shadows marauding through the woods below. She here would not waste three at once but one by one released all the remaining arrows, each finding a mark. Dozens of the bezerkers were disabled, yet the rest came on with renewed fury.

At last Eldril reached the summit. Here was waiting one of the eloquences of her craft: a toboggan perched at the gateway to a descent through the woods, a sleigh ride device to outpace all possible pursuers. She placed herself headfirst upon the vehicle and kicked the sleigh, it pitched forward through the woods down a formed track. Occasionally she dragged her legs to slow and make safe her descent, but she soon had to cease this as arrows and javelins landed in the passing trees. She pitched forward with all her speed, veering first to the right and then to the left and so on down the mountain. Angry oaths of retribution began to fade behind her with her speed, yet she would not hesitate but took the advantage. When she reached the shoreline, at the end of the speedway she had invented, there was a great cliff over the waters. As she flew over she released her grip on the sleigh, and in midair curled up into a little ball for the collision with water.

She collided with teeming, surging surf, and the force of her fall plunged her deep into the water. At first she could not tell which way was up, until, after a few seconds, she was reoriented, just in time to be crashed against the stony shore. Thee stood her tethered white mare, champing at the bits for a return, and there was moored her sailing vessel. Her life on land had ended, temporarily, and she would now return to a life on the dangerous tides. As usual, she was caught between a rock and a hard place, but prudence had again proved the better part of valor. These berserkers, at least, would never find her.

She stripped off her wet furs and traded them for dry ones from onboard, and then her horse on board her modest craft, and swiftly raised sail and debarked. For now, her journey must be to the north. Her failed mission to trap wolves was only a minor setback, as Omyranth had again smiled upon her, but she knew, in her heart of hearts, her life would not meet its full term, for, as her mother men that said, Eldril was not of this world, Eldril was of the world of the Spirits, of the Shades, who only appear at rare junctures of Earth and Sky, and then disappear into the Mists of Time, yet whom might appear again. Eldril cast off the lines as they sailed away, and let out a laugh, fluttering away in the wind like a seagull, as she cast her prayer to the god of triumph, Erubis. Her contingency measure in the event of marauders had been perfectly laid. The waves would be her home again for a while.

CHAPTER THIRTY-SEVEN:
A MEETING WITH MISTER TUTTLE

Eldril spent her spare time, between minding the waves and sail, and feeding the horse wild grasses, in making more arrows. She sailed steadily north about the coastland, until she found one frozen day she decided to land on, as the waters were becoming more treacherous. She tethered the mare to an ancient pine, and trekked inland with her bow. She marked her way with stones as she traversed unfamiliar bare hillocks towards a range of mountains, setting snares as she progressed. A light snow began to fall, and she laughed again.

Away in the distance her dilated black pupils spied an unusual snowdrift, and out of curiosity she followed this direction, along a frozen stream bed. She soon noticed signs of life: frozen over holes in the ice indicated someone had been fishing. Her senses were alerted, yet everything seemed harmless enough. Still, she remembered what her father Gideon had told her as a child, "The easiest thing to deceive his oneself." So she armed her crossbow and approached the unusual drift.

Out of this snowdrift popped a funny little unkempt man wearing clothes woven from sheep's wool. "I thought there would be a visitor!" he exclaimed, and drew on a carven antler-horn pipe, something Eldril had never seen before. Also, of course, Eldril had rarely met a civilized person. Yet she wasn't surprised, only curious.

"You were expecting me?" she asked politely.

"Well, not you in particular," said the funny little man, "but someone, sometime. And it seemed to be in the air, as it were. Are you hungry?"

"No," Eldril replied," the salmon are good here. Perhaps you could tell me what you're doing with that thing in your mouth."

"Tobacco, mind you," said the man. "Can't seem to get enough of it, although I have a pretty plot. Are you sure you wouldn't care for some mushroom soup?"

"Thank you, but no. Right now I am more interested in this tobacco. What a funny word."

"Here, try some. Only the finest, mind you. Bred for ages, don't you know." The man passed the pipe to Eldril as though they were best of friends.

"And what is this called?" Eldril queried.

"Why, that is a pipe." Eldril inhaled through her mouth and exhaled through her nose. "It has a particular taste," she noted, "much better than sage or mint. And it would seem to keep one warm…"

A little bell chimed. "That would be one of my lines getting a tug. Excuse me while I investigate, but go on enjoying. I keep a supply of the stuff drying constantly."

"I see," said Eldril, and her bemusement began to get the better of her. "This is a very funny little man," she remarked to herself as she wandered away to a hole in the ice.

He soon returned with a nice fat trout and introduced himself. "My name is Tuttle, after my grandfather," said he.

"My name is Eldril. My mother Min made me that. Pleasure to meet you."

"Haven't seen a soul in ages. Not since my own parents passed on of the flu, don't you know? Can't seem to count the years, really. I can't say I've ever imagine anybody quite so pale as you. Where do you get it from?

"From the ineffable sky," Eldril tried to explain.

"That is a good answer, although I imagine it's inherited," Tuttle remarked.

"Why, yes. It must be, at that" said Eldril.

"Do you know anybody?" Mister Tuttle pursued conversationally.

"Only the Spirits my mother taught me. Let's see, there's Omyranth, Erubis, Xanth, Zantu, Boabdil, Jerub, Onrehat, Choronzon…"

"Yes, yes, no doubt there are, but do you have any friends?"

"Omyranth has always favored me… and of course my horse is my friend."

"Do you have a horse, you don't say? I once saw a herd of wild mustangs in my youth. Magnificent creatures really. Well, you don't seem to be married."

"That is really a too kind of you," said Eldril, "much too kind. I prefer to live alone with myself."

Tuttle looked away very much dejected. "Well at least stay for a few days and smoke more tobacco, and we shall discuss this and that."

"My worse is tethered in the day. Are there any wild things about?"

"Perhaps up in the mountains," Tuttle replied, "but it's been cold here a very long while."

"Then I will take you up on your kind offer. Some rest is needed. And some tobacco, so I may meditate."

"What is 'meditate?'" Tuttle queried.

"It would really take too long to explain," Eldril abjured regretfully.

"I see. Well, come inside my igloo while I tend to the soup, and we can have a good chat. No doubt you know of the outside world, and I am ignorant."

Eldril thought it a fair offer. "We will chat," said she, "and perhaps I will try some mushrooms soup."

"It has some fine algae in it" Tuttle offered, "and soon, some trout."

The interior of the igloo was lined with bars of polished oak wood, and a spacious dining area was spread with wool. "Why is this stuff?" Eldril again had to ask.

"From sheep, don't you know?"

"I have heard of them."

"I used to have a little pen of such back in bygone days. I don't reckon I'll see one again. They were awfully friendly mind you, much like I imagine your horse is. Disease got the better of them in the end. A dreadful pity, they were my only friends."

"My own time is limited," Eldril commented without emotion. "What should we talk about, and all the high heavens?"

"Well," Tuttle said, and then paused briefly. "You seem like the religious sort. Have you heard of 'God'?"

"Yes," Eldril answered, "long ago. He was a major character in a book I read as a child."

"Well he's much more than that. Why he can do everything, even. But usually he is a voice we hear in our heads, sort of like when we think out loud, only it isn't us. Much of his work is to go about destroying and such but in the end he is considered good. The people of old held to the notion rather fervently, I am led to believe. They said that when you die you might meet him, and spend the rest of your time in his house with lots of folks such as deserve it."

"I prefer to move about," said Eldril.

"Quite so," returned Tuttle. "Otherwise things begin to get a little stuffy."

The air in the spacious igloo was beginning to fill with tobacco smoke, and Eldril felt conspicuously reticent to give the pipe back to Mr. Tuttle. "There's something funny about this herb, Mr. Tuttle," she remarked. Tuttle took her meaning. "I can spare a plant or two for you to cultivate. And I have a spare pipe about here someplace." The igloo was full of decades of flotsam and jetsam which had floated ashore, each a puzzle of forensic deduction. "Do you, by any chance, have anything I might find useful to trade?"

"Well," Eldril responded, automatically in a mood to barter, "all my valuables I must keep and: my astrolabe, my compass, my knives, my first, my books…"

"Aha, books. There we have our subject, for I have only a few. Perhaps you could spare just one, mayhaps?" Eldril could tell that this was a moment of some greed for Tuttle, as was only understandable in his frozen wasteland.

"A fair trade might be Sophocles," Eldril tried.

"Never heard of him. Still, it sounds worth it. The tobacco plants for Sophocles, then."

"It's a deal," Eldril finalized.

"But a poor trade for losing your company," Tuttle interjected.

"You're too kind," Eldril said, sipping some soup. "As an extra to our trade, is there anything good to hunt here?"

"Plenty. Plenty of caribou. But there're trifle skittish," Tuttle explained.

"Not a problem. I shall blend in with the snow."

"Sounds awfully cold."

Eldril stalked the caribou herds without a single fur to cover, starkly naked but hidden by the white of the snow, except for twin pupils of exceeding dark, and a ready crossbow. She kept low and sifted to drifts towards the open tundra. Caribou were grazing, which she pondered some while, never having seen exactly the like, but being familiar with deer. She crawled forward stealthily, but could begin to sense that the Caribou sensed her. She chose the largest buck, and knelt on one knee for balance, then unloosed her deadly volley of three arrows at once, all finding their mark. With a rumbling in the ground the herd scattered away.

Eldril whistled for Tuttle, who arrived with a sled and carving knives. "I never wish to take a life," he declaimed, "but I am positively starving for roast caribou."

"We shall have our fill. Omyranth does not disapprove."

"He doesn't? Well, that's something. Here are your furs. Propriety and decorum, above all else."

Over a feast of a dinner, Eldril asked Tuttle of his parentage.

"They gave me a great education," he replied, "although they were lacking in such. Good fishermen is the most that can be said. Not to impute them, really, it's just that the child is always smarter than the parents, wouldn't you say?"

Eldril laughed like a seagull, in between chewing. "I've never thought about it that way before, exactly. My parents were the rare canny sort. My father Gideon was a great pioneer, who discovered my mother Min in a remote, peaceful township very far away. The greatest gift they gave me was self-determination, because they always insisted I, myself was preferable to being anything else. They told me façades are forms of self-imposed fascism."

"Do you suppose, Eldril, that the people will survive?"

"I do not," Eldril put plainly. "There're things out of balance, and the time is long for many natural disasters to befall. Yet we may assume that, many millions of years from now, should some hardy animal survive, such as the wolf or cougar, it may come to articulate speech."

"Or perhaps the badger," said Tuttle. "I've always had a fondness for badgers."

"Perhaps the badger," Eldril agreed. "When they speak they will say things no mortal human has ever thought."

"Quite so," agreed Tuttle.

The two celebrated for many days of odd talk, but that it came time for Eldril to depart, for she was ultimately solitary by nature, except for her mare. They say goodbye warmly, and Tuttle shed a tear.

"Please return if you can," said he. "I shall be here fishing."

"It was quite nice to meet someone educated," Eldril returned, "but my place is in the south. I await the arrival of a few survivors."

And so it was that Eldril rescued Justine and Alvin one day, and journeyed with them to safety.

CHAPTER THIRTY-EIGHT:
TIME MAKES MAN FORGETFUL

Many more centuries went by from the era of Nicholas and Jenny, who lived on the magic isle before it had sunk, leaving only Eldril's gravesite above the cantankerous waves. The centuries spread out into more millennia, and ever so slowly people ceased to be primarily wandering clans in the north. From the north would come a uniting factor to challenge the marauders of the south, at long last bringing about the true 'war to end all wars'."

For a time there existed a successful clan in the swamps of South Carolina, who made a good living from the natural abundance, with a township made of boardwalks and walkways that penetrated the jungle, and additionally these people welcomed newcomers, seeing that it added to their strength and prosperity. They were ruled over by a just monarch, named Pious, who adjudicated feuds and whose word was accepted. This was to change, however, with the arrival of an abandoned infant, who was taken in by the community, jaundiced and hungry, and was given the name "Mordred."

Mordred grew up surly and ill-favored, quick to laugh a harsh laugh but quick to anger. When necessary, his tongue was sober, and he spoke fair words, reasonable and sound, such that they reverberated with the sentiments of his people. He often spoke of fair meadows for a chosen people, and slowly rallied a band under his allegiance with the aim of departing the swamp for these greener pastures. Ever so slowly, this group grew into a united band, dissatisfied with the life of the swamp, and steadily under the yoke of the malcontent Mordred, who patiently urged them over time to rebel and depart.

Pius summoned Mordred to hear his words, and see if there was sound counsel therein. Mordred keenly modulated his hostility to a quiet righteousness, and explained to his king the nobility of an expedition to expand the prosperity of the people. Pius listened with gravity, and debated that the people already knew a prosperity that was unlikely elsewhere. Then Mordred rose up among the assembled Senate body and with a sharp dagger stabbed Pius to the heart. Amidst the conflagration of protest and denial he cried out.

"The time is arrived for all good people to unite for a better life. Too long have we listened to the counsel of the timid and weak, who would have a subsist under the yoke of mediocrity. Too long has this soft and quiescent tyrant gain-sayed the greater glory we might collectively achieve. Those not attached to our destiny might stay, I grant them this. But those against me must perish for the well-being of our collective. Who here is against us?"

A pall of silence descended upon the throng. Mordred continued. "Now is the time to gather resources and depart. Justly we shall spare the discontent fishing gear and such items as are basic. For the rest, we shall depart for the North and establish a new kingdom, indeed a new kinship, which show value the pursuit of the hunt for mutual sustenance, as always, yet who shall also ban together in a brotherhood united by common philosophy: devotion to industry, to building, and to establishing a great city state in the midst of the wild."

In the end, summoned by overwhelming popular sentiment, few wished to remain. Mordred gathered his community about him, appointing as knights such hardy folk as would best serve their expedition and such wise elders as he could trust, temporarily. With the community's united strength, the way north was a relative ease, and such modest enclaves of people as they discovered were swiftly incorporated by the coercion of indubitable threats and intimidation, or simply slaughtered for their belongings. Mordred would inevitably choose for himself among the young women, under the guise of assembling the sisterhood to govern the ultimate foundation of the city, which gathered even more popular sentiment in his favor.

Finally green pastures were achieved, yet Mordred led his folk further into a mountain stronghold. The first thing he did there was to teach his people how to quarry and cut stone, and as years passed by buildings were assembled, and the buildings represented government, religion, and commerce in one. Roads and marketplaces were layed, and so that people had a place to sell their goods and support their family. Word of this miracle spread far and wide, and soon the population brimmed with people from near and far seeking their livelihood.

Of his chosen women Mordred took one named Drusilla to be his lawful bride, for he deemed her a cunning politician and architect of the law, and while initially one to be loved for a certain graciousness, eventually a queen to be feared for attention towards resolving strife with deadly force.

As Mordred grew towards middle-age, his estate grew as well, swiftly becoming a thriving empire under his yoke, although the people liked and trusted him less overtime.

"Let them hate me, so long as they fear me," he remarks to his wife.

Trails and roads spread out in all directions, and the people submitted to the rule of law, and conglomerated as had not been seen in the many millennia since the Wars. Yet the marauders in the far south gained rumor of this, and perceiving a threat, began to band together with the object of war. The South had thrived yet, and had many fierce some leaders to guide the people in this purpose, and so it was not too long before they rallied in quest for the great city of the North.

This news came to Modred, and he, too, made rightful preparation to meet this challenge to his authority and his empire.

The sky itself gathered in foreboding, and the two armies at last met amidst terrible lightning and thunder, which slashed through the sky and rumbled across the land. Mordred himself, riding a tamed mustang, gathered and led his army in a fateful charge against the marauders of the South, and for generations there will be stories of the opposed rampaging armies, of carnage and slaughter and gore. Beneath the raging sky thousands perished to feed the earth with their blood, as tides of humanity met with swords and battle axes and crossbows in combined calamity.

The sky parted at sunrise to reveal the South in defeat, yet with few from the North surviving, as well. Mordred had led the charge, yet had escaped unscathed, while sending many of the opposing warriors to their end. He received a hero's welcome as he paraded back into the City.

Yet this did not purge Mordred's thirst for death. He was consumed by a death instinct, the desire to make the living inert. While raised to new heights by his victory, he sank to new lows of depravity, and initiated a slow surreptitious campaign to persecute his own people. First petty crimes were met with cruel and unusual punishments, until only a directed suspicion was sufficient to put a person to a sentence of jail, and then eventually to death. The populace lived in fear, and many went back into the Wilderlands. It was nearly the end of the life of the City, as, drained of its manpower, the shifting gears of society ceased to function. It was the end of Mordred, who was poisoned to death by his wife Drusilla.

So would end the final war. Strife among roaming bands of competitors would still occur, as well as isolated peaceful communities would enjoy brief times in the sunshine of peace, yet never again would war afflict the Earth.

"History repeats itself," Jack the hermit had said to Gwynhr over a flagon of wine. The fire burned in the hearth. "So, there is bound to be another war."

"How is this so?" Gwynhr asked in trepidation of his friend Jack's words.

"Precisely because what one generation inherits is passed down to other generations, by force of word and deed and their indoctrination amongst certain people, who must inherently struggle with the same issues, such as war versus peace, gentility versus violence, opposition versus acceptance. It would be nice to say that, over time, there would be a cumulative benefit towards peace. Yet time makes Man forgetful, and Man was ever contentious."

CHAPTER THIRTY-NINE:
THE POLE

Sir Edwin Willoughby was guiding a team of surveyors in the Yukon when the detonations sounded. Their eyes were drawn incredulously in the direction of the Pole that night, as the Aurora Borealis was rudely interrupted by tremendous mushroom clouds which blossomed up into the atmosphere. The sign could only be read as an attempt to annihilate the race as a whole, whomever had initiated it, or whatever, as perhaps it was the automatic response of a computer that had did the deed.

Willoughby was the first to react. "Everybody on board! I can only mean one thing: waves approaching!"

The surveying crew of 12 jostled on the basket of their balloon, pulled up the anchor, and set the gas fire. The balloon lifted off ever so slowly, as a raging crashing sounded from the suddenly liquefied ice. The religious among them prayed to God, to Jesus, to the Holy Ghost for mercy, while the rest merely prayed. Twenty feet aloft, a tremendous gust of wind took their modest craft, blowing it almost perpendicular to Earth, and was followed by seismic jolts below. Then like the Deluge of Noah, tidal waves rolled over the distance, driving more winds before them, and crackling throes of lightning and awesome thunder.

"A few more feet!" Willoughby cried, but in the wind their balloon was barely receiving heat from the fire, "Just a few more feet!" The title waves rushed towards them at gale pace. "All unnecessary weight overboard!" The crew heaved overboard all their surveying equipment, tents, and food. The first wave loomed like a speeding bank of fog, yet made entire of water and pulverized rock.

"A few more feet!" cried Willoughby again. The initial tidal wave peeked above the little balloon, and slammed downwards with all the furious Wrath of God. The balloon exploded with the dullest pop, and the basket was overturned into a rolling, heaving maelstrom. Only Sir Edwin Willoughby managed to grip on to the submerged basket, the captain going down with the ship, while the others were whisked away into the water.

The impact knocked the air from his lungs and drove water into his nose and mouth, yet he clung to his shredding basket with all his strength. He was rolled upside-down, then right-side up, and upside-down again. Then his tidal wave was slammed into the muddy slopes of a remote Canadian mounted, boiled and hung there frustrated, then subsided down the banks, leaving Willoughby coughing and vomiting in the mud. He was covered in mud, but the wave had subsided, taking the forested hillside below him with it. "Dear God!" he exclaimed, although he was not one of the religious ones of his party. He squinted about through the mud in his eyes. "Praise the Lord!" he exclaimed, although only the mud saved him. He was hundreds of miles from any previous civilization, without food, fire, or provisions, and ached all over from the beating he had received. In addition, his mind struggled to grasp his experience, which came with only one explanation yet no prior warning in all his experience, except that as a child in school he was told to 'huddle in place.'" "Damn the fools!" was the next thought his cognizance could utter.

Flocks of birds streamed overhead through a storm wracked sky. At last the clouds broke, revealing the distant stars far away, with fates unknown. Willoughby clawed his way uphill, until he heard a woman's voice: "Is somebody there?"

"Yes!" cried Willoughby. "I came in the wave!"

"You did?" the voice answered. "I'll come down and help you!"

I dark-haired woman could just be seen descending the slope. "How did you survive!? That was sheer murder, what I saw!"

"Sir Edwin Willoughby!" Edwin ejaculated, still short of breath. "At your service!"

"Rebecca. I was on the mountaintop photographing the stars, when everything changed. I don't suppose anybody should see the photos, now." The young woman reached Edwin and helped him scramble to his feet. "Everything below is washed away, for as far as the eyes can see. And all I have is lentils and granola bars. I believe we are doomed."

"Better not to die alone," Willoughby gasped.

"Aye, at that."

"What do we do now?"

CHAPTER FORTY:
BENEDICTUS

Eldril laughed. Justine and Gwynhr were doing a little dance in the mango grove.

It was another warm and humid day in the South Pacific. The waves were at low ebb, and so Eldril proceeded to leave the lovers at their play and hunt along the shoreline and the bay out to the reef, for seashells and abalone and any flotsam and jetsam, and driftwood for the fire. She discovered an old floatation device that was invaluable, especially for Justine, with her useless right arm. The abalone were prolific again, and with her woven vine basket she even caught a lobster on the reef.

The long equatorial day came to a balmy close for the threesome with the feast of seafood, and Eldril lured a goose for that nights special midnight celebration.

"First," Justine said, "let us give thanks to the Bountiful, from whence all arises, and give thanks specifically for tonight's delicacies. But let us also be reminded of serendipity, without which we would not be here, on our magic island. And let us remember love, which feeds our soul even as tonight's feast shall feed our bodies." Justine and Eldril turned to Gwynhr, who cleared his throat and stood with hands clasped behind his back in appropriate recitation posture.

"And may I say," he began, "a brief, and hopefully timely, Benedictus. May all gathered here today not only give thanks to the prime victuals, but also may we thus preform solemn ablutions in regards a certain hygiene of the Spirit, which being accomplished may allow us to take our duly allotted share from life without guilt, but in all due recognition of those people and animals who have allowed us to achieve such a state, and in a general fond remembrance of children everywhere, who grew up in the labors of the Spirit to perform difficult work. And as a solemn reminder to myself, may I add my humble debt to Jack the hermit, who originally inspired me towards my humble knowledge, wisdom, and quietude."

Eldril stood in turn. "With the turning of this page, may we renew our devotion to each other above all else, and may we recognize the profound uniqueness given to each individual, whatever their station in life, and to the peace and freedom that all deserve."

EPILOGOS

Jack the hermit strode forward in his leather boots, pulling the modest cart behind him, stacked with a number of sizable bricks of honeycomb. As he went he sowed flower seeds to the wind.

It was a mild spring day for the desert arroyo, if spring it was, for long ago people had stopped counting, the mysterious weather being what it was. Jack counted his blessings that fine morn, and chewed bread with comb as he walked, the better to think by. Already his flowing hair and beard were nearly white with the years of pondering.

At the abbey he sat over a flagon of wine in the dining hall with one Charles Dutton, later to become Monsignor Dutton, although the title was mainly honorary, in token of his work in the field of sociology.

"The meadows are thriving," Jack there hermit reported, "and the bees are unusually busy at their work!"

"Excellent," replied Dutton. "Things are quiet here, except for a few flirtations."

"You don't say?" said Jack, and nearly choked on his wine as he began to laugh. "Now this is my kind of abbey," he chortled.

"The grapes are turning rosy..." Dutton continued.

"Please stop!" said Jack, enjoying a significant belly-laugh. "What will you do, then?"

"I am merely biding my time," answered Dutton.

Jack chomped on some comb. "Sounds reasonable," he said thickly. "Good things come to those to wait. Or is it 'seize the day.' My learning fails me."

"I am on the lookout for a wink, the abbess told me so," Dutton said with consummate satisfaction.

A page entered to inform Jack that his cart had been loaded with tankards and flagons and amphoras of wine.

The pair shook hands. "Charles," the hermit said, "until we meet again!"

"I'm back to my studies," Dutton replied.

"Don't work too hard," said Jack, "but stop and smell the roses."

Eldril kneeled and sharpened an arrowhead, perched upon the rocky pinnacle of snow, her pupils dilated in a field of white. A stirring, restless wind moved her silken white hair, and she had the intimation that an arrival was imminent. She gathered her work and proceeded through the redwoods towards her sacred grove, where, after many piteous overthrows, would arrive Justine and Gwynhr.

"Omyranth!" Eldril swore.

END